CW00384007

The Long Marriage

*Ellie and Roger's marriage has endured 33 years
but his enforced early retirement
sends them both in a spin*

GILL BUCHANAN

The Long Marriage Copyright © 2020 by Gill Buchanan.

All rights reserved. No part of this book may be reproduced in any form or by any electronic or mechanical means including information storage and retrieval systems, without permission in writing from the author. The only exception is by a reviewer, who may quote short excerpts in a review.

This book is a work of fiction. Names, characters, places, and incidents either are products of the author's imagination or are used fictitiously. Any resemblance to actual persons, living or dead, events, or locales is entirely coincidental.

Gill Buchanan
Visit my website at www.gillbuchanan.co.uk

Printed in the United Kingdom

First Printing: Aug 2020
GB Books

ISBN- 9798670274982

Also by Gill Buchanan

Unlikely Neighbours

Alex and his wine cellar arrive in Lodge lane
sparking some unlikely outcomes

Forever Lucky

For Katie, it seemed like the end but, in fact,
it was just the beginning

Birch & Beyond

The sequel to Forever Lucky: A testing time for Katie leaves her
uncertain about her future

The Disenchanted Hero

Inspired by the true WW2 story of Molly & Guy

To Tony

Chapter 1

*R*oger opened one eye. His grey-haired sleepy head was just inches from his alarm clock. The red-lit numbers were huge so there was no mistake. Realising it was seven-thirty he shook himself awake. Had he slept through the alarm? He sat on the side of the bed and it suddenly dawned on him, as if this momentous change was hitting him for the first time, he didn't have to go to work. He had retired. Or at least they had edged him out. He might be sixty, and perhaps even the oldest in the office, but he was the marketing director. And he didn't look his age, everyone said so. He loved his job; he wasn't ready to go. He was pushed.

He thought back to the leaving do they had arranged for him even though he said he didn't want a fuss. They said that it was important to mark the retirement of a fine man who had worked for East Anglian Finance for twenty odd years. Such bullshit. They put together a dubious buffet and some cheapskate wine: a very predictable Marlborough Sauvignon Blanc and an Australian Merlot. Somehow, they cajoled a few top bods as well as *the team* to come along after five to one of the larger meeting rooms to make polite noises for a painful length of time before they could all go home and get drunk properly.

It hadn't seemed real at the time, like some sort of nightmare where you wake up and think *phew, thank goodness that was just a dream.* It was when his boss, Nigel, said, 'we're going to miss you round here,' in a very unconvincing half-hearted tone, that Roger could almost feel the stab of a knife in his back. The most he could manage in response was a sarcastic smile. That was all they were worth. Except for a couple of his managers, Grant and Melissa; the three of them had enjoyed many a lively meeting laced with laughs. He knew Melissa fancied him despite the age gap. He'd never respond to her flirtations but at the same time it gave his ego quite a boost.

He looked over to his wife now who was beginning to wake up, yawning and stretching, easing herself gently into just another day for her. She'd probably have a coffee with her friend Carol and then the estate agency would likely call and she'd do a viewing or two for them. It was all right for her, life in the slow lane.

He was a marketing director working in the cut and thrust of the financial world, coming up with innovative ways to promote ISAs and loans. They didn't lend money, they made dreams come true: that special holiday of a lifetime; a daughter's fantastical wedding in a castle; a brand-new top of the range motor. He knew his stuff but of course the world had changed. It was no longer direct mail and telephone marketing; it was all about social media: Twitter, Facebook, LinkedIn and many more; there seemed to be a new platform appearing every week. 'I can't believe we're not on Snapchat,' one of the team would say and Roger would ask them to put a paper together on the merits of that particular platform, mainly to buy him time. So, when they started suggesting he was put out to graze and young Dean, can't be any older than thirty-five, would take over as marketing director, it was insulting. Dean didn't have anything like his experience when it came to handling large multi-million-pound budgets. He was all slicked back hair and skinny jeans and had the sort of unassuming manner that left you wondering what they saw in him. In Roger's day you needed to have presence, personality and charm to get to the top. These days mild acne seemed to feature more highly.

So here he was, wondering why he was getting out of bed at all. What was the point? But he was awake now so he went through the motions. He padded to the bathroom reminding himself he must stretch his calves more, cleaned his teeth and had a quick shower. That felt nice, all that hot water cascading over him; it seemed to wash away a few demons somehow. He looked in the mirror as he dried himself with his towel, rubbing his hair so that it was gently tousled over his head. Then he ran his fingers through it, pushing it away from his forehead. He still had a full head and he'd kept his figure pretty much, just a small protrusion that gave away the odd pint of beer.

On his way to the bedroom to find some clothes he passed his wife, Ellie, and they looked at each other rather oddly. This wasn't normal. He should be going to work and she should have the house to herself. She smiled meekly at him and he probably looked confused. He scuttled off and went to find his shorts and a T-shirt. What would he do with all those work shirts he owned? Ellie would probably suggest taking them to the charity shop. But that was hasty; he might get another job. The prospect seemed remote and a wave of sadness came over him. Ellie appeared behind him holding a mug of tea with a look of concern on her face. She offered him the tea.

'All right?' she asked.

'Yeah, course. Takes a bit of getting used to.'

'It will. I'll put your porridge on.'

'You don't have to.'

She just looked at him, said nothing and went off downstairs.

He opened the curtains to let the daylight in. The sun was already bright on this July day, just the odd white fluffy cloud. The Brett Valley river meandered along the bottom of their garden, the water shallow and stagnant. The purple irises which edged the riverbank were at their most splendid and Roger had to nod to his wife's gardening prowess on that score. Not a bad view he thought to himself.

In the kitchen Ellie had breakfast television on and a presenter was interviewing a group of people with northern accents who were looking slightly startled and coming out with random statements about how Brexit was going to affect their lives in some devastating way. A bowl of steaming porridge was at his place on the table with a jar of Suffolk honey and a spoon. He laughed to himself as he thought, *Next stop the care home.* Ellie looked puzzled.

'What?' she asked.

'Nothing. Thanks for this.'

She sat opposite him with her own porridge. It all seemed a bit formal for so early in the morning.

'What are you going to do today?' she asked and his mind went blank at first. 'How about tackling that flat-pack from IKEA; we could really do with some extra storage?' Her expression suggested she thought this was a great idea.

His heart sank. The last time he'd attempted a flat-pack there had been blood, sweat and tears. Literally. And then Jon the handyman was called to rescue the situation as Ellie raised her eyebrows and sighed a lot.

'Ooh.' Ellie suddenly seemed excited and went over to the worktop bringing back two envelopes. 'Here you are.'

'What's this? It's not my birthday.'

'Open them.'

He did. 'Oh God, it's official. "Happy Retirement". What's bloody happy about it?'

'Who's it from?'

'Your mother. I suppose you put her up to this? I mean she's far too demented to do it herself.'

'Roger! That's enough.'

'Sorry. This one's from Colin. It's all right for him. He'll probably plod along as a project manager until he's quite happy for a life of Saga holidays and with a trip to the opticians being the highlight of his week. Have you told the whole world?'

'My mother and your brother. Hardly the whole world. Oh, and the boys, but they won't send you a card.'

'No, too busy living a normal life. Matt will be at work 24/7 and Ben will be producing his next masterpiece to decorate no one's wall.'

'You have got it bad. Don't be such a misery guts. Just think of the possibilities now you have more time.'

Roger's mind went blank. 'I'm sure something will come to me.'

Later that morning he turned his laptop on. Perhaps sitting in front of a screen would help. Microsoft news told him that Boris Johnson was about to become Prime Minister. It sort of added to the ridiculousness of life. He read his five emails (there would have been around fifty at work) and decided he didn't need Viagra yet, in response to two of them, and that he still didn't fancy going on a Scandinavian cruise even if it did include a visit to the Blue Lagoon to melt his stresses away.

As he turned in his chair, he couldn't help noticing that the dreaded flat-pack had mysteriously appeared in the room; another passive-aggressive move from his wife. Right, he'd show her. How difficult could it be?

A quick look at the assembly instructions with virtually no words but lots of pictures told him that in just twenty-seven simple stages the Kallax 5 x 5 unit would be providing all his storage needs. The first image of a single grumpy cartoon man crossed out was opposite three smiling cartoon men looking very pleased with themselves. This was a bad omen but one he ignored. Just below that was a smiling man phoning IKEA. No phone number of course, just the sure-fire certainty that you're going to get stuck and need help.

Ellie appeared. 'You'll have to build it in Matt's old bedroom, against the back wall. It's not going to fit in here.'

'Right.' Roger decided only a woman would place a flat-pack where she didn't want it.

'You okay?' She stroked his head and looked concerned.

'Yeah, yeah, I'm fine.'

'You look a bit peaky.'

'Great. You really know how to make a man feel good about himself.'

'Why don't you walk up to the shop and buy some milk?'

'Do we need milk?'

'Not desperately but you could just get one carton.'

Roger decided some fresh air wouldn't be a bad thing. He had never walked up to the shop before; in fact, he rarely went in. It was only a tiny community shop; what was the point? Apparently, there were people in the village who relied on it, he was told by the self-righteous types. He put on some trainers and set off up The Street, looking around him almost as if this was his first exploration of this sleepy village.

Normally he zoomed through in his car. It was all very pretty: lots of thatched cottages, old houses that were very well preserved, with tidy, appealing front gardens. Pink roses featured heavily. The medieval church tower loomed over the community and apart from the pub and the shop there wasn't much to it. Why had they moved here? It was the house. They really liked the house with the River Brett meandering along the bottom of their garden. Well, Ellie did, anyway. He liked it too and the commute to Norwich from here wasn't too bad at all. It was a good place to relax after a busy week at work.

He got to the shop. The notice board outside told him he could be doing anything from yoga to knit and stitch at the village hall; he'd forgotten about the new hall. How could he after all the hoo-ha that had gone on. Roger had kept well out of it but his wife had kept him up to date with the progress of the two warring factions as they battled out whether to convert an old building or build a new one. He couldn't see what all the fuss was about.

He went through the door and Jeffrey eyed him suspiciously from behind the post office counter.

'Morning,' Roger said feeling alien in this environment.

A woman behind the counter smiled at him. She looked friendly enough but seemed to be watching him. It was a small place so he soon found the fridge and picked up some local farm milk, the label of which he recognised.

'Cash only, I'm afraid,' she said from above her orange tabard, as he waved a debit card at her. He could see now from her badge that her name was Margaret and she was a volunteer. Roger was beginning to realise that a lot of people in this village were already retired and seemed very happy about it. 'Sorry, we haven't got a card machine yet. The shop committee will be meeting next month to discuss whether or not we go contactless.' She tittered as though this might be a touch too radical for Little Capel.

'Not on my watch!' the man behind the post office counter shouted across.

'Jeffrey will be able to give you some cash,' Margaret explained nodding towards him. Why was he wearing a knitted tank top in July?

Roger didn't hide a cynical smile. 'How very convenient.'

Five paces and he was in cash city.

'How can I help you?' Was this man deaf?

'Fifty pounds cash, please?' he said waving his card around.

Jeffrey pointed to the card machine on Roger's side of the glass divide. The cash acquired, Roger returned for his milk.

'You're Ellie's husband, aren't you?'

Roger wondered if he was going to need personal ID to buy his milk. 'That's right. Roger.'

'We don't normally see you in here on a weekday.'

'No, well, I'm normally at work up in Norwich.'

'Ah, yes, you work for that big financial services company.'

'Indeed, I do. Well I did.'

'Oh, sorry to hear that.' You could almost see the cogs of her mind whirring.

'Let's just say I'm between jobs.' An elderly man shuffled in behind him.

'It won't be easy, you know, finding a job at your time of life,' the man said.

'Thanks.' Roger had to laugh. 'I'm not that old, you know.'

'Donald, really!' Margaret said, and then to Roger, 'You're a very attractive man, if you don't mind me saying so. My mother has always fancied you from afar.' Her expression was starry-eyed momentarily. Her mother had to be ninety at least.

'Excellent. Maybe I'll become a model and start advertising Stannah stair lifts.'

'Not a bad idea,' Donald said. 'Or Nordic cruises. They're very popular round here you know.'

'Poligrip dentures,' Jeffrey shouted across.

'I'll bear all that in mind,' Roger said and couldn't quite believe that he waved and said, 'goodbye, then,' as he walked out of the shop.

'Well that was an experience,' he said to Ellie as he put the milk in the fridge. 'I've got my new career mapped out with the help of Donald.'

'What are you talking about?' She seemed distracted.

'Nothing,' he said feeling like he was coming back down to earth.

'Good, because James has called; I'm off to do a viewing in Gem Corner.'

'Right.' It was odd but the thought of her going out to work made him feel even more inadequate somehow. She was staring at him. 'Bye then,' he said in an attempt at normal.

She'd turned and was off. 'See you later. Won't be long.'

He wondered if she would rush back because he wasn't at work where he should be.

Half an hour later, after getting stuck at assembly stage two of the flat-pack, he was on the phone to Jon. 'Not until Wednesday?'

'Sorry, mate. Will Ellie be in on Wednesday?'

'More likely me. I've retired,' he said with disdain.

'Oh, good for you.'

'Doesn't feel like it. Listen it might be better if we can do this while Ellie's out actually. I'll give you a call when the coast is clear.'

'Okay.' Jon sounded perplexed.

'Great. See you Wednesday.'

Roger sank into the chair at his desk and felt thoroughly deflated. Thoughts of signing up for carpet bowls and the history group at the village hall made him shudder. He came to the swift conclusion that he needed to find a job. He wasn't ready for retirement.

Chapter 2

Ellie stood at the door of her son's bedroom and sighed. Roger had been at home a week now and he was beginning to get on her nerves. Perhaps she should find him a project?

The room had the look of an aged cottage with wonky walls, sash windows and wooden floorboards which sat awkwardly with the signs of radical teenager. Ben had done his best to put his stamp on it. She often thought back to his reaction when he first saw the house. 'It's very old, isn't it?' There was no appreciation of its aesthetic: the country kitchen with its large island (Ellie had always wanted an island) and the orangery which they now called the garden room which overlooked a large garden sweeping down to the river.

He'd been allowed to paint one of his bedroom walls navy blue but definitely not all four walls black. There was still a poster of Scissor Sisters up: one chap with a silk neckerchief while another had a rather dubious black stringy vest on. The girl looked quite formidable with her stark leather dress against luminous white skin and a tattoo showing on one arm. A pair of Ben's ripped jeans and a rather ferocious studded belt hung untidily over a chair. Just poking out from under the bed was a crumpled *NME* magazine with the words:

'*Yeah Yeah Yeahs: Show Your Bones*' across the cover. Ellie had no idea what that meant but assumed it was something she'd rather not know about.

Being the youngest, Ben had been the last to go and it had been such a wrench. She worried about how he would make his way in the grown-up world. He wasn't like Matt, all capable and high-flying with what seemed like a new girlfriend every time she spoke to him. But she knew she had to let go of them both, cut the apron strings. Ben was twenty-eight now. And so in love with Bella, as he calls her. Apparently, her real name is Madeleine. Such a pretty name Ellie had thought when she first heard it.

'But it's too long. I can't keep saying Madeleine all the time, Mum,' Ben had protested.

'How about Maddie?'

'Mum, everyone calls her Bella. Right? So that's her name.'

She was beautiful all right. And a natural beauty too with her long dark shiny hair which looked good even when she'd just got out of bed. She didn't need make-up and didn't wear it. Was that what made her look so young? She was only three years younger than Ben but she looked no more than a teenager.

Ellie came out of her trance and asked herself the same question she had asked many times. Was this the day to turn this last vestige of the boys' childhood into some sort of functional room? A guest room, perhaps? But then they had already done that to Matt's room, it being the bigger of the two. And now they had the storage unit in there, she could put some of Ben's stuff away. She strongly suspected that Jon had assembled the flat-pack but hadn't said anything to Roger who had been very quiet about it. Ordinarily when he tackled a DIY job he'd have the scars to prove it. And Roger had turned the smallest bedroom into some sort of office where he spent a lot of time on his computer doing she had no clue what.

Perhaps this should be *her* room? She smiled to herself. Why did she feel a tinge of guilt at that thought? Perhaps she'd take up some sort of hobby? Craft? Art even. Wendy in the village belonged to some sort of art group.

'I'm just off to paint a watercolour,' Ellie said out loud and laughed to herself.

'What's that, darling?' Roger appeared. She still wasn't used to his lurking presence since he'd retired. She had enjoyed having the house to herself during the day.

'Ben's room. What do you reckon?' She nodded into her son's domain.

Roger walked into the room properly and looked around. 'Well that grim poster could go. And it could use a lick of paint. I never did like the darkened wall. Maybe get twin beds; might be more useful for when the boys come to stay.'

'What are you talking about? They both have girlfriends. They're not going to be interested in twin beds. No, I was thinking I might turn it into an art studio.'

Roger laughed unashamedly straight in her face. 'Whatever for? You can't paint and Ben's living miles away in London.'

'How do you know I can't paint? I haven't tried yet.'

'When are you going to find time? You will insist on doing that silly viewings job at the estate agents. Unsociable hours it is sometimes, as well.' He turned away from her now. 'Punters wanting to be shown round posh Suffolk pink cottages on Saturday mornings or weekday evenings even! They should get one of the youngsters to do it.'

'Since when were we out socialising on a weekday evening?'

'When I was working there was a social life attached to the job.' A glazed expression came over his face. 'I enjoyed a round of golf with a client or two.'

'That's your idea of social? While you were whacking balls into the rough, I was stuck with brain-dead wives, talking about permanent hair colour and the escalating price of Pinot Noir since the film *Sideways* came out.'

'That doesn't sound so bad to me. I like a glass of Pinot. That reminds me...' He was about to head off.

'Not one of your precious wines again; don't tell me a Sangiovese perfect for drinking today!'

He looked offended, hurt even, and Ellie realised she'd gone too far. He had suddenly become a sensitive soul.

'Oh, it doesn't matter. I just...' He stopped.

'Just what?' she asked gently now.

'I suppose I just don't know what to do with myself now I've been thrown into this strange retired world against my will.'

'How about getting some consultancy work?'

He thought about it and could see nothing but obstacles, and at the same time the niggling doubt about his ability to keep up in the new digital world pulled at him. 'Well… no, I don't think so.'

'Why don't you ring up Bryan? He's been retired a year or so now. It might help to talk to your buddy about it?'

'I don't think Bryan is the type to do therapy.'

'Well, he knows you better than most. And you could see if he wants a game of golf?'

'Don't know.' He was staring out of the window now. 'Looks like rain.'

'No, it doesn't. It's just a bit cloudy.'

'Bryan doesn't even play golf.'

'Maybe he'd like to start.' It was a feeble response but it felt safe; this was going nowhere. He was beginning to look despondent. At this rate he was going to decline into depression. 'Why don't you help me with this room?' she said thinking the suggestion was a decent enough olive branch to raise his spirits.

'But what are we going to do with it? Won't Ben mind? Shouldn't we tell him first.'

'No, I don't think so. He's twenty-eight and living in a flat in Tufnell Park.'

'A house, he said. 'A big house with lots of other people. Sounds like a commune.' He was looking around him as if his son was a grave disappointment to him.

'No, it's not a commune. They have to share; rents in London are ridiculous.'

'I told him he should go to Norfolk. There's plenty of struggling artists there and house prices are much less if you pick the right place. He'd be nearer to us too.'

'Well yes but young people don't want to live in dreary old Norfolk. Can you imagine the sultry Bella there!' Roger laughed and Ellie was thankful for that. 'No, London is where it's all happening. And they both manage to get quite a bit casual work.'

'So there he is waiting on tables and working in bars just so he can produce abstract paintings that no one wants to buy.'

'Don't be so negative. His art teacher said he had enormous talent. And it takes time to make a name for yourself.'

'You can say that again.'

'He told me he's got nearly five thousand followers on Instagram.'

'And are any of these followers going to buy one of his weird paintings?'

'It takes time.'

'So you said.' He sighed gloomily and sat on the end of the bed.

'Listen, you need to do something positive. Snap out of this low mood.'

'Low mood? I don't have low mood. I'm fine.' He stood up purposefully. He was tall and had kept his figure; he had that going for him.

'I tell you what; let's do it. Let's tackle this room.' Having said that, Ellie suddenly wasn't at all sure about it. Thinking and doing were so far apart in her mind. 'Maybe we'll start tomorrow.'

'You've got to go out, haven't you?' He looked pleased with himself. 'Don't tell me, James Addington have called and want you to do a viewing this afternoon?'

'No,' Ellie said but not very convincingly. 'There was an email earlier, a possible couple from Essex wanting to view in Capel Green.' At that moment the home telephone rang.

Roger fired a sanctimonious smirk at her. Ellie went to take the call in the kitchen. Damn, it was the agency.

Mr and Mrs Ellis from Romford were certainly not the typical customer of James Addington estate agency. For a start they were much younger. They looked round De Vere House with wide eyes and giggles.

'Where we gonna put the flat-screen telly with all those beams?' Mrs Ellis asked.

'We'll have it suspended from the ceiling,' Mr Ellis, shorter than his wife and slightly tubby with a cheerful face, was gesticulating with his arms as his wife let out a high-pitched titter. He turned to Ellie. 'What does Grade One listed actually mean? Could we rip this lot out and modernise it?'

Ellie took a sharp intake of breath. 'Erm, no, no, you wouldn't be able to do that Mr Ellis.'

'Call me Kevin, please. And this is Shazza. So, we have to keep it like this with tapestries on the wall and the dark wood

18

everywhere? These walls look like they need plastering if you don't mind me saying.'

'This house is actually a fine example of medieval and Tudor architecture. Those are wall paintings, not tapestries.'

Kevin was screwing his eyes up now. 'Well they're ancient whatever they are.'

Ellie suddenly remembered something that might resonate with this couple. 'The property was featured in one of the Harry Potter films.'

'Harry Potter! Mega. But darlin' if you don't mind me sayin' we've moved on a bit since medieval whatsits and this isn't gonna work for us and the kids.'

'I see your point.' There was a chance this viewing was over. 'Have you seen enough then?'

'Oh no we want to see upstairs. Blimey we've come all this way.'

Ellie led the way and couldn't help wondering if these people were just complete time wasters. 'Have you looked at many properties?' she asked.

'Just a couple. You see the thing is...' His face had reddened and he looked beside himself with excitement.

'Oh no Kev, we weren't going to say anything. We agreed.' His wife gave him a stern look.

'There's no 'arm. This lady's not going to know any of our lot.'

'Oh, if you must.'

Kevin looked like he might burst before he blurted out, 'The thing is we've come into a bit of money.'

Ellie nodded in acknowledgement fearing what was coming next.

'We've won the lottery!' Shazza shrieked and they were both whooping for joy as they entered the master bedroom.

'Oh yes! Now that's more like it, a four-poster bed. I could live with that.' Kevin didn't hesitate to climb on to the bed, shoes still on, and lie on his back looking up in wonderment as he kicked his heels.

'The property doesn't actually come furnished.' Ellie hadn't met the owners but she could still imagine the look of horror on their faces if they could see this scene.

'I'm sure we can sort something out with them. Negotiate the odd item into the price. I mean there can't be many people who want to buy this, with that Grade One restriction thing.'

'Not sure if the kids will like it,' Shazza said looking doubtful.

'What with a huge bedroom each? And isn't there another wing? Can't believe it; a house with two wings. We could put your old mum in the little one, then she wouldn't have far to come to babysit!' They both seemed to find this hilarious. Ellie grinned through gritted teeth.

When she thought she couldn't take any more and they were stood outside on the pavement, Kevin asked, 'Any good pubs in Capel Green?'

Ellie tried to work out where they'd fit in. She was about to suggest The Cock Horse when Kevin interrupted her thought,

'I hear The Swan Hotel is rather posh. Hey babes, we could get a room for the night!'

'Ah, nah, we've got to get back for the kids. Mum's got her bingo this evening; she won't want to miss that.'

'That's true. Oh well, we might be living here soon.'

Ellie wondered if there was some law against lottery winners buying historic houses and if there wasn't perhaps one should be passed very quickly.

Halfway up Swingleton Hill Roger stopped, panting for breath. This was ridiculous; they had only been on this walk for half an hour or so. Suffolk is supposed to be flat. Bryan was looking smug.

'You out of puff old boy?'

'Less of the old if you don't mind.' Roger waited for his breath to return to something like normal and looked out across a field of rapeseed and a big expanse of blue sky. A giant combine harvester was carefully extracting the seed which flowed out of a large pipe into a trailer.

'Just not used to it, I suppose?' he said when he noticed Bryan was looking straight at him.

'Too much sitting behind a desk.' Bryan did a few star jumps just to be irritating.

'How come you're so bloody fit?'

'I've taken up running. I'm up to 5k now.'

'What? Nah! Whatever for? And what's with the kilometres? I thought you voted for Brexit?'

Bryan was swaying his bald head like a pendulum and he had a stupid grin on his face. 'Everyone uses kilometres these days. Anyway, let's just say I have my reasons.'

Roger was beginning to wish he hadn't phoned Bryan in the first place. But what with Ellie going out he suddenly didn't know what to do with himself. It was silly really but he knew he'd had quite enough of pottering round the house for one day. They walked on and eventually the pathway flattened out taking them across a grassy field as they made their way up to Stackyard Green. A kestrel hovered gracefully above, flapping its wings to stay afloat as it searched for prey below.

'Not far old boy.' He gave Roger's arm a friendly whack. And then for some strange reason Bryan asked, 'Everything all right with you? I mean tickety-boo and all that?'

'Yes! Course. Just struggling a bit with this retirement malarkey. I mean what do you do with yourself all day?'

'Ah yes, I wasn't sure at first but then I got on to the Village Hall Committee and started volunteering for the Guildhall in Capel Green – you know the National Trust place.'

'And that's enough, is it? I mean how does that replace a full-on career? Don't you miss the office banter, the swift half after work?'

Bryan looked thoughtful but said nothing and they walked on in an amiable silence. Roger began to think there was something that Bryan wasn't telling him. Something which had put a spring in his step.

The Capel Rose pub painted in a soft creamy yellow was standing before them. With the village green opposite, it was a perfect example of a country pub.

'Right, my shout,' Bryan said going straight through the front entrance into a cosy bar with wooden beams across the ceiling so that you almost needed to duck. An inglenook fireplace with two leather chairs either side looked very inviting and Roger made his way over there.

Bryan came from the bar with two halves of bitter.

'Halves? What's wrong with the full pint? We're not driving.'

Bryan patted his surprisingly flat belly. 'Sorry mate but got to look after myself, keep in trim.'

'You've never bothered too much before.' This was it; this was the secret coming. Bryan was looking coy. 'Come on, mate, spit it out. It's a bit late for a mid-life crisis. What is it with the abstemious drinking and the keep fit running?'

'This is just between us, okay? I haven't told Carol yet.'

Alarm bells rang. Roger was stunned and said feebly, 'Go on then.' He almost didn't want to know.

'I've met someone.'

'You, bald as a coot, have bloody well met someone! Does she need her eyes testing?'

'Hey, keep it down.' Bryan was glancing furtively round the pub. There weren't many in and the young barman looked more interested in his mobile. 'Actually, she's quite a bit younger than me so I need to keep up.' He sat up tall and puffed up his chest.

Roger was wide-eyed and flabbergasted. 'Am I dreaming this? What the hell's going on? I mean, I know Carol has her moments but this is off the scale. You mean to tell me you're having an affair with a much younger model? You entering clichéd prick of the year or something?'

'Listen.' Bryan was red-faced and looking all serious now. 'Tiffany is no flash in the pan. We're in love.'

'Oh my God. She's called Tiffany. Don't tell me she's a beauty therapist from Braintree.'

'No.' He was sulking now. 'Actually, she's a personal trainer at the gym at Hadleigh.'

'Right.' Roger was nodding at his friend, trying to take it all in. He didn't want to mock. This was obviously serious stuff. And what about Carol? He was very fond of Carol. The four of them had been friends for many years, even shared a French gîte together in Provence. 'But surely your marriage is worth more than...'

Bryan was affronted. 'I'm sorry but my marriage to Carol was over long ago. We've rubbed along, put up with each other but there's no spark any more, no magic.'

'But mate, you can't expect fireworks after almost forty years. More sort of amicable companionship, cosy nights in front of the telly. Someone who's always there for you.'

'That's the trouble. You're happy to settle for that. I'm not. With Tiffany I feel alive, excited even.'

'But it's always like that at first, isn't it? Are you sure this Tiffany will last the course, grow old with you?'

'I can't think about that. I'm in love and I just want to be with her.'

They took the shorter route back, past Boyton Hall where horses grazed in paddocks in the sunshine, and then downhill on the home straight into the village. Bryan was quiet and seemed wrapped up in his own thoughts. Roger blurted out the odd bit of mundane news in an attempt to fill the awkward silence and was relieved when they got back to The Street and the point where they would go their separate ways. But before they did, Roger felt moved to say something.

'Listen mate, I only want the best for you.'

'I know.' Bryan looked downbeat but managed a half smile. 'The best is Tiffany.'

'Right.' It was still shocking. 'Well, I'll see you then.'

'See you Roger.'

Roger wandered in a daze up to Rose Cottage and found himself absurdly pleased to see Ellie's little Ford Fiesta in the driveway. He went through the back door into the boot room where, grinning to himself, he took off his walking boots and went through into the kitchen. Ellie was stood at the island with her reading glasses perched on the end of her nose looking at a recipe book. He went straight over to her. She looked up and over her glasses at him, slightly bemused.

'What's the matter?' she said.

'Nothing,' he said innocently.

'What have you done now?' She moved away and almost threw her hands up in horror.

'I haven't done anything! Can't I smile at my own wife?'

'No! Don't be ridiculous!' Her eyes were bright blue.

'You know you're still as gorgeous and sexy as you were the day we met.'

'You been drinking?'

'One half of bitter. Bryan's on some stupid keep fit craze.'

'Must be the fresh air that's gone to your head.'

'Can't you take a compliment, my darling wife?' She was staring at him, unnerved by his adoration it seemed. Why did marriage have to come to this?

'Right well leave me alone. I'm going to try this Lorraine Pascale recipe and I need to concentrate.'

'What are we having?'

'Fish. Sea Bass.'

'Lovely,' he said as if she'd just promised him food heaven. He moved away slowly, still taking in her elf-like features, the highlights in the soft peaks of her hair, her figure; she still had it; she was still the one and only woman for him.

'Right, well, I'll away to my cellar and select a bottle of white.'

'Wine? On a Monday?'

He took no notice and off he went.

Chapter 3

Carol had sounded quite lacklustre on the phone but, as Ellie was in the middle of showing the Maynards around Brett Cottage, she just had to say, 'I'll call you later.'

Then, as luck would have it, James insisted she went into the office after a series of viewings which had already taken up most of her morning. She quite enjoyed it most of the time; some of the viewers could be a bit monosyllabic but she'd learned not to take offence. It was almost certain that unless they were all smiles from the first room they entered, it was going nowhere.

As she sat the other side of his desk, James insisted that his PA made her a cup of tea which made her wonder if there was a bitter pill to swallow. He asked her how that morning's viewings had gone.

'Fine. I think the Leyton-Smythe's from Surrey might put in an offer on The Manor at Gem Corner.'

'Excellent.' He looked overly pleased. 'We've actually had an offer from the younger couple from Norwich on 3, The Green.'

'Really? Well I suppose they were quite enthusiastic but I must say I'm surprised.'

'It's quite a low offer.'

'Ah. That would explain it. I thought the asking price might be a sticking point.'

'Yes, but two offers out of three viewings is very good going, Ellie.'

'Oh.' She was quite taken aback but then composed herself. 'Thank you.'

He leant in. 'As you know Amanda is leaving us soon and I was wondering if you'd be interested in a full-time permanent position?'

'Whoa! That's a big leap.' All she could see was a look of disappointment on her husband's face. Since he'd retired, he had moaned about her little part-time job. The trouble was retirement had been foisted on him before he was ready and he was like a fish out of water. She was surprised, considering how he clearly felt, that he wasn't trying to get some sort of work. But he seemed to be stifled, stuck in this no man's land wandering about not knowing what to do.

James, meanwhile, was rattling off the salary package she would get with potential commission. 'After all,' he said, 'if she became an agent the viewings she had done today may well have resulted in a bonus.'

'Well yes,' she allowed her thoughts to be spoken out loud not quite knowing where to go with this, 'but there must be a lot more to being an agent.'

He sat back in his chair and smiled at her. He had aged well and was one of those men whose grey hair just made him look more distinguished. Perhaps one too many long lunches but she knew he had a tennis court up at Capel Tye which kept him reasonably fit. 'I'm sure an intelligent woman like yourself will soon learn on the job; there are some training courses we can send you on. So how about it?'

Ellie sat there wide-eyed, dumbfounded.

'What are you afraid of?' he asked with a twinkle in his eye.

'Let me have time to think about it,' she said in an effort to take back control of this conversation.

'Fine. But don't take too long; Amanda leaves in just two weeks. If you're not going to fill the position we'll have to advertise.'

Ellie went home via the supermarket and arrived laden with shopping bags.

'I thought we only needed a few bits?' Roger said as he stood there lamely.

'Are you going to give me a hand?' Ellie asked trying to take the edge out of her voice.

He looked confused before he shook himself and went out to the car to get a couple more bags. When it was all on the kitchen worktop, he picked out a bottle of wine from the cardboard carrier to read the label.

'Organic?' he said looking incredulous.

'Yes, organic. It's a Côte du Rhône; you always say they're underrated.'

'But organic, since when?'

'Just thought we'd try it. I was reading an article the other day and it was talking about pesticides ending up in wine and how bad they are for us.'

'Haven't done me any harm so far?' He stood tall and flexed a bicep.

'How do you know?'

'I've not been to the doctors in years.'

'Exactly!'

'So what's so bad about the wine I drink then?'

'Oh, it was saying you'll get cancer and die or something.'

'Ridiculous.'

'Ooh I must ring Carol,'

'Carol?' He looked worried. Retirement really didn't suit him.

'Yes, our friend Carol. Is that all right?'

'Of course it is.'

Ellie put it down to a *Men are from Mars* moment and dug her mobile out of her handbag. She dialled and realising Roger was staring at her she took the phone into the garden room.

Carol answered straightaway.

'Sorry, darling it's been one of those days. How are you?'

'All right, I suppose. Bryan is out again.' She sounded deflated.

'Oh? Where's he gone?'

'The Guildhall at Capel Green but it's not his day; he normally volunteers there on a Wednesday. He said somebody had let them down so he was covering.'

'Well that's okay, isn't it?' She thought how wonderful it would be if Roger got out more. 'I mean you don't want him under your feet all the time, do you?'

'No, but...' Her voice trailed.

Ellie wondered. Perhaps there was a problem.

'I really wanted us both to go to B&Q to buy some coving,' Carol said. 'I mean I could go on my own but it's Bryan that will be putting it up and I don't want him complaining about what I've bought.' She sighed. 'Although right now I can't see him doing any DIY let alone putting up coving.'

'Is there something wrong, Carol?'

'I don't know. Probably just me.'

'Why don't you ask him outright?'

'Ask him what?'

'Well...' She picked her words carefully. 'Ask him if everything is okay? Perhaps you should ask him if you can go to B&Q tomorrow; tell him about the coving.'

'I could do.'

'I think you should, Carol. It's probably nothing.'

'Maybe.' There was quite a long reflective pause before Carol said, 'How's Roger coping with retirement?'

'Well, apart from a bit of furious pottering he just seems to lurk around the house and resent me going out. And now James Addington want me to go full time! No idea what to do about it.'

'But do you want a full-time job? I mean with Roger retiring perhaps you should retire too or at least stick to part time.'

31

'I certainly don't want to give it up; I quite enjoy it. And I know this probably sounds awful but I need to get out of the house more now. Roger's always skulking around.'

'Perhaps stick to part time then.'

It was funny but as Carol said that Ellie felt mildly irritated. She realised she was drawn to this full-time option and quite excited by the challenge it would present.

'You still there?' Carol was asking.

'Yes, sorry, just thinking about things.'

'Like me then; too much thinking.'

Ellie considered that it wasn't like her at all. 'When are we going out next? The four of us, I mean? It's been quite a while, hasn't it? Have you got your diary handy?' She walked into the kitchen and grabbed the calendar from the wall. The shopping had disappeared; Roger must have put it away.

'Yes, that's a good idea.' Carol sounded perkier. As Ellie put the calendar back on its hook Roger appeared and looked closely at it. 'Arranging something with Carol?' he asked.

'Yes, we thought we'd try the pub in the village again. Apparently, they've got a new chef; Carol saw it on Facebook.'

'But you've put Carol and Bryan.'

'Yes, that's right. You're not busy this Friday, are you?'

'No.' He suddenly looked worried.

'What's the matter?' Ellie asked confused.

'Nothing.'

'Good,' she said happy to leave it at that.

The next day Roger was on LinkedIn and stumbled across a job ad for a marketing director in Colchester; not his favourite place but he read on and found himself squirming at the language they used. *Would suit ambitious self-starter.* Whilst they hadn't actually used the word 'young', Roger was convinced that they were angling for that. He knew all about age discrimination from when he had recruited for his own team. Then he saw the salary. It was half what he was used to. No one his age was going to go for that. He sat back and thought about it. It was a job and would get him out of the house five days a week. Tick. It would bring in some money at least, better than nothing. Half tick. He'd have a reason to get up in the morning. Tick. He wouldn't be bored stiff wondering what to do with himself. Tick. He read it again. No chance.

He went and looked in the bathroom mirror, pressing his face up close to see how badly wrinkled it was these days. He had never really worried about such things up until now. He was obviously attractive to the opposite sex so why bother. He picked up his wife's eye cream and smeared it under his eyes. Far too much; it looked ridiculous so he wiped it off again. Now he just looked greasy. He had an idea and went back to his computer and typed *botox* into Google choosing the option: *botox near me.* When he realised what it was actually made from, the bacteria that causes botulism, and how much it cost, he decided it was one of his more foolish ideas.

A notification popped up on his screen. The Wildlife Trust in Ipswich were looking for a marketing manager. The job sounded idyllic, if very worthy, but the salary was pitiful.

Roger felt depressed. He could either die of boredom or humiliate himself with a job that was far beneath his skill set. There had to be more to life than this. It was at this low point that a text pinged through on his mobile from Ellie. He was pleased until he read it.

Staying on until 6pm. Lots to do. Any thoughts on supper?

How about we drink ourselves into oblivion, consider we've not had a bad life and enter into a pact to end it all. He could see the headline in the local paper now: *Mr and Mrs Hardcastle of Little Capel drank a rather fine claret and listened to Thelonious Monk as they took their own lives.*

He reread the text message and had an idea. He hadn't done much cooking over the years, as his wife was so good at it, but how difficult could it be? He went down to the kitchen and opened the fridge door staring in, his mind going completely blank. He closed the door and walked over to the shelves that housed all their cookery books. It hadn't really occurred to him before how many they had. An absurd number. Looking at the titles of some he was pretty sure that most hadn't been opened; he certainly couldn't remember eating Thai street food in the comfort of his own home. Then he grabbed one that caught his eye. *The Quick Roasting Tin: 30 minute one dish dinners.* This sounded perfect. The picture on the front cover was of shiny looking salmon fillets amongst a bed of green healthiness with some red chilli sprinkled over.

This was the sort of thing that Ellie would order in a restaurant. He opened up the book and found the recipe in the work night dinners section. There it was: sticky soy and honey roasted salmon with asparagus and sugar snap peas. It even sounded quite nice. He looked at the list of ingredients carrying the book back over to the fridge and opening the door again. He couldn't see any salmon; perhaps they had some in the freezer? He rifled in the salad drawers at the bottom. No asparagus. No tender stem broccoli. Ah! He found sugar snap peas and he was pretty sure they had frozen peas. Delving into the freezer he found a packet of salmon fillets and then the peas in the bottom drawer.

Back in the fridge he found a courgette and decided that would be a good substitute for what they didn't have. He looked at his watch and wondered if the salmon would defrost in time. He had about two hours. Looking at the instructions on the back of the packet he decided it was touch and go so he pierced the plastic covering with a sharp knife and put the fillets in the microwave on defrost for one minute. He took them out and prodded them. They were still pretty solid but he decided to wait and see; after all this dish only took thirty minutes.

Ellie found Roger asleep in the lounge with the newspaper over his face. She gently removed *The Times* and laid a hand on his arm. 'Roger,' she said just loud enough to awaken him.

'What? Oh, must have dozed off.' He looked at his watch; it was 6:45pm. 'Oh bugger,' he said, realising his plan had been scuppered.

'What's the matter?'

'Nothing. It's just that I was going to surprise you.'

'With the salmon tray bake?' she asked having seen the evidence in the kitchen. 'Looks lovely. You can still do it; it won't take long. I'll put the oven on for you so it warms up.'

Ellie had been told to sit at the table and pour the wine. Roger had selected an Italian white wine which he said would be perfect with the fish. He insisted that he had everything under control but looked hot and flustered. Finally, two plates appeared. Ellie looked at hers maintaining a thin smile on her face. 'Well, it smells good,' she said effecting a lightness to her voice.

They clinked glasses and tucked in. Ellie was thinking that it wasn't bad; the fish was a bit overcooked and squeaked on her teeth but the flavours were good.

'What do you think?' Roger asked looking all expectant.

'Very good,' Ellie heard herself say.

'Very good? What does that mean?'

'It's lovely. Tasty. You'll have to cook more often.'

'Thank you.' His shoulders dropped. 'So, what's James Addington got you working on now and so late?'

'Ah, well, I've got some news on that front.'

'Oh? You want to pack it in? I don't blame you; especially now I'm, you know...'

'No! No, I don't. Actually, it's quite the opposite. You see Amanda, one of the agents, is leaving and they've offered me her job.'

Roger's eyes were wide. He quickly descended into an anxious stare. 'You're not going to take it, are you?'

Ellie took a deep breath. It was the response she was expecting, although perhaps not so extreme. Why did everyone think she should be cajoled into retirement living just because her husband had been forced into it. She wasn't ready. 'It's not a decision I've taken lightly. I mean, at first, I thought no way. But the more I think about it the more I like the idea. It will be a new challenge for me. James thinks I'm up to it. He's very impressed with my viewings; they're resulting in quite a few offers.'

'Is he now! As if it's not bad enough already, James this and James that. He'll be moving in with us next.'

'Don't be ridiculous.' Ellie took a glug of wine.

There was a charged silence as they both picked out morsels of food from their plates. When the house phone rang Roger sprang up and walked over to the handset to answer it; something he never normally did, considering it an intrusion on their meal time together.

'Carol, how are you? Yes, she's here...'

Ellie gave him a piercing look and shook her head making it very clear that now was not a good time.

'Actually, Carol, we're just having supper, a bit later than usual. Can I get her to call you back?'

Call over, he sat down again, moved some remaining food around his plate and put his fork down again.

'The money would come in handy,' Ellie dared to say.

'Oh, I see, now I've been put out to grass...' He looked deeply offended as he stared into his empty wine glass. 'But there's the redundancy package and my pension's pretty good.'

'Yes, of course it is. We could manage, I agree.'

'If we got your mother out of that outrageously expensive care home it would help. I mean, does she really need to be in there?'

Roger went to refill her glass but Ellie put her hand over it. 'I've had enough,' she said and then added, 'Mum wasn't managing on her own in her Hadleigh home; you know that. And when it came to care homes, well, it had to be the best. I couldn't bear to see her unhappy or mistreated.'

'I agree, but Starling Skies has ludicrous fees. Surely there's something in between neglectful and five-star luxury living.'

'But Roger, it's her money that's paying for it as you well know. We sold number 12, Benton Street to pay for it.'

'Yes, but that's your inheritance that's rapidly draining away.'

'Well that's my choice. I'm not prepared to take the risk of moving her to somewhere I'm not happy with. Starling Skies comes with amazing reviews and an outstanding rating. I'm not settling for less.'

'Right, we'll just have to manage then. Anyway, I'm on the case, looking for a job so it's only a matter of time.'

Ellie bit her lip.

'Don't look at me like that.' Roger sprang up and started clearing their plates. 'I'm only sixty. Lots of people work well into their seventies these days.'

Ellie sat back in her chair with an ironic smile on her face. 'So, *you* should be working but *I* should be at home?'

He wandered back towards her, sheepish now.

'You have a point,' he said reasonably. 'It's just hard for me at the moment. All the employers on LinkedIn seem to want young and fresh-faced.'

'Young equals cheap.'

'Exactly and I'm never going to find a job to match my old salary but I need something to stop me going mad.'

Ellie couldn't see him being successful in his job hunt but she knew it was best to keep quiet and let him do what he had to do, to serve his ego.

'Look, if you really don't want me to take the job...' Why was she backing down? After all, it would be tricky as she'd told James that day that she would take it. 'But what's the point of us both being at home and at a loose end?' she added with appealing eyes.

'Yeah, you're right. You must take it. Perhaps ask if you can do it part time?' His expression lifted as Ellie's dropped.

'No, forget that. It's full time.'

'I'll just have to become a better cook, then.' He smiled and Ellie smiled back at him.

'It was tasty. Just the salmon was a bit overdone.'

'Yeah, probably all that time in the microwave on defrost didn't help. I was paranoid about giving you salmonella.'

'That's chicken! Not fish.'

'Of course it is.' He started to laugh and she joined in.

Chapter 4

'But Bryan and Carol are never late. It's usually us rushing up The Street to get here on time.'

Roger said nothing. His whole demeanour, since Ellie had reminded him about this evening out, was lukewarm.

'Don't you think?' She tried to catch his gaze. Was he in one of his retirement moods?

'I'm sure they'll be here soon.' He sipped his beer. Ellie had opted for a soft drink; she didn't want too much alcohol and they were bound to order wine with the meal. She looked at the door of The Dog and Duck for the umpteenth time and wished she had got a glass of wine.

The pub was filling up; Friday evenings were always popular. Everyone else seemed relaxed and happy while there was an unexplained tension at their table.

'I think I'll text Carol.' She looked at Roger half expecting some sort of affirmation but nothing came.

Hi Carol, We're here. Are you on your way?

'Is everything all right?' she asked Roger.

'Yes, everything's fine.' His voice had an edge to it; there was no reassurance at all.

'Is there something I don't know about?'

He had a strange disturbed look on his face. She knew he wasn't happy about the job with James Addington but he had been making an effort. He was always so pleased to see her when she got home from work and wanted her to talk about her day, just when she wanted to collapse in front of the telly.

Just then Bryan and Carol appeared. Carol looked flustered and was full of apologies. 'Bryan was home late. Our evening out had slipped his mind.' She had a faint look of alarm about her. Bryan had an unconvincing thin smile fixed to his face.

'Well, you're here now,' Ellie said hugging her friend. Bryan seemed rigid, not his usual self. Maybe they'd had a row.

'All right, mate?' Roger said uncertainly, shaking Bryan's hand.

'Fine, yes.'

'Let's order some wine now we're all here,' Ellie said in an attempt to lift the mood.

'Red or white? Shall I get a bottle of each?' Roger said perusing the wine list.

'Just a glass of red for me,' Bryan said as his wife flashed him an angry stare.

'I can't think why you insisted on us walking when you're only having one drink,' Carol said. Bryan didn't react which was somehow more chilling than if he had.

'Come on Bryan, we haven't seen you two together for ages; let's get two bottles and we'll see how we go.' Even Roger seemed to be trying to improve the ambiance.

'We'll leave it up to you, Roger. You're the expert when it comes to vino,' Carol said as she rooted around in her handbag. 'Damn,' she muttered.

'Forgotten your reading glasses?' Ellie asked.

'Not again,' Bryan added unhelpfully.

'I don't seem to be able to remember anything these days.'

'Here borrow mine. I've decided.' Ellie handed hers over.

Halfway through the meal, Ellie couldn't wait for this embarrassing fiasco to end. Making conversation was a laborious task. Bryan was giving monosyllabic answers to any questions and Carol looked close to tears.

'Any holiday plans?' Ellie asked hopefully.

'I fancy Croatia this year. I hear Split is very nice, not too touristy and less expensive than Italy,' Carol said.

'I like the sound of Split, too,' Roger agreed. 'Interesting wine region.'

'Maybe the four of us could go together?' Carol suggested feigning laughter as she looked at her husband's expression.

'There's a thought,' Ellie said thinking that if it was going to be anything like this, it would be a nightmare.

'What do you say, Bryan?' Roger gave him a friendly punch on the arm.

'I'm not sure if we're going on holiday this year,' Bryan said, the words catching in his throat.

'Since when?' Carol turned on him. 'I want to go on holiday even if you're a stay-at-home misery guts.'

There was an excruciating pause. Ellie's heart went out to Carol; she was convinced that tight-lipped Bryan was the villain of the peace.

'Carol tells me you've gone full time at James Addington?' Bryan asked shaking Ellie from her thoughts and surprising her with this sudden effort at conversation.

'Yes, yes, that's right.' They were all looking at her. 'I'm enjoying it, actually. It's very different to doing the odd viewing.' She watched her husband's face carefully as she spoke.

'She gets on very well with James, you know. James Addington. From the same stock they are,' Roger said failing to disguise the malice in his voice.

'Don't be ridiculous; it's got nothing to do with that.'

'Ooh, I don't know. I mean you got the job without so much as an interview.'

'But they know me already. I've been doing viewings for them for a couple of years,' Ellie protested.

'They always say it's not what you know but who.' Bryan had suddenly come to life.

'Too right. And them two both being descended from the upper classes,' Roger sneered, the chip on his shoulder almost visible.

'Not that again!' Ellie exclaimed. The waiter, a young girl who looked very unsure of herself, was hovering. Ellie caught her eye and smiled.

'Everything okay, shall I clear the plates?'

'Yes, lovely, thanks,' Ellie said thinking that her chicken had been quite tasty.

'Would you like the dessert menu?'

'Not for me,' Ellie was quick to reply and the general murmuring around the table was negative to her relief.

Carol was looking wistful. 'I suppose with you retired and Ellie going out to work full time it must feel like role reversal.'

Ellie flinched.

'It's fine,' Roger answered reaching for his wine glass and draining it. 'Actually, I've started cooking the evening meal.'

'You'll be donning an apron next,' Bryan said laughing at his own joke.

'Very funny. Actually, I'm making plans of my own for a new career. A brand-new adventure. After all, I'm still young...ish.'

Ellie raised her eyebrows. 'Oh yes? First I've heard.'

His expression back to her said *Shut up*.

'Don't tell me you're setting yourself up as a consultant.' Bryan sounded sure of himself.

'No, don't fancy that. You'll just have to wait and see.'

'Very mysterious,' Carol said.

'Shall we get the bill?' Ellie caught the eye of the waiter and was relieved to see her come quickly.

Out on the pavement Ellie knew that this was usually the point someone would say, *Come back to ours for coffee,* but there was no danger of that this evening. She hugged Carol hard and said into her ear, 'Ring me.' She couldn't extend the same warmth to Bryan.

'Maybe we should organise a girly weekend, just you and me,' Ellie said with a cheeky laugh. 'Maybe we'll go to Croatia!'

'Brilliant idea,' Carol said and looked brighter than she had all evening.

As they walked away Ellie linked arms with Roger and snuggled in to his side.

'So, what's this plan you've come up with? Sounds exciting.'

Roger laughed easily now. 'I haven't got a clue! I just know I need to do something or I'll go mad.'

'Oh, I see. But you're still looking on LinkedIn, are you?'

'Yes, I am but I must admit it's an exasperating pastime. I'm beginning to become paranoid about my age. They only have to say, "seeks energetic, dynamic individual" and I read that to mean about twenty-five.'

'Perhaps you should give up on the idea of going back into marketing. Think about something that's completely different.'

'Like what? And if I haven't got any experience then I'll be making the teas and sweeping the floor day one. I can't stand that level of humiliation.'

'Maybe you should advertise on the village shop notice board? You know, mature man seeks work, anything considered.' Ellie was amused by her own suggestion.

'Ha, ha, very funny. You know where that will lead; I'll have women after me thinking it's some sort of escort agency.'

'No! Don't be silly. I was thinking more DIY and gardening.'

'Both of which I am distinctly average at. No one's going to be paying me for that.'

They were both laughing as they went through the back door of Rose Cottage. Ellie waited until the kettle was on before she said, 'Do you know what's wrong with Bryan?'

Roger hesitated, avoiding her gaze.

'Come on, you can tell me. I won't say anything.'

'He's sworn me to secrecy.'

'But Roger it's so obvious that something's amiss. I mean did you enjoy this evening?'

'It was strained, I must admit.'

She went right up to him with appealing eyes. 'Tell me. For Carol's sake.'

Roger sighed. 'Bryan's having an affair.'

'Oh my God!'

'She's much younger than him. It's a mid-life crisis and a half but he doesn't see it that way.'

'You mean it's serious?'

'According to him she's the love of his life; his marriage to Carol has been dead for some time.'

'Bastard. Lying cheating bastard.' She tried to take on board the enormity of the situation. 'Carol doesn't know, does she?'

'No. And you mustn't tell her,' he said sternly.

'That's not fair.'

'It's not but it's their marriage and we shouldn't interfere.'

'Rubbish! He can't get away with this.'

'Okay! Okay. I'll tell Bryan he's got to tell her. But it must come from him.'

'You'd better.' Ellie was shaking with indignation. It was such a shock. She'd convinced herself they were just going through a bad patch. After all, a long marriage was full of challenges; she knew only too well. 'Tomorrow morning. Carol can't be humiliated any longer.'

'But when she knows. Then what? They've been married as long as us. She'll go to pieces.' Roger walked over to the kettle. 'Are we making this tea, or what?'

Ellie threw teabags into mugs and poured boiling water over them. 'Oh Roger, how awful. Poor Carol.'

Roger took her into his arms and held her. 'We'll do what we can to help Carol through it.'

Ellie lifted her face to his. 'Thank you,' she said and he kissed her.

The next morning Ellie was actually pleased to be going to work even though it was Saturday. Roger hadn't even bothered to tut at the idea; instead he had a worried look on his face. They both knew what the elephant in the room was but didn't refer to it.

James said a cheery hello to her when she got to the agency, even though he had a nervous-looking young couple sitting in front of his desk and he was pulling out house details from the filing cabinet. He laid them out on the desk.

'We've had an offer on this one already but it didn't quite meet the seller's expectations.'

The woman zoomed in on the pink cottage. 'That's lovely. Very pretty. Can we view this one, please?' She looked at her husband.

'It's a bit small. Where is it? Is it on a busy road?'

'Well, it's on Capel Hill. Busy...ish.'

The wife's face pleaded with him as if to say: don't destroy my dreams.

'Well, no harm in taking a look I suppose,' the husband conceded.

Ellie checked her emails and her diary and saw she had a viewing at nine-thirty arranged by Sarah, the office manager. After a wave of mild panic, she printed off the details of the property and seeing it was in Capel Green knew she could get there pretty quickly. She kept telling herself that she had to take this job more seriously now she was a bona-fide agent; they were putting their trust in her and she had to deliver. Gathering what she needed, she put on some lipstick, and stood up to leave. James caught her eye and came over to her.

'Off to view May Cottage, are you? The Swales.'

'Yes, that's right'

'They've been looking for a while. We're hoping this one ticks their boxes. I'm sure you'll work your magic.' He had a definite twinkle in his eye which was slightly disconcerting.

Ellie flashed him a cynical smile and made for the door.

She pulled up outside the Victorian terraced house for sale in the nick of time but not before the potential buyers unfortunately who were already stood on the drive. They had that resigned, exhausted look on their faces. She rushed over to them. 'Mr and Mrs Swale? Sorry I'm late,' she said wondering why, as she wasn't.

'No, no. We were early.' Mr Swale smiled warmly. Mrs Swale was potentially the stroppy one.

She took them through the front door into a small hallway and stepped quickly into the living room which she had already worked out was the biggest room downstairs. The dimensions of the kitchen had looked like they might disappoint in this day and age when a kitchen-dining room was essential for most.

'A bit small,' Mrs Swale said and Ellie felt doomed.

'But there's only the two of us,' Mr Swale argued.

'Original fireplace,' Ellie pointed out.

'And high ceilings,' Mr Swale added.

'I need to see the kitchen,' Mrs Swale said in a voice of authority.

Ellie let them lead the way and hung back to give the kitchen its best chance. She could see through the doorway that it looked very presentable with cream Shaker units and a lantern window in the flat roof at the front flooded it with light; it was actually quite an appealing space. Beyond it was a conservatory where the current owner had a dining table. Perhaps there was hope.

All eyes were on Mrs Swale awaiting her decision.

'Mm, not bad; quite nice, actually,' she conceded.

'It is, isn't it? Really light; I like that. And it looks like they eat in the conservatory.' Mr Swale was obviously viewing weary and keen to find *the one*.

'Hot in summer; cold in winter,' Mrs Swale said dismissively now.

'We could have an air conditioning unit put in.'

'You could,' Ellie agreed, 'and it already has underfloor heating.'

'I bet the bedrooms are small,' Mrs Swale said.

'Let's take a look,' Ellie said in upbeat fashion. She was the rise to Mrs Swale's fall. 'Actually, why don't you two go up on your own. I will wait here for you.'

She went back through to the conservatory and looked out on to the garden which was not a bad size and had some pretty borders. Her thoughts meandered back to the evening before. She had been adamant that Roger should force Bryan to tell Carol of his shocking betrayal. But now she wasn't so sure. It was bound to have a devastating effect on her friend. But then if the same was happening to her would she want to know? It was all so difficult.

The Swales appeared: him cheerful, her only mildly depressed. 'Would you like to see the garden?'

'Yes, we would,' Mr Swale said.

Mrs Swale actually showed an interest walking round the lawn peering into the borders. Perhaps she was a gardener?

'Is that the garage that comes with the property?' Mr Swale asked pointing to the end of the garden.

'Ah yes, it must be. A garage in Capel Green is quite a find.'

'Yes, I wouldn't like to have to park out on the busy high street.'

Mrs Swale appeared. Was that a vague smile on her face?

'Seen enough?' Ellie asked.

'I think so,' Mr Swale dared as he looked for clues of hope in his wife's expression.

Ellie knew that now she was duty bound to ask the inevitable question: 'So what are your thoughts? Would you be interested in putting in an offer?'

Mrs Swale looked affronted.

'We need a bit of time to think about it but it certainly ticks a lot of boxes,' Mr Swale said.

'Great. Are you looking at any other properties?'

'No. We've looked at quite a few over the months but nothing's been quite right.' Mr Swale flashed her a knowing look.

'Well here's my card, should you have any questions.'

Mrs Swale sighed deeply as if the whole process was something terrible to be endured. But then she said, 'I suppose this will have to do,' her eyes circling in some sort of crazed expression.

Following that Ellie was pleased to have two good-humoured families to show round a small cottage in Gem

Corner; one at ten-thirty, the other at eleven. It was such a beautiful village, making property very expensive, and had buyers trying to work out how they could possibly live in very small spaces. The words sofa bed, bunk beds and IKEA storage often featured. At the end of the viewing they were still scratching their heads.

Viewings over she went back into the agency, but only because James had insisted on it; she was allowed to go home at lunchtime some Saturdays if she didn't have any viewings. It would have made life easier to go straight back to Roger. She felt his pull whenever she was at work since he'd retired.

'Well here I am. Do you need me?' There were no clients in at that moment aiding her in making her point.

'Sit down, Ellie.'

'Sounds ominous.'

'Really, I just want to find out how you're getting on?' he asked with overtones of protesting innocence. 'Oh, and the Swales called for you about half an hour ago.'

'I should call them back.'

'Did it look like they were going to bite?'

'Difficult to say. I think they've just had enough.'

James looked confused. 'Okay, well give them a call and then I'm taking you out for lunch at the bistro, at The Swan.'

'No need, really.'

'I do with all new agents so make your call and we can go.'

'What about manning the fort?'

Just then Sandra walked in. James didn't say anything; just looked really pleased with himself.

Ellie was relieved to see that The Swan was busy and mainly with innocent family get-togethers. All with well-behaved children; that was the middle classes for you. They were sat right in the centre of the restaurant.

'Not the best table,' James complained to the waiter.

'Sorry, sir, we're fully booked.' A raise of the eyebrows by James prompted the waiter to add, 'There are tables in The Gallery restaurant.'

'No! No, this is fine,' Ellie said quickly sitting down and making herself comfortable. She had only eaten in The Gallery once and it was a very formal, five-course affair. Absolutely what she didn't want now.

James sat down. 'Champagne?' he asked.

'Goodness no. I don't drink at lunchtimes normally.'

'Make an exception. Let me buy you a glass of Champagne, Ellie. Please?'

Was she being priggish? 'Oh, if we must; I suppose I did receive my first offer as an agent this morning.'

'The Swales?' He looked genuinely excited.

'Yes, that's right. The asking price too.'

'That's fantastic. Has the owner accepted?'

'Yes, I got through straightaway; I told them they are unlikely to get a better offer.'

'I knew it! You're a natural.' He beamed at her and she couldn't help feeling very pleased with herself. Then she thought that perhaps she was overreacting and she should be more professional so she quickly turned to the menu.

James started talking about the bigger picture for the agency whilst Ellie was trying to second guess what all this was really about. He was going on about how they needed to offer a top-notch service to compete with the online offerings.

'Yes,' Ellie agreed, 'we do charge a lot more.'

'But it's a very different service; I mean the client does everything themselves pretty much, online. But I was thinking we could do more on the social side; you know afternoon tea and a review of the property market, that sort of thing.'

'Interesting. Do you think our clients would like that?'

'Anything with a free drink involved. It's a way of connecting with them, making them feel special.'

'Well it's worth a try.'

'Good, I'm glad you think so. I suggested it to Peter the other day and he looked at me like I wanted to open up a branch on Mars. That's what I like about you, Ellie; you are open to new ideas. We need that kind of enthusiasm.'

Ellie didn't quite know how to respond. She saw herself very much as a late-in-life chancer and certainly lacked the ambition for any kind of dynamic career. Making a bit of extra money was simply a bonus. 'I'm happy to do what I can but you know I don't have any great aspirations, James.'

'Ah! Well, you put yourself down. I see talent and potential; a woman in her prime.' He laughed, thank goodness, at that point.

'Really James, I'm very flattered but...' But what? But she had a husband at home who resented her doing well while he languished in an uneasy state. 'I don't know, I...'

'You underestimate yourself.'

'The thing is, James, as you know Roger's retired now and so...'

'So you feel you have to join him?'

'Not exactly.' He had a point. 'I love this job actually. I like getting out of the house and the new challenge of it all.'

James looked thoughtful. 'I've not met Roger but I'm sure he's man enough to see his wife do well.'

Ellie found it hard to agree with that.

'Look, how about the three of us having a spot of supper one evening. Perhaps if he gets to know me a little better, he might feel differently.'

Ellie considered that the absolute opposite was probably true. 'What about your wife? Wouldn't it be better with the four of us?'

James looked down into his lap and then up again with an air of resignation. 'Mrs Addington has left me. Ghastly business; ran off with the gardener.' His expression remained stoic.

'Oh gosh, that's appalling. I'm sorry to hear that.'

'Probably says more about me,' he said and it was the first time she'd seen him looking vulnerable.

'It's hard. Marriage.' Why did she say that?

James looked longingly at her from across the table and Ellie thought perhaps she'd given the wrong impression.

'Roger and I do very well at it, though, most of the time.'
Why did she have to be so honest?

'So, I'm afraid it's just the three of us, unless I rustle up a plus one.'

Ellie feared the worst. 'Why don't you leave the idea with me and I'll broach it with Roger.'

'If you must.'

Help, Ellie thought to herself and forced a smile. Hopefully he would forget about the idea.

Ellie slipped into the house feeling a little guilty and was surprised to hear voices coming from the kitchen. She burst in. 'So sorry I'm late...' There was Carol sat at the breakfast bar clutching an empty tea mug as if her dear life depended on it, her face red and blotchy.

'Oh Carol.' She rushed to her and gave her a hug.

'You knew, didn't you,' she said bitterly, beginning to cry.

'No! No, I didn't. Not until last night. After we got back. I mean only when I forced Roger to tell me.'

Carol sat rigid, fragile. 'I know. I know it's not your fault that I've got a pathetic excuse of a husband.'

'I thought you'd be back earlier,' Roger said in a disillusioned tone.

'Yes, I know. I'm so sorry. James insisted on this lunch thing. I did text you.'

'So, what was it all about?'

Carol sniffed. 'Do you want me to go?'

'No, don't be silly.' Ellie stayed near Carol's side. Her husband was still looking at her. 'Something and nothing. I'll tell you later.'

'What's that supposed to mean? Did he proposition you?'

'No! You're being ridiculous. It was about the estate agency.'

'You know his wife left him.' Carol helped herself to another tissue and blew her nose.

'What?' Roger looked worried. 'No, I didn't know that. Never actually met the guy although I've seen his photo in the local press. Looks like an upper-class twit. Probably why he fancies my wife. You know there's a lot of inbreeding amongst the upper classes. Ellie threw out the rule book when she married me.'

'Oh, for goodness sake! Put away that chip on your shoulder and start talking some sense. Poor Carol has a marriage in tatters and all you can do is have a dig at James Addington.'

'You're right. I'm sorry. I'm sorry, Carol. Listen why don't you two go and sit in the garden room and I'll bring you a drink. Perhaps something a little stronger than a cup of tea? How about a glass of wine?'

'Just a small one for me,' Ellie said as she put an arm around Carol and led her away.

When they were sat side by side on the sofa Ellie said, 'So, tell me...' and Carol burst into tears. Eventually she summoned up enough strength to give her version of what Bryan had said to her.

'He's such a selfish bastard. Thirty-five years we've been married. Thirty-five years of washing his stupid boxers; trying to come up with something interesting to cook every evening only for him to say "It's lovely, love," like he's totally underwhelmed by my efforts; putting up with him cutting his revolting toenails in the bath. Never once have I complained. I knew. I knew something was up. I said to you, didn't I? The other day about the coving and him being out all the time.'

'I'm so sorry, Carol. I just didn't think it would be anything like this.'

'He had the audacity to stand there and say, "*I'm sorry, Carol, our marriage is over. I've met someone and I'm in love. I feel alive for the first time in many years.*" Can you believe it?'

'What an appalling thing to say. He's hardly God's gift to women.'

'Exactly! But he seems to think he is! This Tiffany woman is a personal trainer at the Hadleigh gym and she's much younger than him. What on earth does she see in him?'

'Money, I expect; perhaps she needs some sort of father figure in her life; it's hard to say but it does happen doesn't it?'

'What? Being traded in for a younger model?' Carol was angry now.

'Listen.' Ellie turned to face her friend and looked at her earnestly, 'Bryan is an idiot. You are a lovely person and you've been an amazing friend over the years.' She pulled her close.

Roger appeared hesitating at the French doors. Ellie nodded to him and he put a tray in front of them with two glasses and a bottle of wine in a cooler.

'It's your favourite, Carol, Chilean Sauvignon Blanc.' He poured for them. 'Sorry about earlier; I was being a bit of an arse.'

They both looked up at him but didn't say anything and he retreated back to the kitchen.

'Here's to us.' Ellie raised her glass. Carol took a large glug of wine. 'We're here for you, okay? You can stay here for a while, if you like? Until you sort yourself out.'

'He should be the one thrown out of his home!'

'Quite right.' Ellie considered what Bryan might do. 'Do you think he'll move in with this Tiffany woman? I can't see it lasting; I really can't. He's such a fool.'

'He's even been on some stupid fitness craze trying to lose weight.'

'Trying to keep up with her, no doubt.'

Carol sighed deeply. 'Oh, Ellie, what am I going to do with the rest of my life?'

'You're going to have a bloody good time. You're going to create a new life for yourself. You can't be destroyed by him and give up.'

Carol looked at her somewhat surprised. 'Do you think so? Do you really think so?'

'I do. You've got a lot going for you. James said today that I'm a woman in my prime!' She giggled in disbelief.

'He does fancy you then.'

'No! No, he doesn't. Well, maybe he does. I mean I must admit I had no idea his wife had left him. He has this way of covertly insisting on things, and before you know it, you're sat in the bistro with him having lunch and drinking Champagne.'

'You had Champagne with him?'

'I didn't want it. Although having said that, it was rather nice.'

'So, what did he want?'

'He was just talking about the agency and some ideas he's got; getting clients in giving them afternoon tea and talking to them about the property market. I went along with it but I thought it was all a bit far-fetched. What do I know? I'm the newbie.'

'What I don't understand is why you feel the need to go out to work; is it because Roger isn't working now and you need the money?'

'It's nice to know that there's going to be a bit more coming in actually but, if I'm honest, it's more about doing something for myself. Roger's been quite difficult to live with recently and it helps me to get out of the house.'

'Perhaps that's what I should have done. Been a bit more selfish; done things just for me. Maybe he would have respected me more, if I had done that.'

'Hey, you can't turn the clock back. You did what was right for you at the time. Anyway, you had your career in teaching; you made an excellent teacher; I was always really impressed with how you handled things, you know, difficult children, awful headteachers, Ofsted inspections; they were a nightmare.'

'Yes, I did really enjoy it. Of course, I took time off to have the children...'

'But you went back as soon as Megan was at school.'

'Yes, I did. I miss it actually.'

'Listen, why don't you stay for dinner? I'm sure we can rustle something up. And if not, I'll send Roger out to the village shop. What do you say?'

Carol sniffed and managed a smile. 'Thank you, yes, I'd like that.'

Ellie held her friend's hand between both of hers. 'You'll get through this. I know you will.'

Carol sighed and tears filled her eyes. 'You know the awful thing is, that, despite everything, I think I would have him back.'

'I know. It's going to take time; it's all so raw at the moment. Such a shock. I mean you've been married for a long time.'

'I was so looking forward to our retirement years. I just can't believe I'm facing life alone now. You said it will never last with Tiffany. But maybe it will.'

'I think you just have to take one day at a time.' She topped up both glasses and handed Carol's to her. 'Starting now,' she said clunking her glass.

Chapter 5

Bryan was pleased it was his day for volunteering at the Guildhall in Capel Green. Tiffany was doing a shift at the gym and he felt a bit strange being in her flat on his own. Her response when he told her that Carol had thrown him out and he needed somewhere to live was lukewarm at first, to say the least. He quickly added that it would only be for a few days but had no idea where he'd go from there. In his dreams this moment was very different to the reality. He had somehow imagined that Carol would go and stay with a friend or maybe one of their daughters and leave him the house.

But Carol had taken the news very badly. He had assumed that she was aware that their marriage had gone stale and thought she might have been reasonable about it. After all, lots of couples split up. It was awful seeing the shock in her face, the tears in her eyes. Worse still was the anger she threw at him. He had never seen her like that before: shaking with outrage, screaming at him almost to get out.

He needed Tiffany to have some sympathy; to reassure him that he'd done the right thing. She had said, yes, he could stay with her but there was a reticence about it. How could she! After all the times they had been together and she had complained if only he would leave his wife.

By the time he reached her front door and she let him in to her domain, with his holdall of rapidly grabbed clothes, she seemed to have warmed to the whole idea. She was even keen for them to go out and celebrate and they went off to a very nice restaurant on the outskirts of town for a romantic meal which of course he had paid for. But then she didn't earn much and he was happy to foot the bill for her to have a more exciting lifestyle.

So now he was happily shacked up with a beautiful woman, half his age. He must be the envy of all his friends, surely? He'd left a world of mundane retirement and entered a younger place which was more vibrant, more fun.

A group of American tourists were making their way through the Guildhall. One of his colleagues was giving them the history spiel, telling them all about the mixed fortunes of the building from its height, when wool merchants became very wealthy through their trade, to the low of it becoming a jail with the gruesome tales that accompanied that era. Bryan simply stood to one side, ensuring the precious artefacts were not touched whilst smiling benignly and remembering how wonderful Tiffany had been in bed last night.

Roger decided to cut the grass. It was a dry August day and there was rain forecast for tomorrow. He had ended up doing some gardening the other day and he remembered feeling better for it somehow. It took him a good fifteen minutes just to find the extension lead for the electric mower and then he wondered if he'd be able to do the bottom section of the lawn near the river. How did Ellie do it? He couldn't phone her as she was at the agency and that had all become a bit serious recently. She'd even brought work home with her last night.

'What are you doing now?' he'd asked, when she logged on to her laptop at the dining table.

'I need to read up on a few things to do with the process of clients making offers on properties.'

'Now? At this time of the evening?'

She had looked at him as if he was overreacting and simply said, 'Yes, now.' She didn't match his raised voice.

Once the lawn mower was plugged in and he was striding over the grass, and there was even a little warmth in the sun, he felt better. This morning's search for updates on LinkedIn for a suitable job had been depressing yet again. The most he ever got was a glimmer of hope. Any jobs he decided were worth applying for, he did so with an unease he couldn't shake off. On reaching the end of the online application process he felt more deflated than hopeful. He couldn't help being painfully aware of his own age as he read the job specs which somehow implied they were looking for youngsters without breaking the ageist rule.

Now, the hypnotic effect of toing and froing across the lawn, occasionally stopping to empty the grass collector, was a comfort to him and he was able to pretend that all was well with the world. Perhaps he should become a gardener? But then he wasn't particularly good at growing plants; Ellie had the upper hand there. And if he did offer his services, he would likely be competing against a number of smart alecs with gardening qualifications aplenty.

He was about three metres from the riverbank when his cord ran out. He was pleased, in a way, that he'd managed to predict this outcome but at the same time he was baffled as to how Ellie managed it. He went back into the house and decided to ring her mobile. It went straight to voicemail and he left a garbled message. He decided to ring the agency direct. Surely a man can ring his wife when she's at work?

There was an answer after two rings.

'James Addington speaking.' He sounded as pompous as Roger imagined him to be.

'Hello James, Roger here, Ellie's husband.'

'Hello Roger, how can I help you?' He sounded genuinely pleased to hear from him. Was he about to mock his lowly existence, his fall from grace?

'I don't suppose Ellie is there?'

'I'm afraid not. Out on viewings. Can I give her a message? Is it urgent?'

'Not really. I've just cut the grass and the extension lead won't reach as far as the river so I'm just wondering how I do the last three metres.'

'I see. How frustrating.' Was he mocking him? 'Do you have another extension lead you could use to add to the length?'

That was a horribly good idea. 'No! No, we don't have another one.' They might have but it had taken him long enough to find the first one.

'I have a gardener chap, Raymond his name is, would you like his number?'

Roger was struck dumb for a second but quickly decided he didn't want to come across as the sort of chap who couldn't afford a gardener. 'Yes, please, that would be helpful.' He lied. 'Then I would have more time for…' He was going to say job hunting but thought better of it. 'Other stuff.'

'Yes, indeed.' There was a disconcerting pause before James added, 'I hear Capel Green Farm are looking for people. Casual work possibly but maybe more.'

How dare he! 'I'm looking for something managerial actually.'

'Of course. They do have quite a nifty operation down there, might be worth a look.'

'Thanks,' Roger said dismissing the idea as his ego received yet another blow.

Carol hated being home alone all the time. The day seemed so empty and time dragged endlessly. Even though Bryan had been going out a lot in recent months, knowing what time he'd be back was enough to put her mind at ease and for her to potter her way through the day. She realised all the things she'd occupied herself with in the past were Bryan related. Cleaning, laundry, ironing, baking cakes, finding recipes to try and please him with, tidying up, making him coffee, talking about the girls and how they were getting on.

Now it was just her. It was such a shock to find herself suddenly facing a future alone. Had she been delusional expecting to grow old with her husband? Separation, divorce even, was what happened to other people. And you would always feel sorry for them, but there was a benign acceptance that these things happen rather than a deeper understanding of the devastation it caused.

Would this ridiculous relationship that Bryan had started actually last? He seemed so sure that he was destined to be with *her*. And the girls, their two precious daughters, what would they make of it all, now that they were from a broken home? The thought of telling them was unbearable.

Would she have him back? If he was truly sorry for what he'd done and she could somehow trust him again, would she let him back in? It pained her to admit she probably would. She would find it in her heart to forgive him for the sake of her marriage and for Rebecca and Megan.

She kept the radio on more to break the silence than anything else and found herself listening to *Woman's Hour* a lot. They featured a woman in her seventies who decided she didn't want to live with her husband any more and divorced him. She said that he had become boring and didn't want to do anything, while she wanted to live life to the full and travel the world. Carol considered that description fitted Bryan very well; at least the Bryan she thought she knew; he was predictable, grumpy and moaned every time she suggested a holiday. And she realised now that when she had wanted them to go to Croatia together, or wherever, she was really looking to rekindle the romance in their marriage that had somehow dwindled. But, of course, she now knew his version of new and exciting was Tiffany.

Carol boiled the kettle to make yet another cup of coffee. She probably wouldn't even drink it. Perhaps *she* was boring? She didn't have any exciting hobbies; she'd always put the children first. She had selflessly worked for the good of all others, rarely with a thought for what she wanted out of life. She might go for a girly lunch, on a day when Bryan was out anyway so he wouldn't have to make his own meal, and she'd still feel slightly guilty. She could remember many times when one of her daughters would interrupt her 'me time,' calling her on her mobile with something that demanded her immediate attention. Her eyes would roll, but still she would suffer the call.

Yes, she had put her own needs last for far too long and look where it had got her? Sad and lonely and wondering what on earth she was going to do with the rest of her life.

Chapter 6

Kathleen looked out through her French doors and across the vast lawn. The sun was strong, just a few white fluffy clouds. Everything was still, not a soul in sight. She particularly liked the symmetry of the oak tree in the distance just to the right of her vision. It was bright green which lifted her spirits. She tried the French door which would free her in to the garden but it was locked. Why couldn't she get out?

There was a knock at the door and Emily walked in. This one always hesitated and said, 'All right if I come in, Kathleen?' Some of them just barged in. Hopeless. Sometimes she didn't even know who they were.

'Who are you?' she'd ask.

And they would say 'Daisy' or some such name and Kathleen would look at them and decide whether or not she liked them.

'Time for your meds,' Emily said now. Kathleen sat down in her armchair reluctantly and Emily put a tray on her lap. She stood there watching her while she gulped them down with a glass of water. She always pulled a face as she took them.

'Well done, Kathleen.'

'Oh, for goodness sake, I'm eighty, not eight.'

'Actually, you're eighty-five.'

'Pedantic.'

Emily was about to leave.

'May I go out, please? It is a lovely day.'

Emily didn't actually groan but she might as well have. 'I'll have to get someone to take you.'

'Yes, you will.' Kathleen looked straight at her with a cynical smile. 'Soon. Please!' she shouted as Emily closed the door behind her.

She must have dozed off. She was sure the pills they gave her made you sleepy. They probably had something in them that reduced you into a state of submission. They'd turn you into a zombie if they could. Maybe she wouldn't take them any more.

Ellie sat on the bed and waited for her mother to wake up. Kathleen's eyes opened gently but then she was startled by her daughter's presence. 'I didn't know you were coming.'

'They said you were asleep when I rang so I just came anyway.'

'Yes, not much chance of me being out.' She looked around her as if trying to figure something out. 'How did they know I was asleep? I was awake when Emily came.'

'They probably put their head round the door.'

'They probably have hidden cameras.' Her head darted from side to side, her eyes wide with shock.

'Don't be silly, Mum.'

'Is it Sunday?'

'Yes, I'm working full time now; I get Sundays off as well as a day in the week.'

'Do you need the money, dear? Why don't you have my money? I can't spend much in here.'

Ellie laughed. 'The fees for this place are eye-watering, Mum. You know that.'

'Well get me out then. It's one up from prison.'

'Mum, this is a luxury nursing home; it was the best we could find for you. Look at this room, it's delightful! Plasma screen; large comfortable bed; you've got some of your things from home with you; an emergency button round your neck and you're waited on hand and foot. These ground floor rooms are considered the best by far; you were lucky to get one. And such a lovely view.' She waved her arm across the French windows.

'But I can't get outside; I can't make myself a drink; I have to wait until four o'clock before I am allowed a cup of tea... and a cake if I want to be the size of Deirdre, two doors down.'

Ellie was laughing. 'Mum, I'm going to take you out now. They've given me the key to the French door and the code so I can turn the alarm off.'

'Write it down! Quick! Write it down for me.'

'No. I'll get into trouble.'

'Spoilsport.'

'It took a lot of persuading, let me tell you. I had to sign some disclaimer form.'

'Probably giving them the right to poison me with their drugs.'

It was so difficult to know if the home were mistreating her mother or if Kathleen was beginning to lose her marbles and Ellie strongly suspected the latter. 'What makes you think that?'

Kathleen wouldn't look her daughter in the eye. 'The pills; they make me sleepy.'

'That's old age.'

She sniffed turning her head.

'Okay I'll ask them about the drugs they give you for your arthritis.'

Kathleen had a look of longing about her as she stared out. She leaned forward and whispered, 'What are we waiting for? Let's make our escape while no one's looking.' Suddenly her eyes were bright.

Ellie hugged her mother, 'I do love you, Mum,' she said before entering the code for the alarm and letting them out through the door. She put the key carefully back in her handbag. Kathleen inhaled the summer air deeply.

'At last,' she said triumphantly. 'Freedom.'

'Such a perfect day.' There was a gentle breeze to give some relief from the heat of the sun.

'Ooh, look! Over there.' Kathleen was pointing to some of the other residents. 'It's Larry. I like Larry. He makes me laugh.'

'Shall we go over there?'

Kathleen started running her fingers through her soft white hair, pinching her cheeks. 'Stop a minute. How do I look?'

'Yes, you look fine. As you always do.'

'Fine, huh!' She threw back her head, unimpressed. 'Never mind. I must get my hair done more often at the salon.'

'I'll do your hair for you if you like.'

'No, you're too busy working.'

'Mum, I'm here now. I do my best to get over here.'

Kathleen wasn't listening. Her eyes were fixed on Larry as she made a beeline for him.

'He's chatting up Dorothy! Outrageous. She never says no to a cake.'

'I'm quite intrigued to meet this Larry gentleman myself now.'

'Good afternoon, ladies,' the smartly attired man said as he rose somewhat shakily from his chair. He wore a tweed jacket and canary yellow cravat, his hair silver and long enough to catch the breeze; he looked straight at Ellie.

'Afternoon,' Kathleen replied doing her best to look aloof.

'We're having our tea out here. Would you care to join us?' Dorothy dared to suggest.

'That would be lovely,' Ellie said before Kathleen could object.

They sat there, Ellie joining in the polite conversation and Kathleen in silent protest pushing away the cake she'd been given. When she got the opportunity, Ellie asked Larry, 'Do you like it here at Starling Skies?'

'It's not bad. Beats living on my own. I was all right for a few years after my Elsie died, but then one day I had a fall and couldn't get up. Turned out I'd broken my hip.'

'Sounds painful.'

'It was, but a spell in hospital put me right.' He looked wistful. 'And then I did go home but my son, Graham, had already suggested that perhaps I'd be better off in a home. A decent one, of course. You see I've got osteoporosis and I have to be careful.' He leant towards Ellie and lowered his voice, 'I used to enjoy the odd ciggie.' He chuckled to himself. 'Anyway they look after me here; can't complain.'

Ellie smiled at him. She liked Larry.

Kathleen looked across to her oak tree. This was a very pretty garden and the weather was just right for sitting out. But Dorothy could be a very annoying character. So full of herself.

Larry got up and came and sat next to her at the end of the table. 'Good to see you,' he said trying to catch her gaze. She turned and eyed him suspiciously.

'Yes, well they don't let me outside very much.'

Larry laughed. 'Nothing to stop you pootling along to the lounge every now and then. I'm often in there, happy for company.'

She said nothing.

'There's a music quiz this evening, name that tune; would you like to join my team?'

Kathleen loved music. She was tempted.

'Lonnie Donegan, Cliff Richard and The Shadows...' He had that faraway look.

'They don't make music like they used to,' they chorused together.

'So you will?' His expression was all expectation.

'Yes, I'd like that.' She decided that if Dorothy was in the same team, she would simply show her up.

Larry looked amused. 'She's lovely, your daughter, isn't she? She seems to visit a lot.'

'She's working full time, including Saturdays.' She rolled her eyes in disbelief.

'Well good for her,' Larry said.

Kathleen leant in and said quietly, 'Roger, her husband, has lost his job. He always did have an inflated opinion of himself.'

'Poor chap. What does he do now?'

'Nothing, as far as I know. He could put in an appearance here every now and then, couldn't he?'

'I hope he does. I'd like to meet him.'

'Don't get too excited.'

'Oh Kathleen, you do amuse me. Such a feisty girl.'

She blushed and decided if Larry wanted to refer to her as a feisty girl, that was all right by her.

'Larry, would you like to go for a walk with me around the grounds?' Dorothy shouted across the table, clearly vying for his attention.

'I'm quite happy here actually.'

Kathleen flashed a smug smile at Dorothy.

The first swipe at the golf ball proved very satisfying. Roger hit it cleanly and watched it head right into the centre of the net in the distance. What a beauty. It was pity that it was a practice shot and not his first attempt on the course proper. Especially as they were playing the Heath today; not for the faint-hearted. But the other course here was only nine holes and considered very much for beginners. Roger had the necessary handicap to tackle the trickier course and he had played it a few times before. So, when he'd got a call from Stuart Adams the other day, inviting him to this golfing event, he didn't hesitate to say yes. It was surely going to be an opportunity to network in his old familiar circle of the financial services world with people who valued his experience. Maybe Stuart himself was interested in him now that he was very much available for work. It was certainly going to be a day which was much more in his comfort zone than his disheartening, faceless search for some sort of respectable job on LinkedIn.

Roger looked at his watch and decided to head into the club house where they were all meeting. The first face he noticed was very familiar.

'Grant, mate! Good to see you.'

'Roger, how's it going?'

Why was he embarrassed? He decided not to bring up his sharp exit from EAI. 'I didn't know you played golf.'

'Well, actually, I don't particularly. Going to be winging it today I think.'

'Interesting. You do know you have to have a bona-fide handicap for the Heath.'

'It was mentioned but then they said not to worry; they would take care of it.'

Roger couldn't help laughing. He liked Grant but surely he was about to make a massive fool of himself.

'Well, good luck with that.'

'Roger.' Stuart bounded up to them looking ridiculous in some yellow argyle trousers and a navy-blue tank top.

'Mr Adams, it's a pleasure.' They shook hands heartily.

'Makes a change being on the same team!' he jested.

'And how are things at Zurich?' Roger asked.

'Excellent. Marvellous. Well, at least we're holding our own and in this over competitive market full of start-ups and online comparison sites that's all you can hope for.'

'Good for you,' Roger said patting him on the back and as he did so his eyes fell on the back of a greasy barnet; surely his nemesis, the jumped-up Dean, was not here too? What was this, a free-for-all, regardless of any golfing ability? The man turned and there he was, in all his tight-fitting trouser glory, and having the audacity to wave and smile at Roger. As if that wasn't bad enough, Melissa was at his side looking very cosy and comfortable. She definitely couldn't play golf.

'Interesting group of people you've gathered today,' Roger said to Stuart as he waved a feeble hand across the room.

'Ah, yes, quite a few youngsters, the future generation; we cannot overlook them.'

'And do they all have the required handicap for the Heath?' Roger simply had to ask.

'Well, in fact, not exactly.'

It occurred to Roger at that moment that this day could prove very entertaining.

'So that's why a few of us are doing the nine-holer,' Stuart explained, 'whilst those more accomplished like your good self will tackle the harder course.'

How disappointing.

Teeing off at the first hole Roger felt quietly confident, despite his handicap being a little higher than most of the seven strong group. Stuart was the only one trying to make up in attire what he lacked in ability.

Roger struck the ball neatly and, although a sudden gust of wind sent his ball off to the left, overall it wasn't a bad shot and it was met with grunts of approval.

By the third hole, Roger had worked out that Tom, or Tiger Tom as he thought of him, was the man to beat. He was a smarty pants with sharp creases in his trousers and a polo shirt and looked as cool as a cucumber despite the August temperature. At this stage he was already one under par.

Roger sized up the fourth hole and decided whatever he did he needed to avoid the large pond strategically placed to the left of the hole. He licked his forefinger and held it up; the wind wasn't doing him any favours. He would over aim to the right to compensate. His tee shot wasn't bad but his second shot had him in the rough. As he lined up for his third shot, to get himself out of trouble, he told himself to keep calm and took a deep breath. Tiger Tom appeared by his side. Surely, he wasn't in the rough too?

'Do you want to borrow my pitching wedge?' he asked offering the iron.

Roger had selected a nine iron which was what he would usually use in this situation. Why was his opponent helping him out?

'Up to you, of course,' Tom said.

'Thanks, yes, I'll give it a go.' If only Tom was not watching him. Focus, he told himself, did some practice swings and whack. Miraculously it was on the green.

'Brilliant!' he shouted with relief.

'Good shot.' Tom was nodding at him.

Roger gave him his iron back. 'Thanks mate.'

Back in the club house they all had a drink before the scores were announced. Roger was pleased to come a respectable second but spluttered his beer when Stuart was declared the winner of the elite group.

For the other group a chap Roger didn't know was considered the winner and there was lots of merriment and chortling amongst them as it was announced. Roger found himself near Dean and Melissa and took the opportunity to ask how they had got on.

'Bit embarrassing actually,' Melissa said. 'I don't think golfing is my forte.'

'Is it your first time playing?' Roger asked.

'I've played a bit,' Dean said.

'It didn't help though,' Melissa sniggered.

'Yes, not my best result.'

'He came last,' Melissa leant over to say.

'Oh, well, experience is everything,' Roger took relish in pointing out.

As he drove home, he considered that he'd enjoyed the outing but sadly there had been very little in the way of job offers. He'd even probed Stuart at one point, despite the fact that it was so obviously an embarrassing recognition of his fall from grace.

'Any jobs going at your place?' he'd asked plain and simple.

'Sorry mate, we're cutting back if anything.'

Roger was convinced that was code for we're only taking on youngsters.

'I hear AXA are recruiting. Tom Sterling is your man. I think it's the health side of things, though.'

Roger hated the fact that he was desperate enough to approach Tom. The man had lent him a pitching wedge; who knows?

'Yes, we are. You looking?' Tom asked. Had he not heard that Roger had been pushed out? Perhaps Tom considered that Roger might be content to accept the retired life. He handed Roger his business card. 'Send me your CV and I'll get it to the right people and put in a good word.'

'Thanks mate. I appreciate that.' It was a crumb of hope in a sea of despair.

Carol could see that her daughter, Rebecca, was calling her mobile but she wasn't sure if she could face answering it. The ringing ended and seconds later a text flashed up.

Mum! Call me!

She always was impatient.

Carol had discussed with Bryan how they would tell the girls on the day it all happened; the day her life had fallen apart. He seemed to think that some elaborate scheme where they got both Rebecca and Megan to come home for the weekend at the same time, so that they could tell them together, was a good idea. But, as Carol pointed out, that could take weeks to engineer at the very least. Looking distinctly put out, he had said that he would have to do it face to face because that was only right.

How could any of this be right?

She couldn't believe how cold he was about the whole thing; how he stood there looking slightly bemused, scratching his head when she suggested that he left.

'Can't you stay with Roger and Ellie for a few days while I sort something out,' he'd had the audacity to suggest.

'Why should I be the one who has to leave our lovely home? You're the marriage wrecker, you go.'

Admittedly he had looked a little worried at that point. He'd picked up his mobile and went outside into the garden, no doubt to call his floozy. It was all so upsetting.

Looking at the missed call on her mobile now, she was pretty sure that he hadn't already done the deed; it had only been a matter of days. Her mobile was ringing yet again; she couldn't avoid her daughter forever. She would have to answer it.

'Hello Rebecca,' she said trying to lift her voice and take away the note of despair.

'Mum, at last. Where are you?'

'I'm at home, darling.'

'Is the signal poor there today? I'm trying to ring you from work. It's not easy. I haven't really got time for this.'

'I was in the garden,' she lied. 'How are you?'

'Fine, but I've had a call from Dad. He says he needs to meet me quite soon. He's even talking about coming down to London in the next few days. What on earth is so important and so urgent?'

Carol braced herself. She really didn't want to cry. 'It's up to him to tell you.'

'Oh my God, Mum. Something terrible has happened, hasn't it?'

'As I said, he wants to tell you himself in person.' Her voice was faltering now.

'What? Not that you're getting divorced? Surely? Why on earth, when you have a perfectly good marriage, do you want to get divorced at *your* age?'

Carol flinched and then shed silent tears. She often felt slightly battered by Rebecca's phone calls but this was off the scale.

'Is he there?' Rebecca was asking. 'Is he there, now? Can I speak to him, please?'

'No,' Carol managed to say with certainty. 'No, he's not here. You'll have to phone his mobile.'

'What, so he's moved out already?'

'I have to go now,' Carol said firmly. 'I'm sorry but I really have to go.' She ended the call. She'd never done that to her daughter before. She always gave them both all the time they wanted even if it wasn't convenient. She would agree to anything when they asked for help. Nothing was ever too much trouble. But now she felt torn apart, wretched and tired; she was getting little sleep. She couldn't quite believe that she had reached this point in her life.

She tried to get through the day in some sort of normal fashion but it was no good. She found Ellie's number and pressed call.

'Carol, how are you my darling?'

'I can't do this,' she answered meekly.

'I'm coming round,' Ellie said without hesitation. 'I'll be there in ten minutes. Hang on in there, darling.'

'Thank you.'

As soon as she arrived Carol fell into her arms and Ellie held her tight.

Chapter 7

Ben wandered into the kitchen holding two paintbrushes in the air and headed for the sink which was full of dirty dishes left to soak. It was a large square room with a high ceiling, a big sash window letting in lots of light, shabby units and barely an uncluttered surface to be seen. He began to wash the paint from the sable bristles under the cold tap, turning the murky water bright green, then yellow, settling into turquoise. He bit his lip as he considered if Brittany was likely to mind about this, assuming it was her who had been cooking. Looking around for somewhere to park his brushes to dry, he realised every surface was covered and there seemed to be a lot of flour around. The oven was on and there was a rather nice smell of cookies coming from it. He peered through the glass.

'Out the way.' Bella appeared putting on oven gloves. She had a serious look about her, her dark hair tied back loosely in a long ponytail.

'You planning on entering *Bake Off* this year?'

She opened the door and slid out a tray of baked blobs, prodding one of them. 'No, silly, I'm doing this pop-up thing...' She was looking puzzled as she poked. 'With Anna, you know.' She seemed frustrated that he didn't know.

'What pop-up thing?'

'It's a pop-up stall. It's going to be on the South Bank. I'm sure I told you.' The blobs went back in.

Ben decided not to ask any more about it.

'What's that?' Bella looked horrified at the turquoise scummy mess in the butler sink.

'Sorry, yes, I've just been working on that jazz portrait; the saxophone one. Green and yellow.'

'Can't you wash your brushes somewhere else?'

'Nicole's in the bathroom.'

'What still? That was a few hours ago.'

'Well, someone's in there.'

'Maybe we should check for squatters?'

Ben was mildly amused. He considered himself one up from a squatter on the basis that he just about managed to pay the rent each month by some miracle. He was still holding his brushes and began to make his way to the door, deciding to take them back to his room.

'Aren't you going to help me? You could at least get rid of this paint mess.'

Ben put the brushes into his jeans back pocket so that they stuck out at an awkward angle. 'I'm off out soon; my shift at Revolution,' he said as he began to lift items from the dirty lagoon and pile them on top of other dirty dishes creating an angular and unstable stack. Bella stuck her hand in the sink and pulled the plug.

'Anna says that Revolution don't pay as well as some bars. I mean it stands to reason as the drinks are so cheap.'

'It's a big place, though. They need people.'

'Yeah, lots of people so they pay them nothing.'

Ben had managed to start washing up, actually making plates clean enough to put away somewhere, which he considered quite an achievement.

Bella was back at the oven door. 'Damn!' She whipped it open, grabbed her gloves and pulled the tray out. They looked quite a bit darker than the first time. She opened the back door and put them outside.

'They're not that bad, are they?'

'They need to cool.' She wasn't helping him with the clearing up.

'Perhaps dry some of these?' Ben held a plate up dripping with soapsuds. She found a tea towel which didn't look very clean.

'Ben, do you think we'll ever have our own place? Or do we have to live in this scuzzy commune forever?'

Forever seemed like a very long time to Ben. It was something he chose not to think about.

The journey down to London wasn't as straightforward as Roger had envisaged. The A12 was hideously busy with an abundance of lorries even though it wasn't rush hour. Trying to park at Marks Tey Station proved a nightmare, with both the main car park and the overflow already full. With no time to spare, if he had any hope of catching his train, Roger abandoned his car along with two others at the side of the road leading down to the car park. At least it had stopped raining; it had been a filthy morning. Then the payment meter was bust with a hand written sign on it telling customers to pay online. He quickly made a mental note of the web address and started to run down the road back to the station in his smartest suit and carrying his briefcase. It started to rain again and he managed to step heavily into a puddle splashing his trouser leg. He cursed his fortune and slowed down so that he didn't get any wetter. He daren't look at his watch.

He arrived gasping for breath, sweating from the exertion and wet. The ticket office had a long queue of people that looked as if they were making a day of it and were just happy to be in the dry. So he got his train ticket from the machine outside and ran through to the platform, accidently knocking into a woman wearing white and carrying a takeaway coffee, just as the London train pulled in. Getting straight on he collapsed in the nearest seat, closing his eyes with relief. When he opened them again there was a rather angry woman sat opposite him, with coffee down the front of her otherwise pristine white mac. By the time he had pacified her by giving her twenty quid to cover her dry-cleaning costs and paid for his car parking, using his phone and some app he would rather not have downloaded, the man next to him was asleep with his head resting on Roger's shoulder. He considered leaving him there until he remembered a previous time when he'd ended up with dribble on his sleeve. So, he gently moved away, and in so doing woke the chap, who simply leant the other way and went back to his dreams.

The AXA offices were tall, brown and shiny on the Broadgate development and near Liverpool Street station so at least he didn't need to get the underground. His trouser leg had dried out by now but looked a little crumpled despite his best efforts to iron the crease back in with the warmth of his hands; something Ellie had taught him. It had taken some time for the receptionist to call the guy that he was supposed to be meeting with and Roger was sat like a lemon waiting for a good twenty minutes. It was at this moment that Roger's thoughts spiralled into negativity, just when he should really have been building himself up.

The chap who eventually appeared to collect him looked far too young to be carrying out interviews. He introduced himself as Cameron, 'I work with Martin.' First names were clearly de rigueur in this place. Roger was rather hoping that Tiger Tom would appear but perhaps that wouldn't be appropriate.

Martin Summers was a good-looking chap in a sharp suit. He greeted Roger warmly but seemed to laugh after most remarks which unnerved Roger. Cameron stayed and they were sat on easy chairs around a coffee table in some sort of café set-up which was a bit odd for an interview. Roger immediately assumed that they weren't taking him seriously; perhaps they were just humouring him because he was a sad-out-of-work-sixty-year-old.

The conversation had the feel of a friendly chat until they asked him about his departure from East Anglian Finance which was always going to be the sticking point. Roger spouted his prepared answer which was, 'I've been at EAI for twenty-three years and now I want a fresh opportunity which I can bring my considerable experience to. And I think health and fitness is such an important issue for us all these days.' It was bullshit and they all knew it but still they nodded politely.

As he emerged from the building, his head was full of questions. Did he really want to commute to London for this job? Did he want to work in this gleaming opulent environment where everyone seemed to be in a hurry and in their own world? In the short time he had spent emerged in village life in rural Suffolk, he had realised that there was a different pace to be had where people had time to stop and chat and ask you how you were. Thinking back to the interview he was already getting a sense of the rivalry between work mates that large organisations seemed to encourage in the belief that this was the way to get the best from employees for the sake of the business, for the sake of profit.

He wandered around Broadgate feeling very much out of place. The cafés were soulless where people only darted in for takeaway drinks and didn't stay to commune with others. The shops were mainly empty of customers with windows full of expensive wares, no doubt with the staff gearing up for the lunchtime rush, when that must-have Armani suit would be grabbed and purchased.

He was soon tired of his surroundings and headed for the station and the train home. His gut feeling was that they wouldn't offer him the job. If they did, would he take it? Was it just a chance to boost his ego, raise his standing back home from retired nobody to working professional? The commute and cut and thrust of office life would no doubt exhaust him so that he needed the generous salary to pay for exotic holidays where he would recuperate for a week or two before the next onslaught. He amazed himself at how philosophical he felt about the whole thing. Until this moment he had seen another high-powered job in financial services as his salvation, the pinnacle of his dreams. Now as he stood on a draughty platform waiting for his train to come in, he was wondering if there wasn't an alternative, a better way.

Carol felt quite liberated as she wandered around Waitrose without a shopping list. Bryan always insisted on a list and stuck to it rigidly. Now she only had herself to think about and could peruse the aisles picking up anything that might take her fancy. Smoked salmon; why not? Bryan was never keen on fish. Now she could eat fish to her heart's content. Aubergine. She was reading just the other day about how good they were for you. She would buy one; maybe make a moussaka. Then it struck her that she would be going to all that trouble just for one. What was the point? Ellie's voice rang in her head: *Buy the aubergine and cook something delicious*; *life goes on*. Maybe she would invite Ellie round and they would share the moussaka together with a glass of red wine. Carol sighed. It was hard work this keeping upbeat. She took a deep breath into the depths of her lungs. Apparently, according to something she'd read, this was enough to make you feel better.

The chap at the meat counter looked jolly and smiled at her. She walked over perusing the meat on offer. It all looked too much like hard work. Perhaps she'd get some chicken?

'I'll have two of your chicken breasts,' she smiled. Force of habit. She'd wrap them separately when she got home and put one in the freezer. A hot flush came upon her. She loosened her cardigan. He wasn't looking at her. She was never quite sure if it was obvious. Did she actually go red?

She was eyeing up the petits pois in the freezer section when she saw him in the corner of her eye. Bryan. How dare he come to her shop. Couldn't he find somewhere else? Their eyes met; an anxious glance. How were they supposed to behave? There'd been married for thirty-five years and now they had to coexist in the same universe or at least in Waitrose.

Bryan came over to her. He looked hesitant, nervous even.

'Hello Carol.'

'Bryan.' Another deep breath.

'You okay?'

'Fabulous.' She flashed him a cynical smile.

'I've spoken to Rebecca.' He looked almost pleased with himself.

'Not before she rang me, unfortunately.' She couldn't take the edge from her voice.

'Yes, sorry about that. I thought we'd agreed that I would tell them.'

'She guessed!' The audacity of this man. 'She asked to speak to you and I had to tell her that she'd have to ring your mobile.'

'Yes, of course.' He looked lost all of a sudden. Every word almost caught in his throat. 'I've arranged to see Megan next week,' he managed.

Carol was sure that next week would be far too late but couldn't be bothered to say anything. The two sisters didn't have the best of relationships but this sort of news was likely to be shared between them with some urgency.

'Right.' She walked away from him and towards the checkouts realising that his presence was irritating her.

'Bye, then,' he called out feebly. Was there a note of regret in his voice?

She recognised the checkout woman; they had exchanged pleasantries on a few occasions.

'How are you today, my love? All right then?'

'Yes, thank you,' Carol said breezily and got on with the business of packing her shopping. If she said it enough times, maybe she'd believe it.

Ellie was reading the details of a property in Little Capel from her screen when she felt a warm presence behind her, leaning in. She looked up.

'James?' Why was she unnerved by this man?

'Lovely little place that one, in Back Lane, isn't it? I remember selling it to the current owners; must be ten years ago now.'

'But the kitchen is quite small, isn't it? Everyone wants a large kitchen-dining room these days.'

'Not everyone. These older properties exude character and for that you pay a premium.'

'Mmm...' Ellie was not convinced. 'But some people have converted; knocked down walls.'

'I agree; it's great when it's done sympathetically. And that would attract a further premium. Don't worry viewers of this little place might see the potential.'

Their eyes met. Ellie was beginning to feel a little uneasy in such close proximity to him.

'Are you free this afternoon? About fourish?' he asked.

She knew she was. 'Not sure. What for?'

'There's an interesting place out at Thorpe Morieux. A piece of land actually with an old barn on it in need of renovation. The owner has asked me to price it.'

'And you want me to go?'

'Yes, would you?'

'I think I might be out of my depth with that one.'

'That's okay. I'll go with you. It will be good experience for you.'

Ellie couldn't help wondering if this was a ruse to get her alone somewhere. But then she decided she was big enough to look after herself and fend off any advances. She would go.

'Okay then.'

'Excellent.' He looked overly pleased with himself.

The barn turned out to be virtually derelict but the surroundings were fabulous and it was a large plot.

'Surely your best bet is to get a builder to take it on?'

'Yes, that would work.' James was pacing one of the larger spaces in the barn which he said might be an open plan living area. The height of the building was vast; it would be difficult to heat.

'It's a beautiful spot,' Ellie said wanting to say something positive.

'Yes, that's what will sell it. We need to find someone willing to take on a project. I think the photographs should be mainly of the land and the view.'

They set about measuring up and Ellie made some notes. They were at the far end of the plot, furthest away from the barn, when it started raining. Ellie berated herself for not carrying an umbrella but it hardly ever rained in Suffolk in the summer. It was coming down hard now.

'Shall we make a run for it?' James suggested and they ran across the field and back into the barn, panting for breath. Ellie felt like she was soaked. She ran her fingers through her wet hair. She must look a sight.

They both giggled.

'Well, I think we've got everything we need. Shall we wait here for the rain to lift?'

Ellie considered that if he was ever going to make a move on her it would be now. They were alone and there couldn't have been another soul for quite some distance. She looked at him. He was calm, meditative almost. Perhaps her drowned rat look was putting him off. Ellie couldn't help giggling.

'What's funny?' he asked.

'Nothing,' she said quickly composing herself.

He was looking into her eyes. She looked away. It was still raining. They were stuck.

'You're happily married, aren't you? To Roger.'

'Yes,' she said uncertainly, more so because she wasn't expecting this question. And then she added, 'Yes, we are happy together.' If only she had left it at that. 'I mean like any long marriage we have our moments. I'm a bit worried about him being out of work.'

'As long as he doesn't stop you from working. I think you're quite an asset to the agency.'

'Thank you.' She was surprised by that and how much it pleased her.

Ben rang.

'Hi, darling, how are you?'

'I'm okay, Mum.'

'Good.' This was the point at which Ellie always thought he should say why he was calling but he never did. She wondered if he called out of a sense of duty? He mainly communicated by text message and seemed to have more to say through the tapped-out word.

'Are you still working, Mum?'

'Yes, yes I am.' Why would he ask this? 'That's okay, isn't it?'

'Yeah, of course.'

'And you, still working at the Revolution bar?'

'Yeah, I'm still at Revolution. Quite like it there actually, there's a good crowd but Bella says it doesn't pay very well. She wants us to get our own place one day.'

'That would be expensive.'

'Too right. Anyway, I thought I might come home at the weekend.'

'That would be lovely, darling. This weekend?'

'Yes. Are you working?'

'Well, yes. But I am allowed to have the odd weekend off so I'll see what I can do. I might be able to leave early.'

'How's Dad?'

'He's all right. Has an interview today down in London.'

'What, so he might be working here?'

'If he gets it.'

'You don't think he will?'

'Who knows. Let's hope so. He's going mad stuck at home. How's the painting going?'

'I've been working on a jazz series: bands, saxophones, that sort of thing.'

'I'd like to see them; will you bring them with you?'

'Not sure, Mum. They're really big. I don't fancy getting on the train with them. I could take photos and AirDrop them to you.'

Ellie had no idea what that meant. 'Great. Will they fall out of the sky?'

'No, Mum, they will be on your phone.'

'Oh, I see. Will Bella come with you?'

'She might. She's doing this pop-up café, gluten-free organic or something next week so she's been doing a lot of baking.'

'Oh, sounds interesting. Is that with a view to opening up a café?'

'I think it will be pop-ups to begin with mainly. Unless she can get some crowdfunding.'

'Well, I hope she does come. What time train do you think you'll get?'

'About elevenish. I'll text you when I'm on the train.'

'Okay, but can you text your dad as well. It will probably be him picking you up from the station. Manningtree, like last time?'

Somehow Ellie missed her son more just after she had put the phone down to him. She so wanted to give him a big hug. She always told herself not to read too much into what he told her, but couldn't help wondering if things were okay with Bella. If they split up would it be down to Bella and would it break his heart? But still, he was coming at the weekend.

Chapter 8

Bryan could taste blood in his throat. His limbs seemed heavier today. Tiffany was ahead, lithe in Lycra; she looked over her shoulder.

'Come on! We're barely halfway.'

It was a lovely September evening. The light was good and there was a cool breeze. He had done this run before and Tiffany had been impressed that he could keep up. They had had great sex that evening; he'd been on top of the moon. But it seemed so much harder today. He felt like he just couldn't carry on. He stopped. Was this what they called hitting the wall? He imagined his wife and daughters laughing at him. Punching above his weight, they'd remark. Tiffany was by his side.

'What's going on?' she asked as if there wasn't a thirty-year age gap between them.

'Struggling today,' he managed as he gulped for breath.

'Oh my God. You're not having a heart attack, are you?'

'No, no, don't be silly.'

She looked straight into his eyes and stroked his head.

'Well if you're sure, I'm going to finish or I'll never be ready for the half marathon next month. Is that all right?'

'Of course, yes, you must.'

'You walk back. I'll see you at the flat.' She gave him her keys.

'Right.' He waved pathetically and watched her bound off into the distance. It was a damning blow. She hadn't actually said it, but he was clearly out of the race now; unable to keep up. When she was far enough away not to see him, he found a large stone to sit on. The relief he felt had him crying out. His heart was still pounding. The trouble was that dressed in this ridiculous Lycra, which Tiffany had insisted he bought for himself, he could be mistaken for a serious runner.

They were on the old railway track that ran from the bottom of Magdalene Road, up Broom Hill and through some woodland. Tiffany knew a circular route that brought you back into the centre of Hadleigh. Her shift had finished at five that afternoon so they were getting the practice run in before the light faded at eight. Thinking about it now, the last time they did it, they had alternated walking and running sections. It was all part of Tiffany's big training plan. As a personal trainer, she embraced the challenge and actually found it all quite easy.

Two cyclists, a man and a woman, sped past him. 'Evening,' the woman said. They rode in companionable silence, their wheels in harmony with each other, probably man and wife.

As soon as he felt able, Bryan heaved himself up and started off back towards the town managing an acceptable walking pace. He was going to be all right. Maybe he'd knock the running on the head. He could always cheer Tiffany on from the sidelines when she chose to compete.

As he hit the high street, he saw Robert, one of the volunteers at the Guildhall in Capel Green, coming out of the Co-op. Damn, he'd recognised him. Bryan quickened his pace and waved with a breezy smile across the road to him.

'You taken up running, have you?'

'Just keeping myself in trim.'

Robert looked quite concerned. Surely, he didn't look that bad? Bryan decided he would simply walk on. He couldn't worry about what everyone thought of him.

Further up the high street he turned up an alleyway at the side of the Kings Head and went through a side door and up a flight of steps to a small landing with two front doors. Tiffany's flat was at the back of the building and overlooked a car park.

Inside Bryan put the kettle on. The living area was open plan with a kitchen in one corner, a small dining table and a sofa in front of a television at the other end. It was full of Tiffany's clutter, not a bare piece of shelf to be found. She seemed to have chargers for devices that she no longer had. 'So why do you keep it?' he'd asked innocently enough. 'Well, you never know,' was her vague answer, a modicum of irritation in her voice.

Being part of a Georgian building it, thankfully, had large windows, although the view left a lot to be desired. There was just one bedroom and a shower room. 'Plenty big enough for one person,' Tiffany had explained when he first saw it. That was then, when he was driven by an urgent desire for sex, and the fact that it was somewhere with a double bed where they wouldn't be disturbed was the only consideration. He'd barely noticed the small size of the flat.

Of course, she'd done well to get this place; her grandparents had helped her out with the deposit and she made it clear that she was indebted to them.

But now as Bryan made himself a mug of tea, and moved a pair of trainers out of the way just so that he could sit on the sofa, it struck him that he really couldn't live here for any length of time. He had so few of his own possessions around him. When he suggested he got more clothes from home, Tiffany's answer was that he should buy a new wardrobe chosen by her, more fitting to his new lifestyle.

When he thought of home, he realised how lovely Carol had made Hill View, how spacious and comfortable it was. He had to admit that he longed to go home and luxuriate in the furnishings, potter around the large garden, have a proper parking space for his treasured Mercedes. Of course, he wanted to be with Tiffany; he was in love with her. But he couldn't live like this.

Roger was persuaded by Jim, who was doing his shift in the shop, to consider the grape harvest at Capel Farm. He'd only popped in to buy some milk.

'How long does it go on for?' Roger could feel his back breaking at the very thought of it.

'It's just the odd day or two here and there. Probably about five days in total.'

'Right, so, if you want to join in this grape picking, what do you do? Just turn up?'

'Well you get on their email list and they let you know when the grapes are all plump and juicy and we're set to go. It's usually the Bacchus grapes first.'

'You seem to know a lot about it.'

'I do it every year, mate. Love it! Out in the fresh air amongst the vines. Not a bad way of earning a few quid.'

'I might give it a try,' Roger said warming to the idea. He still hadn't heard from AXA and strangely he wasn't too bothered.

'Tomorrow morning then. Eight o'clock at the farm. Shall I give you a lift?'

'What tomorrow?' Considering it was one thing; actually doing it entirely another.

'Yes, mate. They don't hang about. I got the email this morning. Weather's set fair so we're on.'

'And you think it will be okay for me to just turn up? Don't I need to apply?'

'No, no. Their view is the more the better. We have to work fast, see. But don't worry, I'll let Joe know you're coming along. He manages the operation.'

As he got back to Rose Cottage the postman was just delivering their mail and he handed a couple of envelopes to Roger. He knew immediately by the thick cream paper of the envelope and the typed address that this would be news from

AXA. He went inside and decided to make himself a coffee before he opened the letter. He wondered to himself, was this coffee manoeuvre so he could prolong the dream of getting back into the financial world just a few minutes longer. He smiled and somehow felt quite relaxed about it all. He wasn't at all sure that he wanted to take on a commute to London anyway. If it was a no, would he give up on the whole idea of renewing his old life?

The coffee made and poured, he sat at the kitchen table and opened it. Of course, it was a politely worded, no. There was even a vague attempt at flattery just to lift his ego a little. It was exactly what he had expected but it still felt like a small part of him had died. What would he do with the rest of his life? He remembered that he'd just agreed to pick grapes tomorrow and, even though it was only a few days a year and not to be taken too seriously, he actually quite liked the idea of it. But it still seemed like an enormous comedown.

Roger's alarm the following morning proved a rude awakening. Ellie had a smirk on her face as he scrambled around to be ready on time.

'What about your lunch?' she asked as he was eating his porridge.

'Oh no! I forgot. Jim said you have to take your own.'

Ellie quickly set about slicing bread. 'Cheese and pickle sandwich okay?'

'Thanks. Lovely.'

She handed him a lunch box as he ran out the door. Jim's car was already outside as he'd promised.

'You up for this?' Jim asked as Roger belted himself into the passenger seat.

'Looks like it,' Roger said wishing he hadn't gobbled his breakfast in a hurry.

It was only ten minutes down the road before Jim pulled in and drove a small way up a track. Roger slowly got out of the car and looked around him. The view was glorious across the vineyard; the sun had just appeared above the horizon giving off an amber glow. There were quite a few assembled, some young, some old, and a hum of friendly banter amongst them. Jim introduced Roger to the group. Some responded. A man who looked like he was in charge appeared.

'Morning Roger, I'm Joe. All right? Done this before have you?'

'No, no, I haven't. Love drinking the end product though.'

This was met with a chuckle or two amongst the assembled workforce.

'Right, well you'll soon pick it up. I'll pair you with someone who can show you the ropes. 'Now,' he turned to the whole group, 'we're starting in Lower Brook Field today, picking the Bacchus grapes. Pay is eight pounds and forty pence an hour.'

'Hoorah,' Jim said light heartedly and there were smiles all round.

'And we finish at four,' Joe continued before issuing them all with yellow plastic buckets, a pair of snips and a couple of pairs of thin blue plastic gloves. It was obvious that some knew the drill and had done this before.

'Roger, you pair with Luke. Is that all right?' he asked the young man.

'No probs. How you doin' mate?' Luke shook Roger's hand.

'Not bad, mate.' It seemed the voice of experience today was a young one.

Each pair was lined up either side of a row of vines. Luke started and Roger watched him.

'You pick the ripe grapes only and cut off the whole bunch,' Luke advised as he dropped a bunch into his bucket.

'Seems straightforward.' But then he saw him cut an unripe bunch. 'I thought...'

'Ah, see, these unripe ones, you throw them to the ground.'

'Right, so why is that?'

'It's so that the birds don't come for them when they've ripened.'

'Interesting.' Roger set to work.

Buckets were filled and run to the end of rows of vines from where they were collected by Joe and emptied into a trailer. As soon as the trailer was full it would be going off to the winery, Roger learned.

As the morning went on, he began to relax and enjoy the camaraderie of the workers. It was obvious that this wasn't about the money, but just the sheer enjoyment of communing with nature and helping a local farmer to bring in his harvest.

By the time they stopped for lunch he was mighty pleased that he had a sandwich. The sun was shining down on them now and they sat round in a clearing, on the ground, some perched on a fallen tree trunk. As soon as he had wolfed down his sandwich he took in the scene and was really pleased that he'd come along today. He felt like he'd made a few new friends and there was something life-affirming about the whole experience. It was a world apart from financial services; here, everyone was out to help you, rather than beat you.

By two o'clock they were back to work and Roger was beginning to feel a bit of an ache in his lumbar spine. He stood tall and curved backwards to stretch it out.

'You all right old man?' Luke asked.

'Less of the old man if you don't mind.' They were both laughing. 'Yeah, it is a bit back breaking for me at least but then I'm tall.' He was looking round the group and decided he was probably the tallest.

Suddenly the air was filled with the loud whirring chuff from a helicopter as its blades sliced through the sky. They all looked up. Painted black with gold lettering across it, it was a striking vision. Roger was somewhat taken aback when it landed in a field on the brow of the hill.

'What on earth is going on?'

'That'll be Lady Rochester,' one of the pickers shouted above the noise.

'Just popping in to see us, is she?' Luke asked, amused by this.

'Let's get back to work,' Joe shouted out and they all dutifully obeyed. Ten minutes later a rather attractive woman in jeans, black polo jumper, a fur gilet and green wellingtons appeared and strode directly up to Joe.

'Good day to you all!' She flashed a smile at them all.

'Lady R, just passing were you?' Joe asked cheekily.

'Actually I've come from the winery. They are ready for the third trailer. Are we full yet?'

'Not quite,' Joe said.

'Chop, chop everyone,' Lady R said. 'We need to get this little lot away.'

'Bit faster if you can,' Joe added.

Roger focused on the job in hand and harvested as fast as he could. Lady R appeared next to him.

'Hello handsome, your first time is it?' Her eyes were lively and she beamed unashamedly.

'Er, yes, that's right.' Roger blushed.

'Good, I like a new boy.' Her smile was flirtatious, her eyes playful as she looked him up and down. She addressed the whole group shouting out, 'Drinks on me at The Cock Inn, when you're all done today.' Then in a lowered tone to Roger, 'You will come along, won't you?'

'Love to,' Roger said deciding to throw caution to the wind. After all, Ellie was always working late. Why shouldn't he have some fun?

Megan had just appeared at the door and when Carol opened it, she hugged her hard. 'Mum!' she yelled.

'Come on in.' Carol couldn't stop the tears in her eyes.

'Oh, Mum! This is terrible! How could he? I hate him for this.' She dropped a holdall onto the hall floor.

'How did you find out?'

'Becks. She said Dad wanted to tell me. Huh! And when was that going to be?'

From the moment her daughter arrived, Carol's day was blissful. It was so lovely cooking Megan's favourite chicken massaman curry together as they immersed themselves in girly conversation talking about their hairdressers, Megan's job, what they'd seen on the telly, how Rebecca's life was all a drama and her job in advertising too important to her.

'She'll never find a man. She's too obsessed with climbing the career ladder. Did you know she's been promoted to account director?' Megan said, animated now.

'Yes, she sent a text when it happened. Apparently, a few of them went for a drink after work to celebrate in some Champagne bar.'

'She's all about the high life. I'm sure she looks down on my petty existence.'

'Don't be silly. You've got some lovely flatmates, haven't you?'

'Yeah, Hannah and Jess are my bessie mates; we get on so well.'

'And your job's going okay at Lazards, isn't it?'

'I quite like it in marketing services but it doesn't stretch me. There's this woman, Fiona, she's a fund manager. She's so good at her job but really lovely too. She's always got time for me.'

'Would you like to get into fund management?'

'That would be brilliant, Mum, but I'm not qualified; I mean my degree in Business Admin would help but...'

'Wouldn't they train you up?'

'They have a management training programme where you study and learn on the job. I think you have to apply each year.'

'Why don't you look into it?'

'Yeah, Mum, you know I think I will. Why shouldn't I? It's not like I'm going to be getting married and having kids anytime soon.'

Carol's eyebrows rose. 'Something you're not telling me?'

'No, Mum, it's just I don't seem to be able to get a boyfriend. I mean I always attract the wrong sort.'

'But you're beautiful and the loveliest girl in the world.'

'Oh, Mum, you would think that about your baby girl but in the real world...'

Carol hugged her. 'There's a wonderful man out there for you; you just haven't met him yet.'

In the evening, curled up together on the sofa, they were watching the second series of *The Crown* on Netflix, even though they had both seen it before. A repeat viewing was something Bryan had always criticised and, if Carol did ever enjoy a programme for the second time, he would hide behind a newspaper for the evening. Carol topped up their wine glasses realising that there wasn't much left in the bottle. 'Shall I get another?'

'I'm okay. Wouldn't mind a cup of tea later.'

Carol smiled; her baby was growing up. A feeling of contentment smothered her. What a wonderful daughter Megan was.

Lady R was quick to put her card behind the bar at The Cock Inn and encourage everyone to order their own drinks. She moved easily amongst the pickers sprinkling snippets of conversation here and there with much gaiety. She reminded Roger of Princess Anne with her brusque manner whilst remaining polite at all times. He couldn't help but admire the way she operated. He had been mightily impressed when Jim had told him that she owned the whole operation at Capel Farm.

'So, Roger, good first day?'

'Yeah, it's funny but I actually really enjoyed it in the end. I felt like I'd sort of been talked into it and, well, it's so different from the financial services world.'

'Is that where you work?'

'Did. Until they gave my job to a young upstart who can't play golf.'

She laughed. 'No hard feelings then.'

'I was livid at first but funnily enough I was down in the City the other day, Broadgate circle, and I didn't feel a pull back to it at all. Quite the opposite actually.'

'What area did you work in?'

'I was the marketing director; big cheese; fifty staff and always lots of balls in the air. It was quite stressful actually. You realise that when you stop.'

She was looking at him thoughtfully. 'So, what do you do with yourself now? Apart from grape picking of course.'

'Well there's the thing. I don't know what to do. But I'm thinking I'd like to stay closer to home.'

'What's your golf handicap?'

'Ten, on a good day.'

She was raising her eyebrows.

'Okay fifteen, if I haven't been playing much,' he added.

'Is this the official score?'

He laughed. 'You play?'

'Yes, when I get the chance.'

Roger was thinking she was probably a top-notch player and modest with it. 'Where do you play?' Why did he ask that? He could see where this was going.

'Stoke-by-Nayland and others.'

'Ah yes, I've heard good things about that course.'

'Fancy a game sometime?' How was he going to answer that? Jim appeared just in the nick of time.

'Just breaking you two up. I'm going to have to make a move now.'

'Ah, my driver.'

'You are back tomorrow to finish off the Bacchus?' Lady R asked.

'Er, yes. Yes, I'll be there.' He was rubbing his lower back as he said it. 'And er, yes, maybe, golf sometime.'

She smiled and quickly turned to mingle with the others.

Ellie was showing a young couple around one of the brand-new houses on the new estate at the top of the hill on the edge of Capel Green. They all displayed a pale grey palette throughout their interiors and were pristine to the point of actually sparkling which always impressed.

'Oh, it's fabulous. I love it.' The young woman, who insisted on being called JoJo, turned to her partner and whispered, 'but can we afford it?'

Mr JoJo turned to Ellie. 'Do you think they would take an offer?' He puffed his chest out and looked pleased with himself.

'There's not a lot of room for manoeuvre I'm afraid. The concern is that it would lower the price of the other properties on the estate.' Seeing the disappointment on his face she added, 'I have to be honest but we could try an offer.'

'We haven't seen the garden yet or the garage,' JoJo pointed out and Ellie unlocked the back door and showed them out into what was most definitely a small patch of grass surrounded by a high orange fence which only emphasised its diminutive size. She walked to a gate at the end, opening it. 'The garage is out here.'

JoJo just stood in the garden with a pained expression on her face whilst her man looked at where they might park their car.

The fashionable grey décor was struggling to win them over, now that they had seen the limited outside space.

'Well I suppose we could put in a low offer and see what happens.'

Ellie attempted a genuine smile and probably failed. 'What did you have in mind?' she asked.

As she drove away from the estate, she noticed a few men in an adjacent field at the far end of the development. One seemed to have a clipboard and one of them looked remarkably like James Addington. Ellie pulled her car over into a lay-by and peered across the field until she was in no doubt at all it was him. What on earth was he up to? Surely they were not building more houses? She remembered how the locals had strongly objected to the new estate in the first place citing that Capel Green was the best-preserved example of a medieval village with umpteen listed buildings. How could they build more of these twenty-first century homes?

Later that afternoon she questioned James.

'Spying on me, were you?' He seemed pleased to have her attention.

'I was just passing in the car after a viewing.'

'Yes, well I suppose it's going to be public knowledge soon.'

Ellie's eyebrows rose as she braced herself. 'Not more houses?'

'No, it's a supermarket looking to build one of their metro-style stores.'

'You're joking! That's not going to go down well.'

'Well, you say that, but think about it; it would be very convenient for villagers, especially as they are building a petrol station with it.'

'A petrol station in Capel Green! I don't believe it!'

'But look at the positives. Now we have to drive five or six miles just to get petrol. They've done similar edge-of-town schemes and they've been really successful.'

'But Capel Green isn't a town!'

'Granted, yes, but from our point of view, selling housing, it's a plus.'

Ellie was dumbfounded by what she was hearing. 'Well, yes, I suppose if all the current residents are horrified and put their houses on the market so they can get out quick, we'll be nice and busy.'

James sat there unruffled; she was beginning to dislike him. Intensely. 'Anyway, what's your involvement? They're not giving you backhanders to support their scheme, are they?' She realised as soon as she'd said it that she'd gone too far.

'Oh no, that's below the belt, Ellie. Really. They are just talking to local figureheads at this stage. They've applied for planning permission and they want to consult with people much like myself, and get us on board.'

Ellie wanted to explode. It was obvious that such a reaction wouldn't do her job prospects much good so she zipped her mouth. It was five o'clock and she was justified in leaving the agency and going home. She stood up and collected her handbag and mac.

'You going home?' James asked. He seemed surprised.

'Yes, I need to go.' She tried to take the edge out of her voice.

'Right, well, have a good evening,' he said as if they hadn't just had a major disagreement.

Roger got home to find Ellie in the kitchen with the fridge door open.

'Hello, you're late,' she said. Was she cross with him?

'Went for a drink after.' He slapped some notes down on the kitchen worktop. 'Sixty quid! Well nearly.'

'Great,' she said sarcastically. 'Now, had you planned anything for supper?'

'Ah, sorry, forgot about that. Been too busy out in the fields.'

Ellie looked unimpressed.

'What's got you?'

'Oh, James and stuff...'

'What? What's he done now? I hope he hasn't been harassing you?'

'No, no, don't be silly. We actually had a bit of a row, more of a disagreement; I don't think it's possible for Mr Cool to get hot under the collar about anything.'

'About what?'

'Some bloody supermarket chain want to build on the field next to the new estate on the other side of Capel Green.'

'Well at least it's on the outskirts, I suppose.'

'Don't be obtuse! Capel Green with a Cost-Cut! It's the last thing we need. What about the local shops it would put out of business?'

'Good point.'

'We have to fight it.'

'But we don't actually live in Capel Green, do we? I'm sure there's plenty of people...'

'We're close enough! Anyway, they need all the help they can get to fight this big supermarket.'

'Right.' He didn't really understand why his wife was getting so worked up about this but knew from experience that it was best to keep quiet.

'And we still haven't got anything for dinner!' she yelled and Roger knew this meant it was his fault.

'I tell you what, I'll take you up the pub. We'll spend my well-earnt wages for today. What do you say?'

'No! I don't want to go out.'

'Takeaway? I'll drive to Hadleigh and pick it up.'

'If we must.'

He grabbed his car keys. 'Won't be long.'

Chapter 9

Ben and Bella were waiting outside Manningtree station. Bella looked cross as if having to wait wasn't something she tolerated. Ben had been texting his father for some time before they decided to phone instead. Roger arrived with a scant apology for his tardiness. Ben had a large art case with him.

'You brought some of your paintings with you?'

'Yeah, just three boards. The jazz set. They're not framed yet.'

They both sat in the back and Roger felt like a taxi driver. They were mute and glued to their mobile screens. Roger turned on Radio 4 and listened to a bunch of people that had nothing better to do than have a go at one politician or another about something they considered: '*a disgrace to society;*' '*the beginning of the end of civilisation,*' often blaming the hapless politician for everything wrong in their lives. Roger was mildly amused by it all.

When they got home he sent Ellie a text.

The commune set have arrived. Do put in an appearance sharpish. Rx

She duly appeared.

'Gosh that was quick. Normally you can't tear yourself away.'

'That's not true. Anyway, I'm not best pleased about Mr Addington's support for this crazy supermarket scheme.'

'Mr Addington! How the mighty have fallen into disrepute. Caught red-handed in a field with a clipboard. He must have underestimated you, darling.'

'Don't darling me. This is serious stuff. I might just have to leave the agency and join Friends of the Earth.'

'Steady on; you love that job.'

Ben appeared.

'Ben, darling, I see you've brought your paintings after all.'

'Yeah, Bella said we'd manage on the train so...'

'Brilliant. I can't wait to see them.'

Ben started to unzip the case.

'Where's Bella?' Ellie asked.

'She's just upstairs on her laptop. Something about this pop-up stall; it might rain next Thursday so they have to make sure the food doesn't get wet. She's trying to source glass cloches but they're a bit pricey.'

'I see. Shall we go through into the garden room where the light's good.'

They went through and Ben took out the first painting. You could just about make out a double bass player from the darkness.

'Interesting,' Ellie said. 'What's it called?'

'*No More.*'

'No more?' Roger asked his tone disparaging.

'Yeah, he's sort of dead.'

119

'I see.' Roger met a look of daggers from his wife even though that last response was reasonable. He had a dangerous smirk on his face; that was enough.

The second painting was of three players, a drummer, saxophonist and double bass, and this time you could make them out and there was much more use of colour but they were faceless.

'This one's called *Live Music*.'

'I see what you've done there, son,' Roger said mildly amused now.

Bella appeared. 'Let's show them the best one,' she said pulling out the third painting and holding it up in front of her.

It was a night time jazz club scene and the female vocalist looked remarkably like Bella.

'It's brilliant,' Ellie said. It seemed like the safest reaction to this one.

Bella let out a giggle. 'Can you tell? Can tell it's me?'

'Well you modelled for it but you're not actually a jazz singer,' Ben pointed out.

'No, but it's still me,' she protested.

'Sort of.'

'I think it's wonderful. He's really captured your beauty, Bella.' Ellie beamed at them both.

'I don't suppose you've got anyone interested in buying one of these, have you?' Roger asked and was met with another stern look from his wife.

'Actually, the Hunter Gallery in Bury want to see them.'

'Really? The one at Abbeygate, that's amazing.' Ellie could have jumped for joy.

'Want to see them?' Roger asked incredulous. He threw his head back. Why did he have such a downer on his son?

'Yeah, so I need to get them up there today, really,' Ben said as if it wasn't three o'clock in the afternoon.

'Today? Are you joking?'

'All right, Roger. Keep your hair on. I'll drive him. We can probably park outside. We'll go now.'

'Thanks Mum.'

Roger was happy to stay behind. When Ellie suggested that he sorted something out for their evening meal he seemed almost enthusiastic.

Ellie dropped Ben and Bella outside the gallery with the art case and managed to find a space in the Angel Hill car park. She paid a ridiculous amount for the maximum two hours and went off to the gallery.

A woman in a red jersey dress held a thoughtful expression as she looked at *No More.* She peered at it up close and then moved away to take in the full painting. Her face wasn't giving any indication as to what she was thinking.

'Let me see the other two.'

Ben took each one out carefully. All three paintings were now propped around the gallery floor.

The woman looked at Ellie.

'I'm Ben's mother, Ellie Hardcastle.' She held out a hand.

'Amelia Fortescue.' They shook.

After a long unbearable silence, she said. 'I like them. Yes, I do like them.'

'Good,' Ben said taking it all in his stride.

Ellie was itching to ask if she was going to sell them and how much for.

'But they need to be properly framed. I can't take them like this.'

'No problem,' Ellie said. 'We can do that. Do you recommend anyone for framing?'

Amelia picked up a card from her desk and handed it to Ellie. 'We use these people but there are other good framers around.'

'So, get them framed and bring them back?' She wanted to be sure.

'Yes, that's right. We take thirty per cent commission.' She smiled now. 'Your son is very talented, Mrs—'

'Ellie. Just call me Ellie.'

Outside the gallery Ellie threw her arms around Ben.

'I knew it! I knew you could do it!'

'But how much will you get for them?' Bella asked. She seemed quite nonchalant about the whole experience.

'Don't know but they charge a lot for the paintings in there.'

Bella clearly wasn't easily impressed.

'The fact is a prestigious gallery is going to take your work. That's made my day! My year!' Ellie skipped back to the car while Ben covered his face with his hands.

Overnight it rained hard filling water butts and the River Brett rose up, gently spilling into gardens. On Sunday morning Megan and Carol walked up to Stackyard Green, on to Swingleton Hill and back down through the causeway where the path had become a shallow stream.

'Thank goodness we put wellies on,' Carol said.

'I'd forgotten I still had these at home.' Megan lifted a foot up clothed in a green welly.

'Do you want to take them back to London with you?'

'Don't be silly, Mum. Anyway, I might be spending more weekends here from now on.' Her face lit up as she smiled at her mother.

Carol put an arm around her and pulled her close. 'That would be lovely,' she said. 'I can't remember the last time I had such a relaxing weekend.'

As they walked up to the back door, they saw Bryan sitting on a bench outside looking forlorn. His face reddened as they approached, like a naughty schoolboy outside the headmaster's office.

'Bryan, what you doing here?'

'Hello Megan,' he said hopefully to his daughter.

'Dad.' She didn't do any more than acknowledge his presence.

'What do you want?' Carol asked and didn't mind if she sounded angry.

'Can I come in?' he asked.

Carol felt confused. This was all very difficult but a situation of his own making. What on earth had happened?

Had Tiffany thrown him out? Was he homeless? She decided she would at least hear him out.

'You can come in for half an hour and have a coffee.'

He looked relieved. 'Thank you, Carol.'

Megan quickly took her wellies off and disappeared upstairs without a word. She had always been one to avoid confrontation.

Carol set about making a cafetière of fresh coffee in exactly the way she had always made it throughout their long marriage. It felt like she had instantly turned back into the compliant wife and she didn't like it. Even though Bryan had only been gone a few weeks, she had begun to acquire new habits that selfishly suited her and her alone. It provided some small comfort.

Bryan was sat at the kitchen table waiting patiently for her when she took the coffee over to him. She sat down.

'So?'

'I'm so sorry, Carol, for all this. I really am.'

She looked at him wondering what on earth was going to come next.

'The thing is, Tiffany's flat is tiny. I can't live there.'

Carol was horrified. Was he really saying that he was coming back to her because his new lover's home was too small.

'I know this might sound unreasonable,' he continued, 'but I was thinking that perhaps I could move back in just for a short while. I could sleep in the guest bedroom and keep out of your way as much as possible.'

'And exactly how long is a short time?' Carol asked, angry now. 'Until you've found a more suitable love nest for you and your latest conquest?'

'That's unfair. I was faithful to you throughout our marriage; it was only the last six months when I met Tiffany.'

'Oh, well, that's all right then!' she mocked.

'Look, I said I'm sorry.'

'Somehow it doesn't help.' Carol was shaking with rage. She realised that she hated Bryan for what he had done to her and she could not forgive him. 'No,' she said emphatically as she looked straight into his eyes, 'No, you can't move back in. The expression, you've made your bed you'd better lie in it, seems very apt right now.'

He looked hurt and had tears in his eyes. But she couldn't muster up any sympathy for him at all. Eventually he said, 'Well, I'm at least going to get some of my stuff.' He went upstairs and after what seemed like a very long twenty minutes, he appeared back in the kitchen holding a suitcase.

'I'll be finding somewhere to rent, probably in Hadleigh, just so you know.'

She said nothing. Just watched him leave. She was staring at his undrunk cup of coffee when Megan appeared and hugged her mother.

'Thank God you're here,' Carol said as tears overcame her.

Chapter 10

Ellie was driving down a narrow country lane towards the village of Edwardstone. All the roads looked the same and she really wasn't sure if she was going in the right direction even though the app on her mobile was instructing her to turn this way and that. She was sneaking this errand in during work time, so she needed to be quick.

Finally, she saw School Green which she remembered was near the picture framers she had spoken to. And there it was. It looked like an old barn but then the chap she'd spoken to, name of Andrew, said it did. They hadn't bothered with a sign outside but she was pretty sure this was it. She parked up, took Ben's paintings out of the boot and went to look for signs of life.

A man appeared in overalls. He came over to her.

'Are you the lady that rang earlier? Three oil paintings?'

'Yes, that's right.'

'Need a hand?' he asked as he took the canvases from her.

Inside, he measured each art work and scribbled down a few calculations.

'Do you know what sort of frame you want?'

'Ben said dark. They are going to the Hunter Gallery in Bury St Edmunds so they need to look half decent.'

He seemed impressed by that. 'Right then, well we're talking a bespoke service so they will be at least...' He scratched his head. 'Do you want wood?'

'What's the alternative?'

He showed her samples. 'This is a composite. It's cheaper.'

'How much for wood?'

'At least two hundred pounds per painting.' His expression was braced for her reaction.

Ellie felt a bit giddy. No wonder Ben had not argued with her when she'd said she would get them framed and pay for them. How on earth did struggling artists get a name for themselves at these prices?

'How much for the composite?' As she asked the question, she imagined Amelia Fortescue giving her a disdainful look.

Andrew was scribbling some numbers down and grabbed a calculator. Eventually, he said, 'If you go with what I consider to be the best option, which you might just get away with at Hunters, you are talking one hundred and twenty per frame. That's including the mounts.'

Ellie felt out of her depth. 'Are you sure I can get away with that?'

'This is obviously your first time framing? Is your son fairly new to this game?'

'Very. This is his first opportunity to sell anything.'

'Then I can understand you going for the composite. I'll do a good job. It will be fine.'

'Thanks Andrew, I appreciate that.'

On her way home that evening Ellie called in at the farm shop at Capel Green. It was something Bella had said about the importance of supporting local farmers that had struck a chord with her. Ellie was impressed to hear that Bella's friend Anna had an allotment and grew all her own veg organically. The first thing she saw at the entrance was a poster alerting her to the proposed new development on the edge of the village. *Say No to Spoiling our Countryside and Destroying Independents*, it read. Ellie couldn't agree more. She picked up a basket and went in. It was good to see vegetables and fruit, loose and not wrapped in plastic. The prices were not bad either; a bit more than the supermarket but the whole experience was so much better. She picked up an aubergine, and a butternut squash remembering a recipe she had done before. Then she saw a cauliflower that looked really fresh and popped that in her basket. This place was a real find. In the dairy she saw they made their own cheese and decided to try the cheddar. The red poll beef was very tempting and she bought two steaks. Near the till they had basil growing in pots and she took one. The girl who served her had a friendly smile. There were flyers on the counter with the same protest message as the poster she'd seen on the way in. Ellie picked one up.

'This wouldn't do you any good, would it?' Ellie said.

'No, we've got to stop it. We really have.'

'Well you have my support,' Ellie said proudly.

'Thank you; we're demonstrating on Saturday. We want as many people as possible to sit in the road going through the village.'

Ellie considered that they would probably be right outside the estate agency. 'Well good for you,' she said. When she came to pay, the girl asked if she had a loyalty card.

'No, but I'd like one.'

She handed her a card, made from cardboard she noted. 'You just go on our website to register it and then you get points every time you spend.'

'Great.'

'Will you join us for the sit-in on Saturday?' the girl asked.

Ellie knew there were at least two good reasons why she shouldn't: she was working in the morning and James would disapprove. 'I'll try and make it,' she said.

It was quiet in the community shop and Carol could see that Jeffrey was stood ready and waiting behind the post office counter. He had a look of anticipation on his face, as if he was expecting customers, even though there were none. He was his usual smart self, even if his fashion sense was a little misguided, wearing a shirt, navy-blue tie and tank top. He justified the tank top by saying that it could be quite chilly when you were practically stationary in the post office all day.

Carol was only halfway through her shift and, as there was a stool behind the counter, she sat down. She tried not to worry about Bryan and all the implications of him leaving her and renting a place in Hadleigh but her thoughts naturally meandered in that direction. Did she need to concern herself with the money side of things? Ellie had even suggested she see a solicitor. So soon. Did she want that? It made it so real.

Linda appeared. 'There's a delivery coming in any minute. Susan's cakes. She just called me.' She flitted around the shop busying herself and giving every detail her attention. It was almost as if she needed to justify her salaried role as manager, while the shop was otherwise staffed by volunteers. In fact, she was held in high regard; managing the volunteer rota alone was an onerous task.

'Okay,' Carol nodded. 'Where will they go?' she asked looking at an already cluttered counter.

'You'll just have to make room. Tell you what I'll move this bread that's past its best. I'll mark it down and put it near the chiller cabinet. If it doesn't go today, Pete's pigs will have it.'

Susan appeared through the door. 'Ah, well done,' Linda said. 'Just here.' She pointed to the limited space.

'Six fruit, three lemon and two vanilla.'

'Yes, the fruit are always popular.'

The cakes stacked, Susan looked up. She pointed to Carol in a gesture of recognition and scratched her head; she looked pleased with herself.

'You know I saw your Bryan the other day. In Hadleigh. He was with some young girl. Was that one of your daughters?'

Carol froze mortified. Jeffrey pretended not to notice.

'Small world, isn't it?' Linda said. 'See you next week, Susan, and thanks again for your cakes.'

Susan looked perplexed but turned on her heels anyway.

As soon as she'd gone Carol's eyes met Jeffrey's; he had a look of grave concern about him but said nothing and shuffled some papers that didn't need shuffling. Linda stayed nearby and Carol found herself saying, 'Thank you,' as a tear escaped from one eye.

'You're all right,' Linda said. 'That Susan's always been a bit of a busybody.'

Carol was then saved by what constituted a busy spell for the Little Capel shop; two customers walked in. Carol busied herself with serving them. Gregory did most of his weekly shop in this little place as he didn't have a car and, being forgetful, he asked where almost everything on his list was.

'The eggs are near the chiller cabinet. Why don't you give me your list and I'll help you.'

'Very kind missus. You're good to me. The Mrs isn't doing so well; it's her chest you know.'

'Sorry to hear that Gregory. How about some fruit today? That might help.'

Gregory pulled a face. 'Maybe some bananas.'

'Bananas aren't fruit strictly speaking,' Jeffrey could never read a situation. 'I saw it in the paper.' They all looked at each other as if this was a shocking revelation.

Gregory raised his eyebrows. 'More fake news,' he said.

Carol smiled and put a bunch of bananas on the counter. 'And a scratch card?' she asked when he had everything on his list.

'No, not today. I don't think I'm doing them any more. I've never won nothing.'

'Good decision,' Linda said.

'Work of the devil,' Jeffrey said and went back to serving a customer.

When all was quiet again Linda came around the back of the counter and bent down to peer at the shelves below.

'What are you looking for?' Carol asked.

'You all right?' Linda said quietly under her breath.

'Yes. Yes, I'm fine.'

Linda nodded and then for Jeffrey's benefit she said, 'I think all the tickets that we've had so far for the jazz evening have sold. John must have been in for the money.' Linda said out loud now.

'Ah, yes, I'm looking forward to that,' Carol said remembering she'd got two tickets and wondering who on earth she'd get to go with her.

'It's not until December. Still time to sell more tickets; I'll let John know we're out,' Linda touched Carol's arm in a caring sort of way before moving away.

'I'm not sure it's my thing,' Jeffrey said and Carol pictured him in his cosy home with his mother and his cat having a TV dinner on a tray.

Still time to find a plus one, Carol considered. Definitely not Jeffrey. Perhaps she'd rent a toy boy for the evening.

Kathleen was reminiscing about her happy days at Benton Street. She missed her Henry terribly. Sometimes she would wake up and forget for a moment that he'd gone and then she felt terribly sad all over again. They'd had a large Georgian house and over the years they had turned it into a very comfortable, lived-in home; not too much fuss and formality. There was a darling kitchen with an Aga at its centre which helped to keep the house warm in winter. And she loved to cook for Henry; he always appreciated her efforts. 'This is delicious,' he would say and smile across the table to her. What a gentle soul he was.

Their neighbours had complained about the houses being right on the road with just a narrow pavement between them and the lorries that would trundle past. But Kathleen couldn't hear the noise of traffic so it didn't bother her. She liked the fact that she was only a few minutes' walk from the high street. She liked to go into the Co-op to do her shopping and then sit in the café, Paddy and Scott's, at the front, while she recovered in one of their nice leather chairs drinking a coffee. Yes, she was better off at home.

She started looking for her house keys, opening drawers, even the bottom of her wardrobe. She couldn't find them anywhere. Perhaps someone had stolen them. Then she saw the mobile phone that Ellie had bought her; for emergencies only and keeping in touch with her, she had said. Kathleen didn't bother with it because she didn't know how to use it. She had got to the age of eighty-five without needing such a thing; why start now? But it would be useful for calling a cab to take her home. She turned it on and a red light was flashing at her. There was a wire next to it which fitted into the phone so she plugged it in and waited. As she sat there it occurred to her that her good neighbour, Betty, had one of her house keys. She would get the key from her and then she'd be back in her lovely home. She felt excited at the prospect. She'd had quite enough of this place.

Something happened with the phone and it seemed to spring to life. She looked at the screen and didn't understand it and then she realised that she didn't know the phone number of any taxi firms in the area where she was. In fact, she didn't even know where she was. She needed to find out. She wandered down the corridor, not sure which direction to go in. One of the carers was passing.

'Kathleen, where are you off to?'

She decided not to tell her that she was going home; she didn't trust the people in here.

'Are you going to the day room?'

'Yes, that's right I'm going to the day room.'

'Do you know where it is?'

'Of course I do, but tell me anyway.'

'Would you like me to take you?'

'If you must.'

The carer took her arm and they walked along turning right at the end of the corridor and then left into a largish room where there were quite a few elderly people and the television was on with the sound very loud.

'Is there a phone box here?' she asked. It would have a Yellow Pages and she could look up a local taxi firm.

'No Kathleen there isn't. Who do you want to phone? There is a telephone in reception which residents can use.'

'Good. Will you take me there?'

'Of course.' The carer looked miffed as if she had far better things to do.

'Who do you want to call?' she asked again, irritatingly.

'It's a private matter,' Kathleen said ever wary of these people.

'Is it your daughter?' The carer wouldn't give up.

'No.' That silenced her.

When they got to reception Kathleen sat on a seat next to the telephone. The carer hovered just a few steps away, keeping her beady eyes on her.

Kathleen looked around her, to the side of the little table the phone was on and underneath it but there was no sign of the Yellow Pages.

'Where are the Yellow Pages?' she asked very sure that she had a right to know.

The carer came over to her with a grave look of concern on her face. 'We don't have Yellow Pages any more, but if you tell me who you want to phone, I might be able to help you.'

Kathleen felt confused and was trying to work out what to do. Why couldn't they have the Yellow Pages; everywhere had them. She felt frustrated and cross.

'Would you like to go back to the day room?' The carer was asking.

'Yes, I would.' She would look for the Yellow Pages there.

The television was so loud that Kathleen couldn't hear herself think so she went over and unplugged it. Everyone was looking at her slightly confused but at least it was peaceful now. She decided to sit in one of the armchairs and put her head back. It was exhausting all this. She'd have a nap and continue her search later.

When she came round, Ellie was sat next to her and the television was back on.

'Is it Sunday?' she asked.

'Hello Mum. No, it's Wednesday.'

'Oh. Do you normally come on a Wednesday?'

Her daughter's eyes were brimming with love. 'I'll come whenever I want,' she said simply.

'Is it time for tea?'

'Yes, would you like to have tea in the garden? It's fresh but the sun has come out.'

Kathleen felt deflated but didn't know why. 'If we must,' she said as she stared vacuously into the distance.

Ellie got home to find that Roger was cooking oven chips and had a couple of sea bass fillets ready to go in the pan to be fried. He turned his attention to her.

'How's your mother?'

'She's okay. A bit confused, I think.'

He nodded in acceptance and returned to the hob. By the time they were sat at the table he'd opened a bottle of Capel Green Farm wine and was pouring her a glass.

'This is the white, the Bacchus grape.'

'And is it a good year?' Ellie teased.

'I'll have you know they've won an award for this wine.'

Ellie smiled and tried to let the tension go from her shoulders.

'So, what happened with your mum; you said they called you.'

'Yes, apparently she was wanting to make a phone call and to find the Yellow Pages.'

'Who did she want to call?'

'She wouldn't say. They said that some residents get the crazy idea in their heads that they can call someone to take them out for the day.'

'Is that crazy?'

Ellie thought back to how her mother had been today. The doctor had said a few months back that there were signs of dementia. He seemed to make light of it saying, 'It's very common in this age group,' and he emphasised that Starling Skies was the best place for her.

'Perhaps her dementia is getting worse. I mean, looking for the Yellow Pages.'

'But it's not that long since they went out of circulation, is it?' Roger pointed out.

'I suppose so. She had her mobile charging in her room but she'd forgotten how to use it.'

'That's no big deal really, is it? I mean I struggle with mine sometimes.'

'We had tea in the garden and Larry joined us; she really liked that.'

'Do you think they'd let her come out for the day if she came here?'

'I doubt it. We could ask. They usually say it's best for them to stick to a routine.'

'Best for the staff, no doubt.'

Ellie felt saddened by the whole situation. 'I wish I could do something.'

'Leave it to me. I'll go and see her tomorrow and see if we can't arrange for her to come here for the day. That will cheer you both up.'

'Might do. Well you can try.' It was a lovely thought.

'Was James okay about you leaving work early?'

'Oh yes, I've told him about Mum. He was very understanding actually. He's been extra nice to me since our disagreement over the supermarket development.'

She clearly had Roger's attention now. Any mention of James and his ears seemed to prick up. 'And this road sit-in thing; are you joining in?'

'Ooh, it's a difficult one. I'm supposed to be working.'

'You could always ask for the day off; tell him you have something special and worthwhile to do.' He was clearly amused.

'Thank you, Roger, I think I can handle James.'

The next day Roger drove to Starling Skies. He had phoned earlier and asked if it would be okay for him to visit his mother-in-law.

'Do you have Ellie's permission?' they had the audacity to ask.

'Of course I do!'

'Thank you, Mr Hardcastle. We will need to get your wife to confirm that.' The receptionist sounded like a jumped-up schoolmistress.

'Well, call her mobile then!' He decided that, far from their rating, this was not an outstanding experience so far. It wasn't long before he had a text from Ellie telling him he had clearance and to be nice to her mother.

It was one of those grey cloudy days where it tries to rain every now and then and the air is damp. Roger parked in the visitor section, deciding that conformity was probably the better option, and went into the reception area.

'I'm here to see Kathleen Hervey, Ellie's mother.'

'Ah yes, I have been informed.' She had a name badge on telling him that she was Angela Hartnell. After he'd signed in, she escorted him to the day room.

'They are doing a meditation session today. We have someone from Inner Guidance here. You may have to wait until they finish.'

'No problem.' Roger was imagining all sorts. They reached the room and there were about fifteen of them sat round in a circle with their eyes closed and their hands resting gently on their thighs. Some of them looked serene, one chap's head was tilting to one side and he let out a snort, others appeared irritated by the whole experience including Kathleen.

The young chap guiding the session had long fair hair held back by a bandana and wore what looked like yoga pants and a T-shirt. 'Deep breath in,' he said, 'and let go... Imagine the sun is shining down on you, warming the crown of your head, your eyes, your jaw... it's all melting away...'

Kathleen sighed unashamedly and opened her eyes. She saw Roger and waved. He waved back. She was smartly dressed, as always, in a pastel green twinset and beige wool skirt. She stood up and started to push her chair back to free herself.

'Sorry, I have to go. I've got a visitor.'

The chap from Inner Guidance broke his faraway stance and looked affronted.

'Remember the commitment we all made to each other at the start of this session, Kathleen?'

'Yes, well that was before I realised it's all a lot of poppycock. Thank you, anyway, I really must be off now.'

She was free and walking towards Roger who tried to hide his amusement at the whole episode.

Half an hour later they were in the reading room sat in tub chairs around a coffee table and Roger had persuaded Angela to get them some tea.

'Tea is at four o'clock,' Kathleen had told him with authority. And she was right; a change to this regimented routine was not welcomed but persistence paid off in the end.

'Not quite the five-star hotel I thought this place was,' Roger said.

'That idea is a thin façade for the reality of the situation,' Kathleen said as she waved to a smart-looking gentleman in a yellow cravat and carrying a newspaper. He came over.

'Good afternoon good people. Larry's the name.' He shook Roger's hand.

'Pleased to meet you, Larry. I'm Roger, Kathleen's son-in-law.'

'Ah, wonderful. Excellent. I hear you got the heave-ho at work. Rotten luck young man.'

Roger was amused by this chap. At least he called him a young man. 'You two know each other then?' Roger asked wondering if romance had blossomed in the confines of Starling Skies.

'Yes, we are fellow inmates,' Larry said with a twinkle in his eye as he sat down with them. 'It's not bad really. They organise various activities to keep us amused; we have a choir coming to sing to us one evening, I forget which.'

'And do you ever go out for the day?' Roger asked.

'Into the garden,' Larry said. 'On a decent weather day, they open the French windows here and out we jolly well go.'

'They don't like me going out; they think I'll wander off.'

'And would you wander away if you could?' Roger asked her.

'It's a nice idea.' She was grinning away.

'The thing is, Kathleen,' Larry was wistful, 'You're special. You know the Queen always has a bodyguard. She can't just come and go as she pleases.'

'Yes, but she has a whole palace to run around.'

Roger was amused by their gentle banter. 'What about if I were to take you back to Rose Cottage, just for a day or maybe a weekend? Wouldn't that be allowed?'

There was a sharp intake of breath from Larry. 'Christmas Day is a possibility. Not sure about the rest of the year. They're big on routines round here: monotonous repetition, over and over, day in, day out.'

Kathleen's face lit up. 'You could help us escape, Roger! Do something useful for once.'

'Now, now, my dear girl, give this chap a chance.' Larry was winking at Roger. 'Tell me, are you planning to go back to the world of work or perhaps you have other ideas?'

'I'm not sure that I'm wanted any more. I need to come up with a plan B but goodness knows what that will be. I did some grape picking recently which I enjoyed but that's only a few days a year and it pays minimum wage.'

'Where were you? Over in France? Bordeaux maybe?'

'Huh! No. Capel Green actually.'

'Amazing what we can do in this country. Is it just white wine they produce?'

'And red. The white wine, made with the Bacchus grape, has won a gold award.'

'Impressive.'

'I'll bring you a bottle, if you like, next time I come.'

'You're coming again?' Kathleen didn't hide her surprise.

Roger laughed. 'Now Kathleen, don't be the archetypical mother-in-law.'

'Ooh no, we might have to start making inappropriate jokes!' Larry was amused.

'So red or white?'

'Kathleen, it has to be your choice.'

'We'll have the one that's won an award; it must be half decent.'

Larry leant in and whispered, 'You'll have to smuggle it in, of course.'

Roger tapped the side of his nose with his forefinger. 'Leave it to me.'

Saturday came around all too quickly. Ellie had mulled over the whole situation repeatedly and all that did was make her more certain that this new development must be stopped. But then she imagined the look of horror on James' face as he saw her sitting in the street, probably chanting something like '*Save our beautiful village*'. Although, on second thoughts she was convinced that James had the innate ability to rise above such situations. She wanted to believe that he was basically a good chap, wasn't he?

On top of all this, Matt had announced the day before that he was turning up, with a girl called Sarah, for the weekend.

'What are we going to do with them?' she asked as she applied her mascara that morning. Roger was straightening out the duvet on their bed.

'Don't worry about that. I'll cook something.'

'Will you? What does she eat? She might be vegan like the last one.'

'Dear Lord, I'm not cooking if she's vegan.'

'Exactly.'

'Maybe I'll book a table at the pub. Saturday evening; they might be full. I'll try.'

'Why don't you text Matt and ask if there's anything she doesn't eat.'

'That's inviting trouble. At least if we don't know we've got an excuse. You never know she might be anorexic and not eat anything at all, just push a lettuce leaf round her plate.'

'That's not funny.'

'True.'

Make-up done, she stood up and Roger smiled at her as he looked her up and down and clocked what had become her go-to-work trousers. 'You won't be sitting in the road in that outfit.'

'I'm taking a cushion,' she said and they both giggled at the absurdity of it all.

Ellie took the car, knowing that she probably wouldn't be able to get as far as the car park. Sure enough, a man in a high-vis jacket was on the corner where she normally turned left for Water Street. He directed her to turn right instead and presumably park on the green. But she couldn't find a space so she just had to keep going following the road round to Back Lane which ironically, brought you out near where the proposed development was. She parked on the new estate which was legal, even if the residents probably didn't like it, and about a ten-minute walk from the high street. As she walked down the hill it wasn't long before she could see and hear the protest. '*Say no to Cost-Cut*,' they chanted. There must have been at least a hundred people. How exciting. As she weaved through them, protesters young and old were smiling up at her, obviously thinking she was going to join them. She met the eyes of the girl who had served her in the farm shop; this was so difficult. Reaching the agency door, she dived in quickly, hoping no one would notice. The noise of the campaigners penetrated through the glass window and filled the agency. James was the only one in and looked uncomfortable.

'Morning Ellie. Well done, you're the only one who's made it.'

'Well actually, I was in two minds.'

'I know, you agree with them. That's your right,' he said and smiled.

Ellie sat down tentatively and turned her computer on. 'Any requests for viewings come in?'

'No. Not a bean. And let's face it if they did, we would be hard pressed to carry them out unless they are outside Capel Green.'

She checked her emails. Then suddenly an eco-warrior type burst through the door in her green T-shirt with slogan, her nose pierced and waving a water bottle around.

'Why aren't you out there?' she shouted at them. 'Sitting here all pompous in your capitalist cocoon. You should be ashamed of yourselves.'

'Well actually...' Ellie felt conflicted; her heart was out there with the protesters.

'It's a free country.' James had got up and was walking over to the girl. 'We have freedom of speech and the right to peaceful protest and hence you are having your say today and believe me we can hear you.'

The girl looked slightly confused. 'So, what are you going to do about it?'

'We will consider carefully the point you make. Obviously as property consultants we have the best interests of the community at heart.'

'But do you support us?'

'We certainly can't ignore you. Now would you like me to refill your water bottle?'

This had a disarming effect on the girl. 'Well, yes, actually. That would be good.'

He took the bottle from her, a false smile on his face. Whilst he was in the kitchen, Ellie said quietly, 'I am going to join you. I just need to clear it with Mr Addington first.'

The girl calmed herself and smiled. 'I didn't expect this,' she said. Her water bottle returned, she left saying, 'See you out there.'

James sat heavily back in his chair. 'I feel beaten today. I think we should close up. I'll divert the phone line to my mobile and take refuge at home.'

'Probably best,' Ellie said massively relieved.

'So, will you join them?'

'I'd like to show them some support and then I'll head home. My son is turning up at lunchtime.'

'Ah, which one is this, the artist?'

'No, it's Matt this time with Sarah, apparently, his latest girlfriend. Him and Ben are like chalk and cheese.'

'Well, have a lovely weekend.' There was a sadness in his voice now and Ellie wondered what James would do with himself all alone up at Capel Tye.

'Now you go first, I'll lock up,' he said.

'Thanks James. Jolly decent of you.'

'I'm a decent chap, believe it or not.'

Ellie went out on to the street, now wondering exactly how she was going to join in. She'd left her cushion in the car as it had felt too silly at the last minute. It didn't fit with the dissenting nature of the event. A guy with a T-shirt which read *Fight to conserve Capel Green* and a clipboard approached her.

'Will you sign our petition?'

'Of course I will.' She added her name, signature and email address. 'How many signatures do you have?'

'About a thousand. There are some idiots who think this crazy plan would be a good idea, but not many.'

There were a couple of police officers keeping a watchful eye but it was all very civilised and there didn't seem to be any trouble. Ellie spotted the farm shop girl again, this time beckoning her over. She smiled and carefully stepped around the sitting bodies.

'Hello! Pleased you came.' She patted the space next to her. There was a long piece of foam under the sitters and Ellie was thankful for that. She sat down. They were all taking selfies with their mobiles and before she knew it, she was in one of them.

'It's hashtag, no to Cost-Cut, hashtag, conserve beautiful Capel Green,' the girl said.

'Where are you posting?'

'Instagram.'

'Right. I'm not on Instagram. Facebook?'

'Post to Facebook. We need to go viral.'

Ellie set about taking a photo and the girl joined in.

'I don't even know your name.'

'Emma.'

'Ellie.' They both smiled for the selfie and Ellie busied herself with putting it on Facebook.

'What were those hashtags again?'

Chapter 11

Bryan tried to lift his spirits as he stood on Hadleigh's busy high street looking up at a large Georgian building which had clearly seen better days. It was a cloudy October day and there was a cold wind. Bryan felt underdressed in a thin jumper and considered that he really needed to go home to get some warmer clothing. Somewhere in this dwelling there was a one bedroom flat for rent that he was actually considering for his next home.

'It's an ideal bachelor pad, close to the shops, pubs and restaurants,' the young naive estate agent spouted. Bryan may have turned his back on his marriage of thirty-five years and taken up with a new love but the word bachelor jarred with him.

The kitchen was tiny; the bathroom didn't even have a shower and the whole place exuded cheap and nasty. They walked into the bedroom where the curtains were closed and there was actually a sleeping body in the bed under a dirty beige duvet.

'Ah, yes, we have a student renting this at the moment. They don't tend to get up before midday.' The body didn't move.

When they were back in the lounge the estate agent added that the current tenant would be leaving at the end of the week and the place would be professionally cleaned. Bryan knew in his heart of hearts that he could not live here even if it was affordable.

'Have you got anything else on your books at the moment?' Bryan asked. 'I can go up a bit with the rent if that helps.'

The agent was thoughtful. 'Not really, in Hadleigh. Maybe one of the new builds on the estate; they are more your sort of family home.' He was scratching his head. 'There's a nice little cottage in Kersey, not far from here. But there you would need to double your budget.'

Bryan's mind was whirring; what would Tiffany think of Kersey? It was a delightful village and only a mile from Hadleigh. 'Would it be possible to take a look at it?'

The estate agent played around with his mobile and made a call. 'You're in luck. I have to pick the keys up from the office but we can go there now.'

They drove in convoy, Bryan following behind, through the ford which always had at least a few inches of water, and up Church Hill which was full of pretty cottages painted in pastel shades. This was more like it. They stopped outside a charming red-brick terraced house with Georgian sash windows. It was not far from the church or the village pub for that matter. He prayed it would be as good inside.

The front door went straight into a largish square living room with an open fireplace; the kitchen too was quite large, reasonably smart and clean unlike the flat. He noticed there was a washing machine there too. The cottage had two double bedrooms and a decent bathroom. He could see from the bedroom window at the back that there was a long thin garden which was mainly lawn and had a small shed, but was not too untidy and could be cheered up with a few pots. The place was unfurnished and Bryan wondered if Carol would let him take a few pieces from their home. It made it difficult, him being the bad guy, to ask anything of Carol. But as Tiffany said, he had a right to half of what they owned.

The estate agent was looking at him expectantly. 'This more what you had in mind?'

'Definitely. I think I'll take it. I just need to do the sums.'

As the estate agent got back in his car, Bryan decided to stay a while and walked down to the pub, The Bell Inn, where he went into a cosy space with a low ceiling and wooden beams. The landlady had a cheery smile. It was the start of the lunchtime session and there were a few punters peering at the pie menu on the blackboard which looked very tempting. He ordered himself a pint of the local bitter and sat near the window in contemplative mood. He thought back to when he'd first laid eyes on Tiffany. She had been handing out flyers in Paddy and Scott's café, promoting herself as a personal trainer. They had got chatting and she was immediately friendly, flirting with him even. He could see that she was tall and had a great body and she had flattered him by saying that if he had a personal trainer it would enhance his already impressive physique. Next thing he knew he was buying her a coffee and by the time he left with his flyer that day, he was in no doubt at all that she fancied him. It was an enormous ego boost. So exciting. And when he was back home with Carol their lives together suddenly seemed quite dull. She kept going on about coving. He'd had enough of DIY to last a lifetime. Why did they need coving?

The Hadleigh flat this morning had left him feeling like he'd made a huge mistake. It was such an enormous comedown from his beautiful home in Little Capel. But the Kersey cottage gave him hope. He wasn't sure how Tiffany would react. She had been uneasy about him looking at places. She couldn't understand why he wasn't happy living in her little flat which she so loved. He tried to explain to her that it was very much her place and he needed his own space. Perhaps she'd fall in love with the cottage and move in with him. The rent was higher than he wanted to pay; he knew it wouldn't go down well with Carol. But he simply had to live somewhere half decent and this cottage was it.

Ellie had to work most Saturdays and so she got a day off during the week. Roger was inevitably pottering round the house, threatening to attempt DIY projects which could only end in disaster, so she looked for excuses to go out.

It had got to eleven o'clock and all she had done was housework. The linen basket was so full she had to put a wash on. Then she discovered the airing cupboard was full of dry clothes so she put those away; not managing to match up Roger's socks as always, she stuffed them in the appropriate drawer. Then she tidied up. With Matt having stayed at the weekend everything seemed to be out of place: newspapers scattered all over the lounge floor and of course his bedroom and his dirty sheets beckoned but they could wait. She suggested to Roger that maybe he could change a bed or two every now and then and he looked at her as if he wouldn't know where to start.

She made herself a coffee and decided to call Carol.

'Fancy lunch out somewhere?'

'That would be lovely. Actually, I was thinking of going over to the farm shop, so we could combine the two. Or are you sick of Capel Green now you work there?'

'Not at all. As long as I don't have to go into the agency on my day off, it's fine. The brasserie at The Swan is always pretty good.'

Ellie insisted on driving and Carol remarked on what a treat it was. They had a table by the window overlooking an elegant courtyard with a spa pool and planters abundant with dahlias in deep purple and cream.

'I think I'm going for a posh sandwich,' Ellie said. 'Brie and red onion.'

'Twelve pounds for a sandwich?'

'Yes, but it comes with fries and salad.'

'Excellent, I'm in.'

As they sipped their wine, they both relaxed back into their chairs. Ellie gently looked at her friend's face for signs of how she was really feeling. She looked slightly nervous; not the self-assured Carol she had known for so many years.

'Bryan is talking about renting a cottage in Kersey, would you believe?'

'I thought you said he was going to get a flat, some sort of bachelor pad?'

'He said he looked at a flat in Hadleigh and it was awful. Run-down without even a shower in the bathroom.'

'Perhaps he's better off staying with Tiffany?'

'He won't. Her place is tiny apparently and she doesn't seem to want him to have much of his stuff there.'

Ellie was shaking her head in dismay. 'What a state of affairs. And how much is this Kersey cottage going to cost?'

'Not much less than eight hundred pounds a month.'

'Well I'm not surprised; it's a lovely village. It doesn't seem right though, does it?'

'That's what I thought to begin with. But then I worry that he'll suggest we sell the house and divide the money in two. I couldn't bear that.'

'You have a good point, but can you really afford eight hundred pounds a month?'

'It's certainly not what I had planned for my retirement.' She took a large glug of her wine; she was getting through it at quite a pace.

'Good job I'm driving,' Ellie teased.

'Sorry, I didn't mean to knock that back. But I've just remembered the other thing he said; this place is unfurnished and he wants to take some of our furniture there. It's either that or he has to buy new.'

'He can't do that! Is Tiffany going to be moving in with him?'

'Apparently she owns her place so probably not.'

'What a mess.'

'You can say that again.'

'Let's change the subject. How's Megan?'

'She's lovely. I told you, didn't I, we had a great weekend together, really relaxing. She is coming again soon but this weekend I've got Rebecca.'

'Oh. On her own or with a man in tow?'

'Apparently she's met a guy called Steve and it's serious so she's bringing him.'

'Well it'll be interesting. Matt was home at the weekend with Sarah and, judging by the way he treats her, I'll give her six months tops.'

'Why do you think he's like that?'

'No idea. I think he's just living the high life in London. He has a well-paid job, a good social life and shares a flat with a couple of mates. He doesn't seem interested in settling down. Apparently thirty is the age they start thinking about it. He's not far off that and I really can't see it but who knows.'

'Rebecca said she wants to take Steve to Bury St Edmunds which she is sure will impress him. Seemingly our village is sweet but boring.'

'Charming. I take it, you will be driving them to town?'

'Of course. Back to being a taxi driver; how I miss it!'

At the farm shop they both filled their baskets with goodies. The man who served them looked like he was in his fifties and was quite good looking, if a little short.

Carol's eyes rested on a poster which was advertising vacancies for staff in both the shop and the café. She liked this place. She had plenty of time on her hands. Her shift at the village shop was only three hours a week and it was voluntary. She smiled at the nice man and asked, 'Are any of the jobs here part time?'

He looked up at her. 'Yes, I'm sure we'd consider that.'

'Oh good. I'm retired really but I do a shift in our community shop once a week.'

'Right, so you have some retail experience.' He seemed mildly amused.

'Yes, I suppose you could say that.'

'Are you sure you want a job?' he asked, almost as if he cared about her.

'Yes. Yes, my circumstances have changed recently and a part-time job would suit me well.' Stop her going stir crazy at home anyway.

'Excellent, I'll get you an application form.'

As he handed it to her he said, 'By the way, my name's Bill.'

As they got back into the car Ellie's mobile rang. Her handbag was on the back seat and by the time she got to it they had ended the call. She looked at the screen. 'The care home; what this time?'

'Go ahead,' Carol said.

Ellie rang back.

'It's about your mother.'

'What's happened now?' It was Stephanie, the manager, so Ellie was immediately worried.

'She's missing. I'm sorry, we are not sure how it has happened.'

'Missing! You mean she's not at the care home? How on earth did she get out? I thought they were all locked in.' As she said that she realised how awful it sounded.

'This isn't a prison, Mrs Hardcastle.'

'When did she go? Have you asked the other residents if they know anything? She likes Larry, have you asked him?'

'We have questioned the residents that were in the day room at the time. One of them did say that she said she was going to call a taxi to take her home.'

'Oh my goodness. Have you called the police?'

'We have notified them.'

'What about local taxi firms; they might know something.'

'We are doing all we can, Mrs Hardcastle.' Stephanie sounded as if the whole thing was a gross inconvenience.

'Right well I will go to where she used to live in Benton Street. Call me if you find her, won't you?'

'Of course, we will.'

Ellie looked at Carol as she turned the ignition; both were horrified.

'Drive straight there,' Carol said. 'Don't worry about me. I'd like to come anyway.'

'Thank you.' It was a moment of small comfort when inside she was terrified at the thought of her mother wandering the streets on her own. She put her foot down and luckily the traffic was light and she got across the Ipswich road with relative ease. Hadleigh high street was busy, though, and she was stopped twice by drivers trying to park and then elderly people crossing the road as if it was pedestrianised and cars didn't exist.

Finally, she reached Benton Street. It was a narrow road with older properties on both sides and parking was allowed on one side only but due to the two-way traffic it was always a chaotic spot. There were no parking spaces. Carol was peering out.

'Can't see your mum.'

'This is hopeless. I'll have to take the first turning and see if I can park there. She turned right into Mill Lane and then again into a quieter road where she could, thankfully, park. They both got out and started walking back frantically to Benton Street. It seemed a lot further on foot. Ellie was beginning to feel like this was a wild goose chase. Was her mother really capable of making it here on her own? But then if she had managed to call a taxi it was quite possible. Finally, they were outside the house where she used to live. It was a large terraced house, painted Suffolk pink and sandwiched with several others to form a row. Ellie had always been concerned about her mother's front door being right on a busy road when she lived there. There was no bell but a door knocker which Ellie wrapped loudly. The two friends looked at each other in anticipation. This felt like a moment of truth. Nothing happened. No one came to the door. She wrapped again as loudly as she could. They waited. Nothing. Ellie felt more anxious than ever. She tried one last time. It was hopeless.

'It was quite an elderly lady who bought the property. She's probably deaf.'

'Is there any way of getting round the back?' Carol crossed the road so that she could look up and further along the row.

'Yes, there is. It's a bit of a walk but there is a footpath that runs along the back of these houses. I think I can remember how to get to it.'

They walked back up Benton Street and down a narrow alley which led to a grassy path with tall hedgerows either side. Neither were wearing suitable shoes for this sort of venture but Ellie was driven by fear. Eventually the path wrapped around so that they could double back on themselves along the bottom of the gardens. The leaves on the trees were beginning to turn to autumn colours and it looked pretty if a bit chaotic as you scanned the bottoms of the gardens. The path had brambles across it in places making it hard work especially in her court shoes. She glanced back at Carol.

'Don't worry about me, I'm all right.'

Ellie stopped and peered into the garden they were opposite. 'I think this is it. I remember this little grey gate.'

They went through the gate. 'Are you sure?' Carol asked.

Ellie looked around her. 'Yes, that apple tree. This was her garden.'

They reached the back door and Ellie knocked as loudly as her knuckles would allow. Still no answer. She wanted to cry. Just as she was about to knock again, she heard a noise. The door was being unlocked and opened slowly to reveal a white-haired woman who viewed them cautiously.

'Yes?' She asked.

'I'm so sorry about this,' Ellie started to explain. 'I'm looking for my mother. Kathleen is her name. I don't suppose you've seen her?'

'Are you Ellie?' the woman asked, a look of realisation on her face.

'That's right.'

'You'd better come in.'

They walked in to what was a cosy kitchen, just as her mother had laid it out. And there, sat at the table, was Kathleen drinking tea as if this was any other day. Ellie was overjoyed. Tears filled her eyes.

'Oh Mum, thank goodness you are safe.'

'What are you talking about, dear?' Kathleen looked at her in astonishment. 'Of course I'm safe in my own home!'

The white-haired lady raised her eyebrows and smiled. 'Would you like a cup of tea?' she asked.

Bryan had been to Waitrose to buy one of their Indian takeaways for two and had read all the instructions, found suitable bowls and set the tiny dining table in good time for when Tiffany arrived home from her late shift at the gym. He'd even got a couple of candles out to light. Since he had told her about the Kersey cottage, she had been very flat with him. Any attempts at intimacy were rebuked with protestations of being busy on her laptop or too tired.

She got in at eight o'clock and seemed to be in a reasonable mood; she was pleased about the Indian food anyway. He managed to serve it up without drama.

'Smells good,' she said pouring the wine.

They tucked in and small talk prevailed until Bryan decided to broach the subject that seemed to be coming between them.

'About this place I've seen in Kersey, I was thinking, as it's your day off tomorrow, we could go and take a look at it together; maybe have lunch at the pub in the village.'

'I thought your mind was made up.'

He had told the agent he would take it and all being well he'd have the keys by next week. He had even told Carol and she'd taken it quite well considering.

'I want to take it but I want you to be happy too.'

'Well, I'll look at it, I suppose. It just seems like a lot of money to spend on another place. I mean, if you moved in here permanently, you could maybe help me out with the mortgage. That makes much more sense to me.'

'Come and look at it and then we'll see,' he said hoping for some sort of miracle.

The following morning Bryan popped into the letting agents and persuaded them that he wanted to borrow the keys to measure up for curtains. Tiffany was ready to go when he got back, wearing tight jeans, a grey T-shirt and a black leather jacket; her hair was loose and she looked stunning.

'You're not wearing that, are you?' she said to him.

He wore a blazer over his T-shirt; was that what she objected to? 'What would you like me to wear?'

She looked doubtful. 'Oh, I suppose you haven't got anything better. We really must go clothes shopping for you.'

Bryan could see his bank balance diminishing to nothing at this rate. He drove her over in his Mercedes – at least she loved the car – and pulled up outside.

'That one there,' he said pointing. She got out of the car and looked around.

'It's a bit quiet round here, isn't it? It's not retirement villas is it?'

Bryan ignored her and walked through the little gate and up the small front garden path to the front door. Luckily, he got the right key first time. 'Here we are.'

She went in. 'There's no furniture.'

'No, well, I've told Carol and she's happy for me to bring some of our furniture here.'

Tiffany had a look of disbelief about her.

'Nice fireplace, isn't it? Apparently, the chimney has been swept recently.' He moved through to the kitchen.

'This is good,' she conceded, and she went up to the window at the back and peered into the garden. 'Is that why you don't like the flat? No garden.'

'No, no, but I suppose it is an advantage of this place. We could have barbecues in the summer; you could invite your friends round.'

She still didn't look impressed. They went upstairs and she nodded in agreement that there was a lot more space than her flat. As they came out of the front door and Bryan locked up again, she said, 'But it's not Hadleigh. Nice place if only it was in Hadleigh.'

Bryan cringed and nearly showed it. 'Come and see the pub,' he said praying that they would have some punters by now and some of them under the age of forty.

They walked in and his first impression was favourable; there were quite a few in. He saw on the blackboard that it was *Fish and Fizz Friday* but then he realised that apart from a woman on a laptop in the corner they were all pensioners.

He ordered some drinks, a half of bitter for himself and a glass of Sauvignon Blanc for Tiffany. At least he knew what she liked. When he turned round, drinks in hand, he saw that Tiffany was making friends with the laptop woman. He sat down and smiled at them both.

'Do you live in the village?' he asked ever hopeful.

'No, I live in Hadleigh actually.' Damn.

'Caroline works in social media. She's doing a promotion for the pub,' Tiffany explained.

'I see.'

There was an awkward moment as they all worked out what was happening here.

'Well we mustn't keep you,' Bryan said looking pointedly at Tiffany. She returned a look of disappointment.

'What brings you to The Bell? Caroline asked.

'I'm thinking of renting the cottage just up the hill.'

'Oh, how lovely. Kersey's a darling little place.'

'Do you think so?' Tiffany asked. 'Isn't it full of pensioners?'

'Mainly. But you'd be surprised how many are on social media these days. This village even has its own Facebook page.'

'Don't suppose it's on Instagram, though?' Tiffany asked.

'No, but I'm working on that.' The two women giggled in unison and Bryan suddenly felt depressed.

Chapter 12

It had broken Ellie's heart, seeing her mother rebel against her return to the care home. There had been a long tea at Sylvia's, the current owner of the Benton Street house. Ellie had thanked her for her generosity of time and her understanding. Sylvia had even gone along with her mother's determined belief that it was still her home. She even told Kathleen that she would stay behind and look after the house for her so she had nothing to worry about.

It was a relief to get her mother in the car and next to her on the passenger seat. Carol sat in the back.

'Are you sure you're okay with this, Carol?' Ellie asked again. 'I could drop you home first.'

'No, don't worry about me.'

A glance at her mother told Ellie that she was frustrated and confused. 'You'll be back in time for your evening meal,' she remarked hoping that would help.

'Not hungry,' Kathleen said defiantly.

'I hear the food is very good at Starling Skies,' Carol chipped in.

'Don't know. I can't remember.'

Ellie was relieved to pull up outside the home; the rest of the journey had been in stony silence with her mother looking less than pleased. She parked the car right in front of the entrance. Signage everywhere told her she couldn't, but she didn't care. Together, they managed to get Kathleen through the doors but she dragged her feet as much as she could. The receptionist came over with a wheelchair.

'That's a good idea,' Ellie said. Seeing her mother's obstinate expression, she added, 'Look Mum, you can have a ride. You must be tired after your day out.' Kathleen reluctantly got in.

'No control over my own destiny,' she spouted.

Carol signalled that she would wait in the car. Ellie ignored her mother and began to wheel her down the corridor.

The manager of the home, Stephanie Tilston, appeared. She was tall and slim with high cheek bones and looked like she had just run a brush through her hair and didn't bother with make-up. Standing there in front of them, her fingers woven together and sitting on her rib cage, her smile was disingenuous.

'We'll take her from here,' she said with an air of authority.

'I'm going to see her to her room and settle her in,' Ellie said using every ounce of patience she had left.

Stephanie looked doubtful. 'If you must but we know what's best.'

'Is that how you lost her in the first place?' Ellie asked and Stephanie at least had the decency to look embarrassed.

When they got to Kathleen's room, the manager stood around simply watching.

Ellie went straight up to her. 'Please would you leave us. I want to settle my mother in. The whole experience has been quite traumatic.'

Stephanie averted her eyes to the floor. 'I'm sure it has. Would you come to my office before you leave, please? I think we need to talk.'

'Yes, if I must.' She felt like a naughty schoolchild but she would say anything right now to get rid of the woman. She turned to see her mother staring out vacantly; it was as if she'd suddenly aged, her skin grey, her eyes sad. In the kitchen at Benton Street she had come alive and now she'd been torn away yet again and forced back into this home where you had to conform to the rules. Residing here meant fitting in, not rocking the boat in return for a congenial atmosphere and a *we're all having fun* ethos.

Stephanie offered Ellie a cup of tea. At least her demeanour had warmed.

'I think I've drunk enough tea for one day.'

'I'd offer you something stronger...'

'I'd be tempted but no. Carol is waiting outside for me so let's get on with this.'

Stephanie smiled. 'We are very sorry that this incident has happened. It has obviously caused us all a lot of worry.'

'Have you let the police know that I've found her?' It had just occurred to Ellie.

'Yes, we have. Also, I've had a staff meeting to try and work out what went wrong.'

'And?'

'We can only think that Kathleen was aided by other residents, so determined was she to get to the place she truly believes is her home.'

For a moment Ellie was almost pleased that her mother had been successful in her mission, given that she had not come to any harm. For perhaps an hour or so she had lived in the past and, thanks to the kindness of Sylvia, she had been able to enjoy being back in what was her home for many years.

'We think your mother's dementia has got worse.' Stephanie was leaning forward now across the desk as if to add emphasis to her point.

'She gets confused at times but she has days when she's fine. I don't think she's that bad yet,' Ellie jumped to her mother's defence.

'Whatever stage she's at, our priority must be to keep her safe.'

'I would have thought it was the duty of any care home to keep their residents safe.'

'Yes, and that is why I have to insist that she moves to the first floor which is more suited to dementia residents. We can't risk her wandering off again.'

'How exactly is the first floor more suitable?'

'The wing is secure.'

'So, they are locked in?'

'It's for their own good.'

'I'm sorry but I'm really struggling with this. I don't want my mother locked in anywhere.'

'Think about it. You've had a long day. I'm sure you'll see sense tomorrow.'

'I am thinking about it and I'm thinking I don't like it.' Ellie's mind was whirring. 'I mean what about Larry? They get on so well.'

'Relationships are a difficult area at this stage of life.'

'Oh for goodness sake! You can't stop people enjoying each other's company.'

'No, but where will it lead?'

'I don't mind where it leads; I think it's really sweet.'

'If you don't mind me saying, Mrs Hardcastle,' she had clearly dispensed with calling her Ellie, 'you are somewhat naive when it comes to the care of the elderly.'

Ellie stood up. She had tears in her eyes. 'I don't care. I know what's best for my mother!'

'You're obviously getting very emotional. I think we should talk again tomorrow.'

'Of course, I'm emotional!' Ellie wagged her forefinger at this incorrigible woman and shouted, 'She stays where she is. Non-negotiable!' and left Stephanie with a look of horror on her face.

*

Bryan had tossed and turned all night and then finally slept through Tiffany leaving for work. As he came to, he still didn't know what he was going to do. He showered, dressed

169

and decided to walk along to Paddy and Scott's for breakfast where he had his heart set on a pain au raison with an espresso – forbidden fruit in Tiffany's world where her body was her temple.

The café was quite buzzy but there was a leather tub chair by the window free, so armed with his goodies he headed for it and sat down. First, he enjoyed the pastry as he watched the world go by and then he downed his espresso. Somehow, he felt better already. He decided that whatever he did, he had to follow his heart. The trouble was the only thing he was certain of, was that his life was an unbearable mess. A mess of his own making. Living with Tiffany had not lived up to his dream of the start of a new life. Increasingly he couldn't help thinking that she saw him as some sort of Sugar Daddy, a money provider and not the love of her life. If he signed the contract on the Kersey cottage today, he would be committing to making the relationship work somehow. He'd also be bound to paying twelve months rent. It was a lot of money and he knew Carol would be very unhappy about it. He couldn't do it. As he looked at the screen of his mobile, he could see that the letting agent was trying to get hold of him. He stood up, popped his phone back in his pocket, and made his way down the side of the Co-op to the street that ran along the back of Tiffany's flat, to where his car was parked. He got in and drove to the house he'd called home for a very long time.

When he got there, he parked on the drive. Carol's car was missing. With no particular plan, and despite still having a key, he rang the doorbell. There was no answer. She must be out. He decided to move his car and park it on The Street; he didn't want to antagonise Carol in any way. So, he parked outside the pub and walked down to Roger's place. He'd pay his friend a visit.

Roger looked surprised to see him. 'Hello mate, you all right?'

'Is Ellie around?' He didn't want to face her wrath.

'No, she's out at work. You're lucky to catch me in actually.'

'Oh, well good.'

'Come in,' he said more welcoming now. 'It's good to see you.'

'Thanks Roger; I really appreciate that. I'm only too aware I'm the demon of the piece round here.'

'Let me make you a coffee,' Roger said putting the kettle on.

'Thanks. Not too strong, I've just had an espresso.'

'To be honest you look like you haven't slept too well.'

'That's because I haven't.' It felt good to speak the truth.

The coffees made, they went into the garden room and sat opposite each other.

'Sorry, do you have stuff you need to do?' Bryan felt like perhaps he was intruding.

'Don't worry about it. Nothing that can't wait.'

They sat in amiable silence for a while during which Bryan wondered where to start.

'How's it going with Tiffany?' Roger asked.

Bryan felt a fool. 'Not so good,' he said, eyes down.

'Sorry to hear that, mate.'

'Her flat's tiny. I simply can't live there. But moving into rented is pretty bleak too. I found a half-decent place in Kersey but Tiffany doesn't like it. She said Kersey was very pretty but like God's waiting room.'

'Harsh.' Roger looked thoughtful. He went to say something and stopped himself.

'What?' Bryan picked up on it.

'Well it's just that you said she was the love of your life.'

'Yes, I did. What a fool I've been.' He was staring into nothingness as if that was his fate. 'Carol hates me. I got a really frosty reception from her when I turned up the other day. And from Megan. My whole family hate me.'

'You've got a hell of an apology to make to get back in their good books. Does Carol know how you feel?'

'No. I don't really know myself. I was going to talk to her, see if she'd let me move back in.'

'I'm no expert but I know you've really hurt her. She's not going to just welcome you back with open arms.' He rubbed his chin. 'Why don't you stay here for a few nights. Ellie might be able to smooth the ground for you.'

'That would be brilliant but what will Ellie think? She probably hates me too.'

'I'll talk to her. Don't worry about her.'

Bryan's mobile bleeped and not for the first time.

'Someone trying to get hold of you?' Roger asked.

Bryan looked at the screen. There were three messages from the letting agent. 'Shit, I better get back to them. Damn, I'm going to lose the deposit money probably.'

'That cottage you mentioned the other day?'

'Yes, I'm not going to take it now. No point.'

'What about your stuff that you had at Tiffany's? Did you pack a bag before you left?'

'No! Gosh yes, I better pop back and pick up my clothes.'

'I take it Tiffany doesn't know about all this?' Roger asked.

'No, I haven't told her. Well, I didn't know what I was going to do when I left hers.'

'Perhaps you should go back and tell her to her face?'

'God, I don't think I can take that today.' He was standing up fumbling for his car keys in his pocket; suddenly a man in a hurry. 'I'll just pop back now while she's still at work. She doesn't finish until four.'

'But mate, you've got to tell her.'

'Yeah, you're right. I'll leave her a note.'

Roger couldn't help being amused. 'A note!'

But Bryan was making a speedy exit, slipping out of the back door.

When he got to Tiffany's flat, he was practically shaking; this was ridiculous. He stood at the front door for a while listening hard for any sign of movement. He couldn't hear anything so he slipped in and searched for the suitcase he'd used to get his stuff here. It wasn't on top of the wardrobe. Tiffany must have moved it. Where could it be? There was only one built-in cupboard in the flat and, when he opened it, it was so full that towels, pillows, cushions, even a teddy bear fell out. Ah, there it was right at the back! More items tumbled out as he grabbed the case. He left the mess and started selecting his own possessions from the mayhem in the living room. Then the bedroom and his clothes; he thought to check the laundry basket; his laptop; books; the weekend papers (Tiffany didn't read them); then into the bathroom for his toiletries. Every time he heard a sound he froze; his heart skipped a beat. Everything was bunged into the suitcase, no order to it; that would come later; he needed to get out of here. He wasn't entirely sure if he had everything as he went to leave and decided to keep the key, just in case. Seeing the fall-out in the hall from the cupboard he decided to shove it back in otherwise Tiffany might think she'd been burgled. Damn! The note! He needed to write a note. He found a scrap piece of paper in the kitchen but couldn't find a pen. This was ridiculous. Maybe he'd go and buy a pen and put the note through the door? He decided to leave anyway; this was far too dangerous. As he closed the door, one of Tiffany's neighbours, a young chap who always seemed to wear a hoodie and be in a hurry, grunted at him as he whizzed down the stairs. Bryan followed him out into daylight and what seemed like an uneasy freedom. Back in his car he decided to text her. That was what young people did these days; they didn't leave hand written notes. He felt dreadful to be ending the relationship in such a cowardly way. Tiffany deserved better. But the sudden realisation that he had made an enormous mistake was so strong. He had been trying to make things work for them both for some time but it was desperate. Hopeless. He had to get out. And he feared her reaction. She would definitely be mad at him. He had to run.

Ellie felt physically and emotionally spent by the time she got home. It had been a particularly busy day at work, ending late. Stephanie had called more than once and she had just decided to ignore her. She really didn't want to talk to her anyway; it would likely lead to an argument. As she came into her village she noticed Bryan's car outside The Dog and Duck and she thought, of all the pubs in all the world, why did he have to drink at this one?

Home at last she dropped everything where she stood. 'I need a glass of wine!' she yelled out unashamedly.

Roger appeared. 'Good day?' he asked hopefully.

'Dreadful. Non-stop and Starling Skies on my back.'

Roger went straight to the fridge and took out a bottle of wine that was chilled. He poured her a large glass.

'Are you having one?' she asked as she raised her glass.

'Bryan and I have got one already.'

'Bryan?'

'Yes, darling. Don't be cross; he's waving his white flag.'

'It will take much more than that to pacify me! What's he doing here?'

'Calm down will you? He's my friend. Our friend.' Roger was walking towards her; she was leaning away from him, 'Come on, give him a chance.'

'Why?'

'Listen, I think it's over with Tiffany. He realises now he's made a big mistake.'

'I can't believe this.'

'I said he could stay here for a few days.' Roger was obviously telling himself he had done the right thing.

'What! What were you thinking?'

'You are at work most of the time. It will be me here, stuck with him.'

'But this is my home!'

'Listen, I know you've had a trying day what with your mother and everything. How about we get a Chinese takeaway and just relax and enjoy the evening.'

Ellie sighed deeply and took a large glug of wine. 'Do I have any choice? Oh... I'm too exhausted to argue with anyone.'

That evening Bryan got a long text message from Tiffany. A quick scan read of it told him she was very angry. He decided to read it properly the next day and picked up the newspaper for distraction.

Chapter 13

'You see, Steve, this village is all very twee and picture-postcard pretty but full of retired oldies, like my mum.' Rebecca gave her a playful nudge as she sniggered.

Steve looked embarrassed as Carol cringed and glared back at her daughter. Why was she behaving like this? 'Less of the old, if you don't mind. I'm still the right side of sixty.'

'And you look amazing,' Steve said but it was so token that Carol could have wept.

'Anyway Mum, what you are good for, of course, and I'm saying pretty please now, but as you did promise...' She was twirling around like a bashful child, 'Will you give us a lift to Bury St Ed?' She fell short of fluttering her eyelashes.

Carol was tempted to plead forgetfulness due to her advanced years, but knew it was futile. 'No problem, darling.'

'Oh and no need for you to stick around if you don't want to; I mean we will probably see what's on at Abbeygate.' She turned to Steve. 'There's this dear little cinema; I mean it's tiny, really, but quite good fun and they show pretty good films every now and then.'

Carol was about to say she quite fancied the cinema herself, when she decided that a few hours without these two could only be a bonus.

After she'd dropped them off, she decided she'd park at Ram Meadow and walked back through the Abbey Gardens. The sun was coming through the tall trees and it was so peaceful as she wandered up and through the flower beds which didn't disappoint whatever the time of year. Reaching the bottom of Abbeygate she was tempted into one of the designer boutiques and had a carefree browse. She thought back to the early days with Bryan when they were dating and he would indulge her in a shopping spree whenever she chose. How times had changed. She wondered if he went shopping with Tiffany, and if he did, was it willingly or begrudgingly? Stop! She reminded herself to bring a halt to the negative stream of thoughts that plagued her. Live in the moment, enjoy today, she told herself and the shop assistant was smiling at her so she smiled back.

'Looking for anything in particular?' she asked.

'Inner peace, I think.'

'Ooh yes, we have that and just in your size too.' They laughed together and the assistant picked up a silk blouse in an animal print. It was just the sort of thing that Bryan would hate.

'Do you know I like that. Perfect for a night out.' She had the jazz evening in mind; she didn't have a plus one yet but Ellie and Roger were definitely going so she wasn't going to miss out.

'Would you like to try it?'

She went off to the changing room and slipped it on. She looked at herself. There was a difference; she looked younger somehow. She loved it! It felt like a new Carol. Sexier and more sassy than the old Carol. She would buy it. She looked at the price tag and thought, whoops, but what the heck. She kept it on and came out of the cubicle and the assistant simply said, 'Perfect. Do you need trousers to match?'

'What have you got?' Carol asked.

'How about black velvet?'

'Ooh yes!'

'These are straight leg and I can see you are slim enough to wear them.'

'You say all the right things, darling.'

Carol left the shop feeling a bit naughty about the amount she had spent but excited about her new look.

Bella quite enjoyed the walk from Tufnell Park and wore her earphones to tune into her sounds and a cute little rucksack on her back. She went through quiet residential streets lined with Victorian houses, much smarter than the one she resided in, and she wondered if she'd ever live anywhere as nice as this. When she got to an entrance for the park, she took the footpath that ran along the edge of Hampstead Heath and up to Nassington Road before reaching the allotments. She could see Anna in her green wellies and old denim jacket tending to her leeks.

'Hey,' she called across and when Anna looked up, she waved. There was a sort of scruffy order to this place. Neat rows of vegetables amongst wilder more overgrown patches with some areas covered with netting held up precariously with bamboo canes. Some had painted sheds, their allotment homes, where they tended to sit to eat their sandwiches and drink tea from flasks. Most of the residents were quite a bit older than Bella and Anna but they were very friendly, almost paternal, and there was a camaraderie that made you feel good. A railway line edged the plots but after a while you didn't really notice the tube trains.

'They look good. Are you picking some?'

'No, I think they might get a bit bigger. I'll leave them for a week or two. Did you bring a flask?'

Bella opened up her rucksack and held it up.

'Great. I've got a couple of stools in the shed.'

They walked over to Anna's pale-yellow shed and were soon sitting drinking tea in the autumn mellow sunshine.

'So, lovely girl, when are we doing another pop-up? I think we should do vegan street food; what do you reckon?' Anna loved to clown around and stroke your hair. You could be forgiven for thinking she was a lesbian but she wasn't.

'I suppose the last one went quite well but all that baking. Too much.' Bella removed a leaf caught on a strand of her dark hair.

'Yeah, the profit wasn't great. Probably because I burned two batches of cookies before I managed a decent batch.' They both laughed.

'Vegan street food. That would fit well at Camden Lock. We could do a market stall. They don't cost much.'

'Sounds like a plan.' Anna looked impressed.

'Trouble is I don't have any money right now. I never seem to have any money in this city.'

'I could ask Jason again, I suppose.'

'Is that not embarrassing? I mean he's your boyfriend, not your dad.'

'He's cool. Let's face it he got me this allotment and that's down to having a Hampstead postcode. There's no way I could afford to live here if I wasn't with him.'

'You're a lucky girl.'

'But you've got the sweet boy, Ben.' She put an arm around Bella and pulled her close.

'He is a babe but a bit of a hopeless one. I mean he's still working at Revolution for no money.'

'Well that's better than not working, isn't it?'

'Actually, he's got these paintings in some gallery near where his parents live. Apparently, they are going to try and sell them for over a thousand pounds each!'

'That would be brilliant.'

'If they sell.'

'Listen, the boy's got talent.'

'Mm, let's hope so. Anyway, the gallery take thirty per cent and his mum had to pay loads for the framing so...'

'But it's a start.'

'Suppose so.'

'Right.' Anna stood up decisively. 'Damn, I need to pee now.'

'Such a weak bladder,' Bella mocked.

'Listen, I've got a bucket in the shed. You keep guard at the door.'

Anna was mid flow when Bella shouted out, '*There's someone coming,*' in an urgent tone that wouldn't fool anybody. Anna finished her pee and took the bucket out with her to dispose of the contents over the railway track.

'How come you don't have smelly pee?' Bella asked looking dubiously at the empty bucket.

'Don't know. I drink lots of water.'

'And tea,' they chorused together and laughed.

'Now, lazy girl, time to dig up some potatoes and... I think we'll plant up the garlic and broad beans over there.'

By the time they had finished the sun was low in the sky and giving off a pink glow. Bella looked up and took in the autumnal view. She always felt better after some fresh air and a commune with nature. 'Better get back to Tuffers before it gets dark and the loonies come out.' She went cross-eyed and tilted her head to one side.

'Oh, stay. Jase will give you a lift back in the car later.'
Bella was thoughtful.

'Or do you have to rush home to Ben?'

'No, he's doing a Rev. shift tonight.'

'Sorted then. Let's go and get some food, I'm starving.'

Bryan was sat down with a cup of coffee and read the text message from Tiffany, properly this time. He felt the odd stab in the chest but mainly he just felt bad, guilty even. He had ended it the coward's way. But his justification was that he hadn't particularly decided to end it. He'd just felt stuck between a rock and a hard place and there was no solution that he could see. He had been in love with her, he really had. She was amazing. But he was kidding himself that the age gap between them didn't matter. Look at Harrison Ford and Calista Flockhart; that was a relationship that endured. But perhaps being rich and famous somehow made it all right. He knew that he felt more like a father than a boyfriend when they went out with her friends. And he daren't even suggest that they went out with his friends. Did he even have any friends now that he'd done the dirty on his wife?

Tiffany would calm down. She would realise that it was for the best in the long run and that she should find a man more her age. Although the line, *You could of at least told me to my face, don't I deserve that*, troubled him. Would she seek him out? He would give Hadleigh a wide berth for a while. It would all be okay in the end.

Bryan just had the small problem of being homeless and having a wife who hated him.

Ben had a text message from his mother. It sounded urgent. He had to call Amelia Fortescue from the Hunter Gallery. He decided to finish his lunch first which was some chilli con carne left over from last night. It was pretty good. Bella wasn't a bad cook.

Then he called the number as per his mother's instruction.

'Ah Ben, yes, I have a buyer for your paintings.'

'Really? Which one?'

'All three actually. There was another client interested in *No More* but then one of my contacts, Jonathan Glover, well, he wants all three.'

'That's amazing. Who is this guy?'

'I've done quite a bit of business with Jonathan over the years. He has a gallery in London, Islington actually, but he has family in Suffolk, his mother I believe, so he took an interest in what we do here.'

'That's good. I'm in London.'

'Anyway, he's willing to pay five thousand pounds for the three.'

'Five thousand pounds?' It seemed ridiculous to Ben.

'Yes, that's right. Is that okay?'

'Yeah, of course it is.'

'And he wants to meet you.'

'Really? Why's that?'

'Well sometimes buyers do want to meet the artist and we arrange it if we can.'

'Could I meet him in London then?'

'Ideally, I'd like you here, tomorrow, when he comes to collect. Is that possible?'

Ben couldn't see how he could do that. 'Not sure about that. You see, I've got a shift at this bar I work at.'

Amelia was laughing gently at him. 'And how much do they pay you at this bar? Minimum wage?'

'Yeah, probably.'

'Well, Ben, darling, this chap is paying maximum wage so if I were you, I would get here tomorrow for three o'clock, if at all possible.'

'Yeah sure.' She was quite insistent but she had sold the paintings which was pretty incredible.

'So, can I assure Jonathan that you'll be here?'

'Let me just talk to my mum, first, and make sure she can give me a lift. I'll call you back.'

'Okay, Ben. Please be quick about it. I don't like keeping clients waiting.'

Ben rang Ellie. It went to her voicemail so he left a message. Then he decided to try his dad.

'Hello son, everything all right?'

'Yeah, Dad, good actually.'

'Don't tell me you've sold a painting?' His tone was mocking as usual.

'No Dad, not one, all three for five thousand pounds.'

'Bloody hell, son, well done you. My goodness, that's incredible. Five thousand pounds. Brilliant. Hats off to you my son.'

'Yeah, but that Amelia woman wants me at Hunters tomorrow at three o'clock to meet the client, some guy apparently, and he has a gallery in London but wants to meet me up your way.'

'No problem at all, Ben. We'll get you there one way or the other.'

'Thanks Dad.' He had his moments.

'Just let us know what train you're on. And Ben...' He stopped mid-sentence.

'What Dad?'

'I'm... well, I'm really impressed with what you've achieved. I know I go on a bit sometimes; I don't mean to but the art world, well, it's not easy for me to understand. But I really admire what you've done, so well done that man.'

'Thanks Dad.' Ben put his mobile down and let this momentous moment sink in. The world was a strange place and often difficult to make sense of. But sometimes things seemed to go right and it gave him hope. Maybe Bella would stick with him after all. He decided to go and start a new painting.

Chapter 14

The article on the front page of the *East Anglian Daily Times* read like an absolute travesty. Ellie couldn't believe it. The protest that she had taken part in was played right down, while all the supposed benefits of this proposal were there in technicolour glory; how so very convenient it was going to be for the people of Capel Green to have a store they could drive to, park outside and purchase their weekly grocery shop. Then it went on about bringing employment to the area. The journalist failed to mention the dent it would inevitably make on local competing businesses making people unemployed. The article even went as far as to say that Cost-Cut was not trying to outdo the farm shop, simply supplement their offering with convenience foods at cheaper prices. Parish councillor, David Harrison, was quoted as saying, *'We are reviewing this proposal and consulting with interested parties but I have to say the idea of a petrol station on the edge of Capel Green is very appealing.'*

Ellie looked up to meet James's gaze across the agency.

'Well at least they haven't got a quote from you!' She dropped the paper on his desk so he could see for himself.

James was his usual measured, unruffled self. 'There's a meeting about the development at the village hall tomorrow evening.'

'Really? They've kept that quiet. Are Cost-Cut daring to show their face?'

'Yes, I believe they will be there. They are aware there is some local opposition and they want to give people the opportunity to ask questions.'

'Excellent. I certainly have a few questions for them.' She picked up her mobile and texted Emma at the farm shop asking her if she knew about this meeting.

She replied, *No! Outrageous that they haven't advertised. Will be there defo Emma x*

Ellie headed straight to the farm shop after work. Emma had said that she finished her shift at five o'clock but she would wait for her. They sat in the café with a pot of tea.

'So, are Cost-Cut definitely going to be there?'

'James, my boss, thinks they will be.'

'Is he with us, on our side, now?'

'He's sitting on the fence a bit because he knows I'm so outraged by it. Apparently, he is going to the meeting but planning to keep a low profile.'

'Can't we persuade him to join our cause? It would be great to have someone like him.'

'The trouble is, he's an estate agent through and through and he can't help thinking that this new development will attract people to the area.'

'But it's going to spoil Capel Green. People want to live in the village because it's such a beautiful place, a conservation area, not because there's a horrible Cost-Cut on their doorstep.'

'I agree wholeheartedly.'

Emma was thoughtful. The man who had given Carol an application form appeared at their table.

'This is Bill, he's the manager here. Do you mind if he joins us?'

'Not at all.'

'Thanks,' Bill said as he pulled up another chair and sat down. 'And we appreciate your support, Ellie.'

'It's the least I can do. I love this farm shop and even if they do build a Cost-Cut express store I certainly won't be shopping there.'

Bill smiled. 'I think their offering is going to be very different to ours. We have done some digging and it looks like they're going to be selling mainly high margin convenience foods. Sweets, crisps, chocolate, biscuits, fizzy drinks and processed foods.'

'All the things that are bad for you,' Emma added wide-eyed.

'Too right,' Ellie agreed. 'Perhaps we should focus on that. You know, how these foods are contributing to the obesity crisis in this country.'

'Yes.' Bill was enthused, 'That will have wide appeal in this area. They're quite a health-conscious bunch in Capel Green.'

'Great. And what about the additional cars that will come through the village?' Emma asked pouring herself another cup of tea.

'That's another really good point. If there's one thing that gets the villagers' backs up it's traffic! Especially down Water Street which is a real bottleneck.' Bill looked around as if he wanted something.

'Shall I get you a tea?' Emma asked.

'Wouldn't mind.'

While she was gone, Bill turned to Ellie, 'It's your friend, Carol, who applied for the job here, isn't it?'

'Yes, that's right. I think she's been for an interview.'

'She has. We've offered her the job.'

'That's great. Just what she needs right now.'

Bill's eyes widened with curiosity. 'She alluded to some sort of change in her life.'

'You could say that. I probably shouldn't gossip but it's her husband, Bryan, having some sort of mid-life crisis and going off with a girl half his age.'

'Oh dear.'

Emma appeared with another big pot of tea and a cup for Bill. 'What time does this meeting start?' she asked.

'Seven-thirty, apparently.'

'I think we should aim to get there well before then,' Bill said.

'Yes, and we really need to spread the word. I will get it out on Facebook now,' Emma said as she fiddled with her mobile.

'We haven't got long.' Bill was thoughtful. 'We've still got some flyers left over from the road sit-in. Trouble is they've got the wrong date on them. I think it would be worth knocking up a new flyer and just printing out some copies. I'll get on with that as soon as we are done here.'

'If you want me to hand some out in my village, I'm happy to do that,' Ellie said pleased to help.

'Great. It will probably take me an hour or so to knock them out; if you want to give me your mobile number, I can let you know when they are ready.'

They exchanged numbers. Ellie felt excited to be a part of a campaign that could really make a difference.

Bryan was home alone. Ellie was at work. Roger had gone to the supermarket. He had offered to go with him but Roger seemed to want to go on his own.

He had found out just last night that Carol had applied for a job. That surprised him. Maybe he should get a job; part time, of course. He tried to turn his laptop on. Nothing. He tried again and again as if the outcome would be different. Still nothing. The battery was dead. He searched through his belongings. Surely the cable was somewhere? He went through everything, over and over, in what was Ben's old room and had become his temporary refuge. It wasn't there. The realisation that he'd left it in Tiffany's flat gripped him and made him feel sick. Perhaps he could get a replacement cable. He grabbed his mobile and did a quick search only to find that it was going to prove difficult. People didn't buy cables without laptops attached. He cursed the size of Tiffany's flat; the untidiness which made it hard to find anything. How could she live like that? It was no good; he was going to have to carry out a rescue mission.

He racked his brain to try and remember what her shift pattern was. Of course, it changed from week to week but she only had one Saturday off in three. But it wasn't Saturday. This was hopeless. He decided to head to Hadleigh and take the risk.

From the main street Tiffany's flat looked dark and gave away no clues. He went down the alley at the side of the pub to the back of the buildings. He couldn't see her car. He looked and looked; it definitely wasn't there. What did that mean? She was definitely out? She often walked to work; it was no distance. But the fact that her car wasn't there was a good sign. Or was it? He decided to go in and let himself into the main door at the side and then crept furtively up the stairs and stood outside her door, his ear against the wood. All was quiet. The main door opened and closed. Footsteps came up the stairs. Heavy steps. Too heavy for Tiffany. A middle-aged woman appeared with two bags of shopping. She glanced at Bryan with a puzzled expression. Bryan flashed a cynical smile at her but realised he couldn't stand there any longer without looking suspicious, so he found his key in his pocket and quietly opened the door. The first thing he noticed as he walked into the living area was that it was warm. Tiffany wouldn't have left the heating on if she'd gone out. And then she appeared from the kitchen and was standing in front of him looking dishevelled, no make-up, a red nose. Was that shock or surprise on her face?

'Bryan. You've got a nerve.'

'Sorry, I'm so sorry about everything. I thought maybe you were out.'

'So, what are you doing here? Going to burgle me?'

'No! Of course not. I left my laptop lead here. My mistake.' He glanced around the room; it was more cluttered than ever.

'So, you thought you'd sneak back in to get it. You weren't man enough to face me?'

'Listen, I'm sorry about what happened, I really am.'

'How could you? Did I not mean anything to you? Is my flat not good enough for you? I would have lived with you in that god-forsaken Kersey place if that's what it would take. But you just ran back to your wife without even a discussion.'

He decided not to put her straight on that last point but to focus on the laptop lead. 'I've said I'm sorry. I don't know what else I can do.'

'Arrgh! You're pathetic.'

He didn't respond. She was a wall of anger stood between him and his power cable.

'You're a sad old man living a sad old life with that boring wife of yours.'

He looked at her and for the first time wondered what he'd seen in her. They were poles apart in attitudes, taste, everything! And that was apart from the age gap.

'Please may I look for my laptop lead?'

'No! Bugger off! Too bloody bad. Buy another one.'

'Actually, it's not possible to just get the lead.'

'Don't be ridiculous.'

'Please Tiffany. Let me look for it and then I'll be out of your hair for good.'

She collapsed on her sofa and started to weep. 'You don't care about me.'

His eyes furtively darted around the room. Where could it be? Without rummaging through her stuff he'd never find it. He moved, slowly at first, towards the IKEA shelving unit and scanned it for the prized item. No wires. He started to move towards the door. He checked her bedroom while she was preoccupied with her wailing.

'What do you think you're doing?' She had sprung up and confronted him. 'Prowling round my flat!'

It was no good; he'd have to make a run for it.

She disappeared back into the living area. He hesitated. He really wanted that lead. Then she emerged surprisingly quickly holding what he'd come for. She threw it at him. 'I hate you,' she said but was somehow calmer now. Why did women need to make such a drama out of everything?

'Thank you,' he said and turned to leave.

'My keys,' she demanded holding out her hand.

And he handed them over. 'I am sorry,' he said yet again.

Ellie got home to find Roger was in the kitchen cooking.

'Where's Bryan?' she asked trying to hide the irritation in her voice.

'He's only just got in. Looks a bit shaken actually. Bit of a contretemps with Tiffany apparently.'

'That's still going on then, is it?'

'Er, no, I think that is well and truly over now.'

Ellie's eyes rolled. 'Come to his senses at last, has he?'

'Oh, come on, Ellie, darling, he is really sorry about everything.'

'Mm...' She was not convinced.

'You could help smooth the waters with Carol for him, couldn't you?' He turned to his onions, 'Shit, they're burning.' He moved the pan off the hob and the indicator light started flashing at him. 'I can't get used to this induction hob.'

She went over to him and peered into the pan. 'They're okay. Caramelised, I think they call it.'

'Good.'

She turned the heat down. 'What are you making?'

'Risotto.'

'That's adventurous for you, isn't it? When will it be ready? I'm going to have to pop out again later to pick up some flyers.'

Bryan appeared. 'Evening Ellie. What's this about flyers?'

'Would you believe there's a meeting at Capel Green village hall tomorrow evening about this Cost-Cut development? And they are going to be at the hall to answer questions from the public.'

'Isn't that a good thing?'

'Well yes, but they've kept very quiet about it so we need to get the word out.'

'Right, well.' Bryan looked like he was thinking fast, 'I'm happy to support the anti-campaign and I'm free tomorrow evening.'

'You're free every evening, mate,' Roger chimed in and Bryan looked vulnerable, hurt even.

'Anyway, I'm picking up the flyers this evening and need to get them distributed around the village before the meeting so there's not much time.'

'I can do that,' Bryan said surprising everyone especially Ellie.

'Will you? That would be really helpful, Bryan.' This was definitely one small step in redeeming himself.

'So, where are you picking up the flyers from?' Bryan asked.

'A chap called Bill, at the farm shop, is producing them and printing them out. So as soon as I get the call on my mobile, they will be ready to collect.' She suddenly remembered her earlier indiscretion when she'd told Bill about Bryan's misdemeanour. 'Actually, it's probably better if I pick them up; you can help me distribute them round the village; that would be great.'

'No, don't be silly. I'll pick them up,' he insisted, 'you've been out working all day.'

Ellie couldn't help smiling as she considered the consequences of Bill being faced with the errant Bryan. 'Okay.

Thanks.' What was that expression? Don't sweat the small stuff.

Bryan found himself an apron to put on and said to Roger, 'How can I help?'

'Brilliant, mate. Would you make some chicken stock?'

'Er...'

'That cupboard for the stock cubes.' Ellie pointed him in the right direction. 'You'll need to boil some water in the kettle.' She smiled knowing full well his culinary skills were non-existent; Carol even said he couldn't make toast without burning it.

The risotto was good and by some miracle Bryan's help had speeded up the preparation of it. Ellie appreciated being able to relax in the garden room with a magazine and by the time they sat down to eat together, she found herself telling Bryan all about the campaign to stop the development. Whether he was interested or not, he was on his best behaviour and made all the right responses. He even offered to ask a difficult question at the meeting the following evening.

'I'll do some research, if you like? Find out a bit more about Cost-Cut and their expansion plans.'

'That would be great. And if you could check out what sort of produce they stock at their other express stores that would be ammunition for our argument about unhealthy foods.'

'Got it.'

True to his word, he picked up the flyers and delivered them in the dark. Ellie couldn't help being impressed. He even seemed cheerful when he got back late into the evening.

'Do you want a cup of tea?' Ellie asked.

'Thank you, yes.'

'How did it go?'

'No problems. I had two hundred flyers and they are all delivered.'

'Well done. Hopefully that will boost attendance at the meeting.'

'I think Bill was expecting you. He seemed quite put out when I turned up.'

'Oh really? I did tell him on a text that it would be you, not me.'

'Anyway, I said that I was only too happy to help and I'd see him at the meeting tomorrow evening.'

Ellie was amused but made sure she didn't show it. 'It's going to be an interesting meeting.'

'Yes, I'm looking forward to it.'

Ben had worked non-stop all evening serving at the bar at Revolution. The demanding punters had come thick and fast and it was difficult to keep up.

'Who else is on tonight?' Ben asked Terry, the manager.

'Robbie called in sick. Sorry mate.'

'Can't you text round. Lofty always says he's up for extra shifts.'

'Three Lonewolf gins, soon as you're ready, mate,' a chap called from the bar and Ben set to serving him.

'Oy, I was here first.'

'You're next,' Ben said decisively nodding towards the complainer. He had watched and learned how to deal with this crowd.

By the end of his shift he was sweating and felt done in; he went straight into the back to get his rucksack and jacket.

Terry appeared. 'Can you stay a bit longer? Help with the clear up.'

'Sorry mate, got to get home.'

'I'll pay you double.'

Ben thought about the three and a half thousand pounds from the sale of his art sitting in his bank account.

'No can do, Terry. I'm knackered and Robbie didn't even turn up so I've done double the work for the same money.'

Terry came right up to him in a slightly menacing fashion. 'You're right mate. I can do something about that. Organise a little bonus for you. I just need you for one more hour.'

'The answer's no.' Ben held on to the thought that Bella would be proud of him.

Terry looked affronted now. 'You want to keep this job or not?'

'Not bothered,' Ben said.

'Honestly, young people today, they don't know how lucky they are.'

'Oh, I do mate. I know exactly how lucky I am,' he said and grinned as he walked out of the door leaving Terry confused and fuming.

Bella and Anna were at the kitchen table when he got home. There were papers all over the place and they were both swigging happily from bottles of Peroni.

'Benny boy, you're home.' Bella reached out to him with an arm as if she was tied to her chair.

'Yeah, back. Crazy tonight. Robbie was a no-show.'

'Oh, baby, baby. Let me get you a beer.'

'Don't mind if I do.'

Anna gave him a random hug. 'Benny, you're special! Quite the pro artist these days.' She always seemed slightly mad to Ben but he quite liked her.

'So, what have you guys been up to? Planning something by the looks of things.'

'Yeah, we're doing vegan street food at Camden Market. How cool is that?' Bella explained as she took the lid off a bottle of Peroni.

'Awesome.'

'My Jase is financing us.'

'Even better.'

'Yay!' Bella handed Ben the bottle. She sat down and picked up a piece of paper. 'What do you think of vegan pad thai – made with tofu?' She spoke very deliberately.

'Obvs,' Anna chimed in.

'And veggie curry.'

'Always good, especially with sweet potato,' Anna added.

'Good choices,' Ben said and tried to stifle a yawn. 'Sorry that place is just knackering me.'

'Jack it in,' Bella said without hesitation.

'I think I may have done just that.'

'Excellent, you're an artist. A proper artist.' She beamed across at him.

They all clunked their bottles and cheered. Ben took a swig, created a pillow with his arms on the table in front of him, lay down his head and fell asleep.

'Bless,' Anna said.

Chapter 15

The hall was filling up nicely, there was a gentle hum of voices, and the organisers were having to put out more chairs. It was a cold but dry night, and so enticed well-wrapped villagers out. A long table at the front of the hall had five chairs behind it – so far empty – and there was a projector and screen set up.

Bill smiled and waved across the room to Ellie. Emma bounded over.

'Brilliant isn't it? We've done amazingly well to get the word out. Bill said he heard one of the Cost-Cut guys saying he couldn't understand the number of people here.'

'They're so arrogant these businessmen.'

'But are all these people on your side?' Roger asked. 'Some of them might welcome this development.'

'Well, we'll just have to put them off, won't we?' Bryan said, waving some papers he held in his hand. 'I've got some stats here that will alarm them.'

Emma raised her eyebrows.

'Bryan's been researching all the factors that support our case,' Ellie filled her in.

'That's brilliant. Do you live in Capel Green, then?'

'No, actually, same village as Ellie.'

Bill appeared with a folder. 'Evening all. Have you all got questions ready to ask?'

'Bryan, here, has,' Roger said.

'Great, well,' Bill opened his folder and started handing out sheets of paper, 'Here's a list of ideas in case you're stuck and depending on how the meeting goes you can shout one or two out.'

'Great, thanks Bill.' Ellie smiled at him. 'And what if they don't answer them properly like politicians?'

'It's always a problem but we will just have to keep pushing and hope they break. Of course, we don't know what they've got up their sleeve.'

Carol appeared from the back of the hall. She looked great, wearing a pretty autumnal scarf and a brown leather jacket over tight hugging jeans.

'Hi Carol, good to see you,' Bryan said nervously meeting her bemused stare.

Ellie was dreading this moment; she felt awful about Bryan staying with them. She hadn't managed to find the right moment to tell Carol yet.

'I have some seats reserved at the front,' Bill said specifically to Carol. Bryan looked anxious.

'Good to see you, darling,' Ellie grabbed her friend's arm. 'Shall we both sit at the front with the farm shop contingent?' She led Carol away and Bill and Emma followed, leaving Roger and Bryan to sit at the back.

The five seats were now filled with men in suits, three with ties and two opting for an open neck shirt. They looked out on to a crowd of jeans' wearers, with lots of padded gilets. The man in the centre was clean shaven with chiselled features and an anxious look behind his eyes. David Harrison, chair of the parish council, shouted above the melee for people to be seated for the start of the meeting. He held his hands up and spread wide asking for hush.

'Thank you for coming out on this chilly evening,' he started. 'We have here various representatives of Cost-Cut and they would appreciate your attention while they share with you their plans in a short presentation before opening the floor up to questions.' He nodded to Chisel Features who stood up.

'We are delighted that so many local residents have joined us this evening—' *No, you're not!* 'I am the regional manager for this area, Derek Dunhill, and I hope you will indulge me as I show you a short film about Cost-Cut.' He nodded to a young woman who was stood at the projector and she started the film.

Of course, it extolled the virtues of convenience shopping and talked about serving the residents of Capel Green. It showed an artist's impression of the proposed store which had the building blending in with the landscape and talked about every consideration having been given to the beauty of this conservation area whilst also pointing out that the proposed development was actually outside the protected zone. Eyebrows were raised as viewers muttered to their neighbours in the audience. Then came the icing on their cake, a petrol station, allowing residents to fill up without having to make the epic journey of over six miles to Sudbury. This fact met a stony silence. Ellie was hoping that people were simply so appalled by the idea that they were dumbfounded. By the time the video was over Ellie was enraged and couldn't keep still. She was itching to tear down their propaganda. Bill leaned in and put a hand in front of her before standing up. David Harrison gave him the nod.

'The people of Capel Green are already served by a Co-op store for convenience and a farm shop for fresh produce, so why do we need a Cost-Cut?'

Derek stood up. 'We believe people should have a choice. Competition is healthy and helps to keep prices low for the customer.'

'The people of Capel Green choose not to have a Cost-Cut in the village,' Bill retorted. 'The recent protest, when over a thousand people signed a petition, made that very clear.'

Another suit stood up. 'We are aware of this, of course, we are. And this is why we have been very careful to adapt the architecture of the store so that, far from being an eyesore, it is a pleasant building forming part of the landscape.'

'What about the car park and all the cars you'll attract!' Bryan shouted from the back and many turned to look at him. He continued, 'I have some figures here of the sort of footfall you are expecting for this size store and it suggests that the proposed twenty car parking spaces might very well be used throughout the long day you are proposing to open for. This means much more traffic through the village.'

'And through Water Street which is already a bottleneck,' a senior lady stood to declare. 'The last thing we need is more traffic!'

This was met with 'hear, hear!' from around the room.

Emma was on her feet. One of the suits also stood, but Emma shouted loudest. 'What about the convenience foods, sugary treats and processed foods that are so bad for our health?'

Chisel Features went bright red at this point. The standing suit gave a feisty reply, 'I understand there is a contingent from the local farm shop here this evening and I think you should know that we have no intention of treading on your toes.'

Emma was incensed. 'You're missing the point. We stock healthy fresh foods that locals want. You are planning to stock the sort of produce that is contributing to the obesity crisis in this country!'

The tubby suit at the end of the long table sank as low into his seat as he possibly could simply drawing attention to himself.

Feisty Suit stood up again. 'We have done our research and there's a strong indication that the express store we are proposing is what many residents desire.'

'Rubbish!' Bryan yelled from the back. 'Who are these people?'

Everyone was looking at Bryan again, even Carol this time.

'A survey has shown that there is a market here in Capel Green for our product; we wouldn't be going ahead otherwise.' What a patronising twat.

This met boos from the audience and Bryan, still standing, shouted out, 'Let's have a vote on it then! Here and now. Those in favour of this scheme, please stand up.' Bryan sat down. No one stood up. Or perhaps no one dared.

Chisel Features was moved to intervene. 'Really this meeting cannot be used as some sort of referendum. I can assure you Cost-Cut have carried out the necessary surveys and they have met with our satisfaction.'

Ellie thought she might explode and sprung to her feet. 'What survey? Show us this survey where this community have apparently said they want an unhealthy food store, a car park and a petrol station to blot their beautiful village.'

Other members of the audience cheered her.

A man stood up and introduced himself as Farmer Derry. 'What Cost-Cut don't seem to realise is that supermarkets are the bane of a farmer's life.' He spoke in a strong Suffolk accent and the suits were obviously struggling to make sense of what he was saying. 'We want to sell to farm shops and local butchers where we get a decent price for what we do. We don't want to sell to the likes of you.' Point made, he sneered and sat down.

Feisty Suit responded. 'We are not planning to stock farm produce so you have nothing to fear.'

'No! Just unhealthy rubbish to make our kids obese,' a young mother shouted out. 'And what about schoolkids buying sweets instead of healthy snacks. It's difficult enough being a mother without Cost-Cut.'

'Let me ask you,' Feisty Suit began addressing the mother directly, 'would you like the cost of your weekly shop reduced?'

'No!' she yelled emphatically, 'not at the expense of my children's health.'

'Well, you are an exception to the rule,' he continued but the boos got louder until he was forced to retreat.

Chisel Features had lost his composure and looked positively angry. He stared at David Harrison as if this was all his fault.

Farmer Derry was on his feet and stomped to the front of the room so that he was right in front of the enemy. 'We don't want you here!' he bellowed. 'Are you stupid or something?' The crowd were cheering. 'Go and blight someone else's village.'

All the suits looked terrified. David Harrison came forward to intervene. 'Now Rodney, I think you've made your point. Perhaps you should sit down.' The farmer growled at him. 'I want these know-it-alls out of here.'

'We need to have an orderly debate. Please would you sit down.' The crowd were all cheering him. There were shouts of 'Say no to Cost-Cut' and all the suits, with a look of horror on their faces, collected their papers, got up and started to file out of the room but this meant getting past the crowd. David tried to form a barrier between them and the protesters and they kept close to the side wall. Bill got up to face the crowd and signalled for quiet. It took at least a minute for order to prevail by which time the Cost-Cut group were safely out of the building.

'I know how strongly you all feel and thank you so much for coming this evening. Let's keep this civilised. We've made our arguments and will continue to do so at every opportunity. Capel Green Farm Shop have a Facebook page where you can also post your support. Oh, and there are flyers for you to pick up on your way out. Thank you and goodnight.'

As they shuffled out, the inevitable happened and Carol came face to face with Bryan again. He had a sadness in his eyes as he looked at her.

She remained composed with her head held high. 'Since when have you been fighting the forces of evil?'

'I...' It was obvious that he was pleased that she had at least spoken to him. 'I, well, I know you're working at the farm shop now and...' He still had her attention and it was making him nervous. 'Anyway, Ellie was getting involved and I just wanted to help.'

She looked as if her feelings were confused. Bill appeared.

'Thanks everyone. I think we can safely say that was a success.' He was looking at Bryan, but then added, 'Really, it's great that we've had so much support.' He handed flyers out to them all. 'This tells you how you can object to the development on the council's planning website.'

'I shall be sure to do that,' Bryan said. Carol looked conflicted.

'Carol, do you have a minute?' Bill said to her and started to walk away. To Bryan's horror she followed him willingly.

'What's going on there?' he asked, his eyes darting from Ellie to Roger and back.

'Nothing, mate,' Roger reassured. 'Probably something to do with when her next shift is, at the farm shop.'

'When is her next shift?' Bryan asked as if he had a right to know.

'Come on, mate, let's go home,' Roger said steering him out. Ellie sighed and thought, what a dreadful mess it all was.

Chapter 16

Ben had his easel set up in the kitchen with his paints all over the kitchen table apart from one end where he'd swept his arm across to bundle an array of random things including unopened mail, mobile phone chargers and flyers for local gigs letting them form a messy pile. He contemplated his palette. So far it was pretty dark, but then his jazz paintings were generally on the dark side. Maybe he'd use some yellow ochre, even some ruby. Bella appeared and flopped around looking agitated.

'What?'

'Are you painting?' She said it in a long drawn out whingeing sort of way. He decided it didn't warrant a response and squirted some yellow ochre oil paint on to his palette well away from the dark shades.

She came over and threw her arms round him. 'Ben!' she demanded.

'What?' She kissed him. He didn't want to be kissed right at that moment.

'I want to try out some vegan recipes but I can't with all your stuff in here.'

'Too bad then.'

'Can't you paint in our room?'

'The light's better here.'

'Why don't you rent a studio now you've got all that money?'

'No, I don't want to waste it.'

'Is this Mummy and Daddy saying you've got to save it?'

Roger had made noises about spending it wisely but he wasn't heavy handed about it. Use the time to paint more was his advice and now he wasn't working at Revolution that seemed like the best thing to do.

'Okay, so you've got your painting and I've got my pop-up cafés and we both want the kitchen.' Bella slung herself into a chair now and gave him a hard stare.

'Look I just need to create right now. That Jonathan guy who bought my jazz paintings, he rang earlier.'

'Does he want more from you?'

'He might do. He likes the jazz theme and he wants me to take some work to his London place.'

'That's good. At this rate we might be able to afford our own place soon. With an art studio and a big kitchen.'

'Maybe,' Ben said.

Bella was texting and after less than a minute she said, 'Right, I'm off to Anna's to cook.'

The couple, who must have been in their mid-thirties, were holding hands and virtually skipping along together with joyous grins as they approached Ellie outside an unassuming two-bedroomed house on Spring Road. Ellie's mobile phone rang and a glance at the screen told her it was the care home.

'I'm really sorry, I'm going to have to get this.' They looked surprised but as if nothing would burst their bubble. Ellie negotiated finding the key in her handbag and let them in to the property while she stayed outside and took the call.

It was Stephanie and they seemed to be on first name terms again.

'I'm sorry, Ellie, but your mother is upsetting the other residents in the day room.'

'Oh dear. Has something happened to bring this on? Is Larry there?'

'We've tried that. It's so difficult with dementia; one day can be very different to another. Listen, I am sorry our discussion the other day didn't end well but we really do need to talk again.'

Ellie sighed. 'Listen, Stephanie, I'm going to have to call you back. I'm at work and in the middle of a property viewing. I should be able to call you in about fifteen, twenty minutes.'

'Okay.' She sounded as if it was far from okay.

James called these houses starter homes meaning they were slightly more affordable than a lot of the houses in Capel Green and very small. Consequently, viewings didn't take long and usually disappointed. Following a look round the downstairs, her clients' bonhomie had been replaced with a slightly anxious confusion.

'Sorry about that.' Ellie shook both their hands and they introduced themselves as Scott and Laura.

'Have you been upstairs?' Ellie asked.

'Not yet. It's smaller than we were expecting,' Scott said frankly.

'The kitchen's tiny,' Laura said as if it almost offended her. 'Could we knock through?'

'I suspect so; you'd need to get an architect to look at it.' Seeing their disappointed faces, she added, 'Open plan is all the rage now.'

She let them go upstairs on their own rather than take up much desired space herself. By the time they came back down Laura looked depressed.

'So,' Ellie turned to the couple, 'any thoughts?'

'I think it's too small,' he said reluctantly.

'But it's all we can afford in Capel Green and this is where I want to live,' Laura asserted.

'Is this really the only option on our budget?' he asked.

'There are some bungalows on the far edge of the village, the church end, that come up for sale from time to time. They all tend to need a lot of work; people buy them and do them up. But the good news is that they cost less than these places and they are bigger.'

'A bungalow,' she said looking as if all her hopes and dreams had just been shattered.

'Are any of them on the market now?' He was more determined to get the square peg into a round hole. 'Can we view one?'

'We have been asked to value one of them but they haven't given us the go-ahead to market yet. I could make sure you are the first to know about it, if they do.'

'Would you, please?' He wandered off back into the kitchen having another desperate look round and knocking on partition walls. She followed with a look of total disillusion. They muttered to each other.

'Right, if you could let us know about the bungalow,' he said.

'I will.'

'And if anything else comes up in the meantime.'

'I will be sure to let you know.'

Finally alone, Ellie didn't really know what to do. She knew that Stephanie was on a mission to get her mother locked up on the first floor. It was such a dispiriting prospect. The thought of her mother being amongst others whose dementia could be much worse than her own was unbearable. The thought of her life of lucidity being over was the saddest realisation of all. Ellie sat in her car and tried not to cry.

Her mobile rang again and this time, surprisingly, it was Bryan. Ellie considered ignoring it but then thought what the heck and took the call.

'Ellie, the care home has been after you. They rang here and I said I'd let you know.'

'Yes, I know. They've already got me on my mobile.'

'Everything okay?' he asked. 'You sound a bit down. Is there anything I can do? I mean it must be difficult when you're at work.'

'Not really,' she said before adding almost as a desperate joke, 'unless you want to go to Starling Skies and persuade

Stephanie, the manager there, that my mother must stay where she is and not move to the dementia floor.'

'I can do that,' he said causing Ellie's eyes to widen in disbelief.

'Are you sure?'

'I'd like to help. And let's face it I haven't got a great deal else on right now.'

'I'm not sure how they will react as you're not next of kin.'

'Well, there's not a lot they can do, is there? I mean if I turn up and say you're at work so they've got me or no one.'

Ellie decided it was worth a try. 'Okay, I'd better fill you in then.'

'I'm locked in!' Kathleen shouted to the carer who had just appeared in her room. 'Is this a prison?'

The girl who stood before her had a vacant expression as she made Kathleen's bed. She didn't seem to feel the need to answer her. Kathleen rose to her feet and went straight up to the girl so that she was right in her face. 'Please, I'm saying please will you let me out of this room. I just want to go to the day room.'

'That's okay. I'll take you after you've had your medication.'

'I don't want my medication.'

'Well, that's the deal.'

She sat back in her chair defeated and took her meds.

Kathleen was stood at the French doors of the day room looking out on to an autumn scene, the trees in the distance with a canopy of rich earthy colours were glorious; if only they would stay like that forever. It might not be the warmest of days but she longed to be free to roam the garden. Being trapped in this place, she had no control over her destiny. She just had to do as she was told, eat what she was given and put up with whatever company was on offer. How she longed to be back at Benton Street, even if she was about to end her days; at least her final moments would be where she felt most alive.

Larry came over to her. 'Good morning, Kathleen.' He had a cheerful disposition; he seemed to cope with this place better than her.

She turned, smiled and replied warmly, 'Larry.'

'May I say you are looking particularly lovely today.'

She giggled. 'Don't be silly.'

'I'm not,' he said. 'Shall we dance?' No sooner had he asked her, she was in his arms, waltzing around the room. Amazingly her legs seemed to work better today. She glided as he led her, this way and that.

'But where's the music?' she asked excitedly. He began to sing a Frank Sinatra song, *Come Fly with Me*, and she joined in loving every second, transported to another time and place. They twirled around the room, the other residents joining in the singing. It was a magical moment; Kathleen felt light on her feet; her spirits were lifted. She would never be locked in that horrible room alone again; she would dance with Larry for evermore.

Eventually, but not for a long time, she began to feel a bit dizzy. He led her to an armchair and bowed to her as he held her hand and she sat down. Larry fell unsteadily into the chair next to her.

'Thank you, kind sir,' she said. 'Are you all right?'

'Bit shaky on my pins. Probably shouldn't have done that but I don't care. Anyway, I didn't fall over so no harm done.'

Kathleen put her head back on her chair.

'The old ones are the best.' Larry was out of breath but had a broad smile on his face and a twinkle in his eye. 'It was a simpler age; life was good.'

'The whole family huddling round the coal fire in the winter.' Kathleen loved to reminisce.

'Ice on the inside of the bedroom window!' They laughed together.

'Oh yes, we had proper winters then.'

'Drinking pop delivered by the pop man.'

'And dandelion and burdock.'

'Ooh, you were sophisticated,' Larry teased.

'Listening to the wireless or playing music on the gramophone.'

'Wouldn't it be wonderful if we could have a gramophone here? Perhaps I'll ask my boy to buy one for us and bring it in.'

'Will he?'

Larry leant in so that he was close to Kathleen's ear and whispered, 'We'll have to get it past matron.'

She squealed with delight but then the reality of their situation enveloped her and her face dropped.

'What is it, Kathleen?' He looked concerned.

'Wouldn't it be lovely if we could get out of here? Just for one day.'

'It would be perfect! Just you and me.' Larry always managed to lift her spirits.

There was something quite sexy about Stephanie Tilston. She was tall and had a good figure under that buttoned-up cardigan and tweed skirt. She reminded Bryan of a headmistress in a school for well-behaved girls and he suspected she didn't suffer fools gladly.

He was already on dodgy ground, not being a relative of the resident he was here about, and it had been quite a battle to get past the steely receptionist. Stephanie was already looking down on him disparagingly before he'd even opened his mouth.

'Thank you for seeing me,' he said and tried to meet her glare with a smile.

'I'm just not quite sure why you're here.' Her eyes widened.

'I'm a good friend of Ellie's and, as you may know, she's at work at the moment, so I'm here as her representative to talk about Kathleen.' He was quite pleased with that term but sadly Stephanie maintained a look of disappointment coupled with mild irritation.

They were sat either side of her desk. Stephanie straightened her back, took a deep breath, causing her not inconsiderable chest to rise, and shuffled some papers before looking up to speak.

'I don't know how well informed you are about Kathleen and her situation...'

'Ellie has filled me in,' he interrupted. 'And I know Kathleen managed to make her way back to where she used to live.'

'Right, yes, and that was a very concerning incident for us all.'

'Well, yes, but she came to no harm.'

'By some miracle it is true that she survived the incident unscathed although settling her back into Starling Skies proved difficult. Sticking to a routine is very important for our residents.'

'For your residents, or for you?'

She looked horrified but seemed to check herself. 'Both, if I'm honest. Calm, happy residents in a daily routine makes our difficult job a little bit easier.' She was preaching what sounded liked well-rehearsed words.

'But are they happy? I understand that Kathleen feels trapped at times. There are times when she's certainly not calm and happy.'

Stephanie sighed deeply before saying, 'Since the incident we are locking her in her room for her own safety. We can't have her going AWOL again.'

'It seems a little extreme to actually lock the door of her room. Could you not just lock the external doors of the home?'

'It's difficult, because other residents can be trusted not to wander too far and on good weather days we like to open up the day room to the garden.'

Bryan was thoughtful. She wasn't totally unreasonable but seemed to be putting safety above all else. 'May I see Kathleen?' He might as well have asked if he could see Stephanie naked.

'I would need Ellie's permission.'

Bryan rang Ellie on her mobile and got through.

'Please would you tell Stephanie that you are okay with me visiting your mother.' He handed the phone over and the deed was done, Stephanie thwarted and out of excuses.

As they walked down the corridor to her room Stephanie started to explain that, as Kathleen had dementia, she couldn't be relied upon to be totally accurate about anything. This sounded like a damage limitation exercise to him.

They reached her room and it turned out that the door was open and Kathleen wasn't there. Stephanie looked more annoyed than embarrassed but simply turned on her heels.

'She must be in the day room.'

And there she was chatting to one of the male residents, their heads close together.

'Thank you,' Bryan said walking over to her. 'You can leave me here; I'm sure I can make my own way out.'

Stephanie's parting shot was an instruction to Bryan to be sure that he signed out at reception before he left.

Kathleen didn't recognise him at first.

'I'm a friend of your daughter, Ellie,' he explained as she peered at him.

'The name's Larry.' The man leaned forward and shook hands.

When Bryan got back to Roger and Ellie's he opened up his laptop and did some research on the internet. He had enjoyed talking to Kathleen and meeting Larry and what had come over more than anything was that they still felt young inside. They both had a lively spirit and seemed to want to enjoy life, even if their minds and bodies were not quite what they used to be.

Larry was perhaps a little more lucid than Kathleen but then he did repeat himself and Bryan had sat patiently through the story of the night of the floods when his son was born, which he regaled twice. Bryan managed to maintain the same expression of surprise both times.

By the time he sat down for dinner he had some notes he had made.

'That looks a bit official,' Roger said in a jokey fashion.

'Oh, just a bit of research I've done after visiting Kathleen this afternoon.'

'What are you doing visiting my mother-in-law?'

'They rang and Bryan offered.' Ellie felt awkward.

'Fair enough. I suppose I didn't get very far.'

'Doesn't matter; I had an interesting trip.'

'So, is she being mistreated or just losing her marbles?' Roger said meeting a look of disapproval from Ellie as she put three bowls of pasta on the table.

'Sorry, I'll shut up.'

'Good idea.' Ellie turned to Bryan. 'How did you get on?'

'They do a decent job, the care home, but I just sense that Kathleen isn't really happy there.'

Ellie's expression was pained now. 'I feel responsible. She's often a bit disgruntled when I visit but I just thought that was her reaction to me.'

'The elderly do tend to take things out on their nearest and dearest. But I don't think that she's as content as she could be.'

'That's awful, isn't it Roger?' Ellie nudged her husband.

'Yes, of course it is. But are you sure? Her and that Larry chap seem to rub along okay.'

'Perhaps we should have her here?' Ellie said with an air of desperation, her eyes meeting a look of horror from her husband.

'That would be a huge commitment on your part,' Bryan pointed out.

'Do you think she'll be better off somewhere else; I mean I haven't a clue where but...'

Bryan turned to his notes. 'There's a place I found on the internet called The Beeches. It's up near Bury St Edmunds but they specialise in dementia care and seem to have a different philosophy to most. They use reminiscence therapy which apparently has had some good results.'

'That sounds like a good idea.'

'Quite a bit further away,' Roger pointed out.

'It's about forty minutes.'

'Yes, but that's not the only consideration. I mean if Mum was happier there.'

'Ah, yes,' Bryan leaned forward. 'You might want to consider her friendship with Larry. He seems like a nice chap and they were talking about running away together.'

Roger laughed.

'I think it's sweet,' Ellie said always mindful of not writing her mother off.

'Anyway, you might want to look at this Beeches place online; maybe make a trip up there.'

'Thank you, Bryan, that's really helpful. I must admit when you said you'd go to Starling Skies for me I was sceptical. In fact, I didn't think you'd get as far as seeing Stephanie.'

'Yes, I did have to do battle with the receptionist, but when I got in front of Stephanie she succumbed to my charms,' he said lightly.

'You want to keep those charms in check, mate.' Roger gave his friend a serious look.

'I don't mean like that, silly! I was finding out how things operate for Ellie's sake.'

'And what did you uncover?' He obviously wasn't convinced.

'Well, what struck me most was that they lock Kathleen in her room at times. They told me it's for her own safety.'

'That's awful.' Ellie frowned with despair. 'We need to get her out of there.'

*

Bella's mobile woke her up. It was still dark. It was Anna.

'What the hell?'

'Sorry, babes. I'm all out of tofu. Have you got any?'

'I'm in bed. What the hell time is it?'

'Six. It's six o'clock. You need to get up anyway.'

'Arrrgh!'

Ben half opened one eye and shut it again.

'So, have you got any tofu?'

'Don't know. Don't care right this second.'

'Will you take a look, babes, please?'

'I will look. I'll call you back.'

'Okay but Bella, don't go back to sleep.'

'No, course not.' She yawned.

'Bella!' She didn't trust her.

'No need to shout.' Bella stuck her little feet into furry slippers and pushed her arms into a dressing gown.

'Yes need, I know you. Is Ben up?'

'What planet are you on today? He's an artist, so no! Call you back.' She ended the call this time. Her long dark hair was all over her face and she pushed a bit of it out of the way

225

but not too much. She made it downstairs without tripping and falling to her death. She was good at seeing in the dark.

In the kitchen she turned the lights on and blinked until she could get used to the brightness. She tried to engage her brain and decided to put the kettle on. She needed coffee. Her mobile rang again.

'Anna! Give us a chance.'

'Sorry babes.'

She opened the fridge door, stuck her hand in and magically pulled out some tofu. 'Yes.'

'Yes, you've got tofu?'

'Yes.'

'Thank God for that. Now, Jase and I are picking you up at seven.'

'Brill.'

'You did do the pad thai veg, didn't you?

'I so did.'

'See you at seven then. Love you.'

'Hate you.'

Free from Anna's paranoia she made some strong coffee, had a shower (keeping her hair dry), put on some jeans, a khaki T-shirt and Ben's big black jumper. Then she sorted out the cool box and carefully packed in all the fresh food from the fridge. Finally, there was the other bag of food, noodles and stuff, that was already packed. She got everything in the hallway by the front door and just as she grabbed her rucksack and stuck her feet in her ankle boots the doorbell went. She opened the door. Anna was wearing a big white fluffy jumper over jeans and boots.

'Impressed,' Anna said and they both set about getting Bella's bags in the boot of the car.

'Morning.' Jason looked weirdly wide awake.

'Yuk to everything,' Bella said and slunk into the back of the car.

They arrived at Camden Lock all too soon and getting out of a warm car was not easy. Jason looked as if he was very amused by the whole thing as he drove away. Bella thought her fingers might freeze off as she helped to set up the stall. It was a clear day and the sun was out but bitterly cold. 'I can't believe we're doing this,' she yelled suddenly as she hopped from foot to foot.

'Calm down.' Anna stopped trying to get the induction stove to work and squeezed Bella's clasped hands between her own which were gloved. 'No mitts, silly girl.'

A chap opposite grinned and came over to them. 'Here, you can have mine,' he said handing over his gloves.

'Awesome,' Bella said. 'Thanks massively. I owe you.'

'So, what are you girls peddling today?'

'Vegan food. Street food obvs.'

'Shame you're not doing burgers.'

'We are. Tofu burgers. You can have one later, on the house,' Anna said.

'That's right just give our food away.'

The guy laughed and shouted out, 'the name's Ricky,' as he went back to his stall where he was selling wood carvings.

227

A few hours later and Bella was laughing and joking with the punters as she served up pad thai in paper cones with little wooden spoons, veggie curry in paper tubs and she even took a burger over to Ricky when she returned his gloves. His mate made some sort of infantile noise indicating there was more to this simple gesture than there was.

Apart from the odd short lull, they were kept busy and they had run out of food by three o'clock.

'We should have brought more,' Anna said looking at her watch. 'There's three hours to go.'

'Not sure we could have really. Anyway, I'm knackered!'

'You guys run out of food?' Ricky shouted across.

'Yeah. It's the first time we've done hot food.'

'You've done well. Even the burger tasted good.'

Bella and Anna turned to each other. 'We did good!' Anna said and they hugged each other.

'Now let's go and get something to eat, I'm bloody starving,' Bella said and they both threw their heads back and laughed.

Chapter 17

'What do you think, Carol?' Bill was looking at her directly across the table and he had a half smile on his face but Carol could still feel the red flush that crept up her neck.

'I think, perhaps, some customers aren't quite sure how to cook some of the vegetables. I mean, butternut squash isn't the easiest to prepare.' This was the first time she'd been to this end of the week meeting at the farm shop and it was quite a daunting prospect.

'I'm sure you're right,' Emma agreed. 'I hear customers commenting on them and then they go for the onions and peppers that they know and love.'

'Mm, a lot of younger people aren't eating meat any more and I found this recipe...' Carol realised that she was thinking out loud and probably going on a bit too much, as she looked round the room, but Bill's expression was encouraging her to carry on. 'Anyway, it was for butternut squash with garlic and rosemary and fried haloumi and, well, I tried it and it is really good.'

There were mutterings of approval amongst the staff.

'So, do you think, if we came up with some recipes, printed them up on flyers and put them next to the appropriate

vegetables it might encourage customers to buy them?'
Emma suggested.

'I think that's a good idea,' Bill said and he was smiling broadly at Carol now. 'Well done, you two.'

'Oh, it was Emma really.'

'We could keep them vegetarian,' Carol added, 'as that's the trend.'

'Yes, I think we should,' Bill agreed, 'they can always do it as a side dish and have meat with it if they want.' He was thoughtful. 'May I ask you, Carol and Emma, to come up with the recipes and then I'll get them printed.'

'What fun!' Emma exclaimed and there was laughter round the table.

The meeting was over in an hour and Carol was surprised how much she'd enjoyed it in the end. There was a great camaraderie in the room and everyone was so positive about everything. Bill had talked about the shop sales figures at the start and, apparently, they were on target. He gently cajoled for even higher sales by praising them for their efforts and saying he knew they could do more.

As Carol picked up her coat and handbag, Bill was at her side. 'Fancy a drink?' he asked casually.

'Oh, is everyone going to the pub?' she asked assuming it was some sort of Friday evening ritual.

'No,' he said lightly and looked at her expectantly.

'Yes,' she heard herself say. 'Yes, I'd like that.' And she was pleased she'd put on one of her favourite blouses that morning and she had her leather jacket with her.

The bar at The Swan was pretty full but there were a couple of seats in the corner. 'You grab the seats and I'll get the drinks.'

She couldn't believe this was happening. She'd decided early on in the job that she quite fancied him but that he'd never be interested in her. He must be younger than her and he definitely had muscles in all the right places. She watched as he made his way over carefully with a half pint of bitter and her glass of wine. He had an unassuming nature but a quiet confidence which she admired.

'Made it,' he said with a broad smile and bright eyes.

After the first glug of her drink Carol felt brave enough to say, 'So, do you buy all your new recruits a drink?'

He laughed under his breath. 'No, actually.' He wasn't shy and leaned in towards her. 'Only the attractive ones,' he teased. It was one surprise after another. Then he straightened his back and looked serious. 'Actually, I like you. Is that all right? I mean I know I'm your boss and all that but...'

'Please don't apologise. This is turning into the highlight of my week.'

They smiled unashamedly at each other.

'I hope you don't mind me saying.' He was staring into his drink now avoiding her gaze, 'I did hear that your husband has left you. Bryan, isn't it?'

'That's right.' Carol was beginning to prefer it that people knew. Somehow it made it less of a drama as life just went on for her as well as everyone else.

'What a fool. Some men don't know how lucky they are.'

'Thank you,' she said and meant it. 'Yes, he left me for a younger woman. Much younger apparently.'

'Do you think it will work out?'

'I don't know. All I know is I have to look after number one.'

'Good attitude.' He was thoughtful. 'And your daughters, how have they reacted?'

'Ah, well, chalk and cheese. Rebecca managed to make me feel like it was all my fault; something on the lines of why couldn't I hold on to a perfectly good marriage at my age!'

'Ouch.'

'But Megan is an absolute sweetie. We had a wonderful girly weekend when she turned up unannounced. It was such a lovely surprise.'

'And what does girly fun comprise of?' He had a mischievous look.

'Watching *The Crown* on Netflix, even though we've seen it before.' He laughed. 'We made her favourite Thai curry and drank a bottle of wine.'

'Are you a good cook? It sounds like it?'

'I suppose so, never really thought about it. Bryan was never one for enthusing at my efforts. Funnily enough I've started to enjoy cooking a bit more now I can simply please myself. I can eat all the things that Bryan didn't like. But it always seems a bit sad, cooking for one.

'You seem to be coping really well considering all you've been through.'

'I'm trying really hard. My job at the farm shop is really helping. Anyway, tell me about you. Why haven't you been snapped up?' As soon as she had said it, she wished she hadn't. Was that hurt in his eyes, pain even?

'Lisa,' he said simply. 'Lisa was the love of my life. The girls weren't even teenagers when she died. Cancer. They didn't catch it in time.'

Carol put her hand over Bill's. 'I'm so sorry. Me and my size nines.'

'You've done nothing wrong.' He had a small tear in his eye. 'The girls are at uni now. Naomi is at Sheffield and Elise is in her final year at Bristol. It was worse for them, really. I threw myself into work while my mother helped me to bring them up.'

'What an amazing mother you must have.'

'Yes, she is.'

'Tough though, even so. For you, I mean.'

He took a deep breath and seemed to pull himself together. 'Another drink?'

'I'd love to, but I'm driving.'

He nodded acceptance. How disappointing the prospect of just going home to an empty house seemed suddenly.

'I suppose we could get a cab home?' she thought out loud.

'Excellent idea. Listen, are you hungry? We could get some food here or there's the bistro?'

'That would be...' She was thinking amazing, she said, 'lovely.' This was exciting.

Ellie was disappointed to get home and find Bryan in her kitchen, even if something did smell good. 'Hello, where's Roger?'

'Roger's going to be home at seven-thirty so any minute now.' He looked pleased with himself. Ellie was beginning to find Bryan's mission to help out in the Hardcastle home, at every opportunity, a bit invasive.

'Right. I think I'll change.'

'Okay, I'll pour you a glass of wine.'

'You been cooking?' she said feeling she couldn't ignore his efforts completely.

'Chinese takeaway; it's keeping warm in the oven. Had to go to Hadleigh to pick it up; dangerous territory these days but I managed it unscathed.'

Ellie didn't hide her disapproval.

When the three of them were sat round the table eating and Ellie had a glass of wine inside her she played with the thought that this might be a good time to say something to the semi-permanent lodger. Just as she opened her mouth, Bryan spoke.

'Listen, I just wanted to say how so very grateful I am that you two have put up with me for so long.'

Where was the but? Ellie looked at him hopefully.

'No problem, mate, is it Ellie?' Roger chimed in annoyingly and Ellie knew full well she was donning a cynical smile.

'The thing is, Bryan, what are you going to do?' Ellie was trying to take the edge out of her voice but failing. 'I mean are you getting back together with Tiffany?' It was a perfectly reasonable question.

'No! No, really, I'm not. She was a big mistake.'

Ellie looked at Roger. Had the two men talked about this?

'So, what are your plans?' Roger asked; he wasn't totally clueless at reading her after all.

'Well, I'm interested in what you both think about this, particularly you, Ellie, because you see...' He realised the bottle of Montepulciano was empty. 'Hang on a minute, I've already opened another bottle, I'll just get it.' He went over to the kitchen and came back with it filling all three glasses.

'It's good this takeaway,' Roger said meeting his wife's scowl as she willed him to shut up.

'Yes, it's from the Happy Garden. Not bad. But getting back to what I was saying...' *Alleluia*, thought Ellie. 'Well, I'd really like to get back with Carol. I was wondering, Ellie, if you could talk to her. I mean sound her out. Perhaps you could tell her that it's totally over with Tiffany.'

Right at this moment Ellie would do anything to move him out. 'Of course, I will.' But what did Carol want.

There was a thoughtful pause around the table before Ellie said, 'I do think you're going to have to convince Carol that you still love her if you expect her to take you back.'

'Of course. Of course, I do. I know I've been a fool now. It will be so nice for us to be back together in our own home; I won't take her for granted any more.'

Roger looked sceptical. 'Something tells me you've got a lot more to do than that. Perhaps you need a grand gesture.

What about booking that holiday she wanted to go on? Croatia, wasn't it?'

'What a brilliant idea. Split she was talking about. Yes, I'll do some research tomorrow.' Bryan looked almost relieved.

'Probably best to wait until I've spoken to her before you book anything,' Ellie said nervous about what the outcome might be.

Bryan deflated like a balloon but picked himself up to say, 'You're right Ellie, I should wait.'

*

'I don't want to go via Stowmarket!' Roger shouted at the voice coming from his mobile app.

'But that's the quickest way,' Ellie said despairing as the satnav repeatedly told them to do a U-turn.

'I knew the traffic would be bad today. It always is on Mondays.' Roger was already worked up and they had only been in the car for ten minutes.

'It was the only day off I could get this week; you know that.' The voice from the app was telling Roger to turn right.

'What does that thing know?' Roger waved a disparaging hand at it. A large farm vehicle turned from a side road ahead of them on to the route that he was stubbornly following. Ellie sat tight and said nothing.

'Bloody farmers clogging up our roads. Why can't they travel at night? What time did you say we would be there?'

'I said we'd be there by three, well before it gets dark.'

Roger was seething in his seat as he followed the farmer going a steady twenty miles an hour. Finally, after a lot more swearing and berating of the satnav, Ellie exclaimed, 'The Beeches! There.' Roger slammed on the brake and swerved into the gateway coming to a halt just outside a large elegant-looking Georgian building.

'Looks nice, doesn't it?' Ellie sounded uncertain.

'I seem to remember you saying that about the place your mother is at now.'

'Well, it's a good start anyway. I mean I couldn't bear the thought of her going somewhere grim.'

'But where is the village? I thought it was in the centre of a village.'

'Well, it's probably further up.' Ellie waved a hand in the general direction of up the road. 'Up there somewhere.'

They walked into a warm and airy reception where a woman, who turned out to be the manager, quickly appeared with a smiley cheerful face.

'Welcome to The Beeches. My name is Pauline,' she said warmly and Ellie had a good feeling already. 'Would you like to have a look around first?'

'Yes please.'

'Then I can answer any questions you may have.' She led the way into the dining room which was painted a bright yellow and had wooden tables and chairs. It was more like a casual restaurant than a canteen. From there they went into the living room where all the armchairs were covered in the same floral fabric and the room was decorated in a soft musky pink.

Ellie said, 'Wow,' as they entered the orangery which looked out on to a beautifully kept garden. There were several residents sitting together and enjoying the view. 'This is really lovely.'

'The place she's in now is pretty good too.' Roger somehow ruined the moment.

'I think you'll find we do things a bit differently here,' Pauline explained with no edge to her tone. 'Would you like to see one of the bedrooms? You are actually in luck as one of the rooms has just come free.'

'Really, but don't you have a waiting list?'

'Now, we don't operate on that basis. We did once, but it didn't work out. If people want to go into a care home and we are full they just have to find somewhere else.'

They followed Pauline up the stairs and she took them into a room which was perhaps not as large as the one that Kathleen was currently in but it overlooked the garden, much to Ellie's relief.

'There's no telly,' Roger pointed out.

'We encourage residents to watch television together in the lounge downstairs; they can provide their own televisions in their rooms if they wish.'

'Seems reasonable. I'm not sure how much telly Mum watches.' Ellie had a look in the en-suite bathroom.

'Shall we adjourn to my office?'

Pauline's office was quite large with an informal seating area where they sat and were served tea in mugs and several cookies looked at them from a plate. Roger succumbed almost immediately and got crumbs down his jumper as he ate.

Ellie ignored him and turned to Pauline, 'So, you were saying that your ethos here is quite different to Starling Skies?

'Yes, that's right. We focus on giving our residents a good quality of life; reminiscence therapy is one of the techniques we use and we also focus on the positive aspects of life.'

'Is it true that your residents can roam freely in the village here? And where is the village?' Roger asked looking bemused.

'We do have a policy of allowing our residents to integrate with the local community. The shop and café owners are all fully aware of The Beeches and our residents. This is actually a designated dementia-friendly place'

'But is it safe?' Roger asked clearly thinking that it was a ludicrous idea to allow elderly people with dementia on the streets.

'Any trips out are planned with two or more residents and, as I said, the local community are very aware of our presence and very capable of helping any residents if they require it.'

'Do they ever get lost?' Ellie needed to ask.

'Occasionally we get a call from a café owner telling us they have a couple of our residents and they feel it would be a good idea for one of us to come and collect them and return them to the home. Sometimes they just get a bit confused.'

'I'm struggling with this idea; I don't mind telling you.' Roger fidgeted in his chair. 'I just can't see how it can be safe to have elderly people with dementia wandering the streets.'

'The answer is that it's not totally one hundred per cent safe.' Pauline's tone was a blanket of calm. 'But it means they are free and they can enjoy what time they have left. Would you prefer it if they were locked in and miserable?'

'I think it's wonderful,' Ellie enthused. 'I think you've got it absolutely right. My mother hates being locked in her room.'

'But she escaped and went back to Benton Street. You were beside yourself with worry,' Roger pointed out.

'Well, yes, but as it turned out there was no harm done.'

'We underestimate these senior citizens and what they are capable of; they deserve dignity at all times.'

'Thank you,' Ellie said simply. 'So refreshing to hear.' Ellie decided she liked this Pauline; she talked a lot of sense.

Ellie couldn't get to Starling Skies over the next couple of days but on Wednesday evening she knew Roger and Bryan were going to eat at the pub so she went over after work. She was anxious to see how her mother responded to the idea of a change of home. As she drove over there in the dark, the rain lashed her windscreen and her wipers screeched as they moved the water around. By the time she arrived she was hunched into a ball of tension.

'Kathleen is getting a lot of visitors these days,' the receptionist said pointedly.

'Am I not allowed to visit my own mother?' Ellie lashed back in no mood for snide remarks.

The receptionist seemed to ignore her. She was looking at her computer screen and said, 'Would you wait here for a moment or two; I'll just find out where your mother is.'

'Surely you haven't lost her again?'

'Just wait here please; you can take a seat over there.' The receptionist nodded in the direction of a small sofa and avoided Ellie's amazed glare.

Ellie sat there quite exasperated by this new charade that she was being put through. A few minutes passed and Stephanie appeared.

'Hello Ellie, how are you?'

'I'm fine.' If bemused. 'I'd just like to see my mother.'

'Of course, and I'll take you there. She's in the day room.'

'I do know where it is; is an escort entirely necessary?'

'I'm going that way anyway,' she made light of it, 'and I just wanted to mention that we don't encourage relationships between our residents, not of an intimate nature anyway.'

'Are you suggesting that my mother and Larry have been intimate?'

'Not exactly but they have spent quite a bit of time together in the day room.'

Shock horror, Ellie thought. But on a more concerning note she was about to suggest to her mother that she moved to The Beeches without Larry.

When they reached the day room it had a subdued air about it. Some of the residents had nodded off; others stared blankly into the distance. Kathleen and Larry looked like they were plotting. Stephanie's chest rose with a deep breath.

'And here you are,' she said in what felt like a patronising tone.

'Thank you, Stephanie; I'll be fine from here on my own.'

Stephanie turned somewhat reluctantly and walked purposefully back down the corridor.

Ellie smiled at her mother as she approached her, but she looked non-plussed. Larry stood up.

'Good evening Ellie, how lovely to see you.'

'Hello Larry. Keeping my mother company?'

'Indeed I have been but I will leave you two to spend some time together; I have a game of backgammon arranged with Arthur.' He winked and walked away blowing a kiss towards Kathleen.

'What a nice man,' Ellie had to admit. 'How are you, Mum?'

'So, so.'

'Are you happy here?' she asked simply as she looked sympathetically into her eyes.

'No, I'm not. But don't worry; Larry and I are planning our escape.'

Ellie smiled at her mother and took her hand, holding it gently. 'Mum, would you like to move to another care home? It's very different to this one and, well, it's lovely and I think you'd be better off there. Would you like to go and see it at least?'

Kathleen's expression was one of delighted surprise. 'Can Larry come too?'

Chapter 18

The farm shop was busier than usual and there were four tills open, but still a queue. Carol was concentrating hard not wanting to mess up again. She'd only mis-weighed some heritage carrots but it would be at the precise moment that Bill walked in. She knew she was blushing and it was infuriating that she couldn't do anything about it. She avoided his eyes and got on with correcting her mistake. The customer was sweet and laughed it off. By the time the transaction was completed and another satisfied customer was on their way, Carol looked up only to realise that Bill had disappeared. This was silly. She felt like a lovesick teenager. She didn't want to feel like this but it was no good. Bill was charming, he was good company and she was totally flattered by the attention he paid her. The other evening had turned out to be delightful and they had chatted easily as the hours slipped away. When it came to going home, he was the perfect gentleman, getting the cab to drop her first and looking into her eyes and kissing her lightly on the lips, leaving her to float dreamily into her home.

Serving customers was proving to be a good distraction. Finally, there was a lull and the queue disappeared. When this happened, the other staff disappeared to the back of the shop where they worked in the kitchen and store room. But it was Carol's job to hold the fort. Bill appeared with Emma.

'Carol, can I have a word with you in the office? Emma is going to cover for you out here.' Emma was beaming at her; did she know?

'Okay.' She felt flustered. What on earth was this about?

'Nothing to worry about,' he said as if he could read her mind.

When they got to his office he offered to make her a cup of tea.

'Are you sure? Don't you want me to get back to the tills? I'm sure Emma has better things to do.'

'She's fine for a few minutes.' He came tantalisingly close to her face and said, 'Relax.'

How could she? She laughed nervously. With a mug of tea in front of her she took a sip and told herself to keep calm. Bill sat down and looked at her unabashed.

'I know I've asked you this before but you didn't really give me a straight answer; are you a good cook?'

'I suppose so. I watch a lot of those chefy programmes on the telly.'

'The thing is, I was wondering how you'd feel about working in the bakery. We make bread, pizzas and cakes. And I was thinking that you could try out the recipes for the veg that you and Emma are doing; we could sell them in the café. You know, sort of try this butternut squash dish and then buy the butternut squash.'

Carol's mind was whirring. 'I like that second idea; I could definitely do that. I have been trying them at home anyway. I've done some baking but not much, so not so sure about that.'

'Carl, our chef, would be able to teach you. They are tried and tested recipes. But how about you start off with the veg recipes for the café?'

'That sounds like a good idea; I'd like that.'

'We are organising an event here at the farm shop one Saturday where we get the suppliers, farmers et cetera to come with their produce and invite customers to tastings. So perhaps we could incorporate the veg recipes into that?'

'Certainly.'

'Great. Well, I'd better let you go now.'

Carol stood up. It was undeniably strange this situation. At times she didn't quite know how to behave.

'Oh, I forgot to mention.' Bill was smiling at her. 'I think it's important that I try some of your home cooking before we let you loose in the kitchen here. So how are you fixed on Friday evening?'

She could feel her cheeks reddening. 'I'll have to check my diary; I'll let you know.' She smiled back.

*

The village of Box Hill had a sleepy aura to it this unremarkable Thursday morning. Ellie parked in the small market square behind the monument and observed Carol who was sat next to her in the passenger seat. She was wearing an animal-print silk blouse under a brown leather jacket. Her chestnut bob had a sharper cut to it and her make-up was carefully applied; was that green eyeshadow? Overall, she looked younger and certainly brighter and she seemed to have a permanent serene smile on her face. Was working at the farm shop part time really making such a difference?

They linked arms and headed down Duke Street which was a narrow lane lined with attractive timber-framed houses painted in varying shades of the Suffolk palette: pink, terracotta, yellow, pale green and white. Eventually it became Church Road and it felt as if they were heading into countryside as the landscape turned green with trees either side of the road. At the end and past the church they saw a sign for the art gallery they were looking for and turned right into Consent Lane which was bordered with arable land. Silwood Barns housed a family home as well as this small pop-up gallery and boutique.

'What a lovely place to live,' Carol said as she twirled around to take in the view of endless fields and a big pale blue sky.

Ellie found the door to the gallery and they went into a warm space with large panelled windows letting in lots of daylight. A woman with a cheerful face wearing a grey tunic and pretty pink scarf welcomed them and offered them coffee.

'Ooh, yes please,' Ellie said.

'Me too.' Carol agreed.

The gallery owner wandered off to a kitchen at the side and Ellie and Carol perused the abstract paintings on the walls. There were four square landscapes depicting the seasons.

'I like autumn,' Carol said pointing to the one depicting earthy tones.

'But it doesn't actually say it's autumn.'

'No, but it must be.'

They became playful and decided which of the seasons the other three paintings were, laughing at how they disagreed.

In the entrance area there were, what looked like, various hand-picked items for sale including stylish lamps and objet d'art. Carol honed in on a funky pair of earrings.

'These are fun.' She held one up to her ear.

'A bit much with that blouse you're wearing,' Ellie advised.

'Well yes, but with a plain jumper they would be just the job.'

Ellie took one in her hand and looked at it more closely. 'Not really you, though, are they?'

Carol smiled with surprise. 'Interesting. Maybe not the old Carol but definitely the new.'

'Well good for you,' Ellie said somewhat taken aback.

'I love these,' the woman said, as Carol handed the earrings to her to pay. 'By the way your coffees are through there in the kitchen when you're ready.'

'What a fabulous shopping experience this is,' Ellie said. She walked towards a table lamp with a heavy ceramic base painted with bright pink flamingos and a plain pale green shade. 'I do like this,' she enthused and looked at the price tag.

'It's fabulous,' Carol said, 'Why don't you buy it?'

'Mm. Not sure. Seems extravagant.'

'But all that money you're earning at Addingtons; surely you can treat yourself once in a while.'

'You're right. I'll take it. Ooh, how exciting!'

The interior of the barn was elegant and luxurious throughout. Even the kitchen had an autumnal display of dried grasses and leaves hanging above the Aga. There they found two coffees in French style dark green cups with gold rims and a plate of tempting cookies. Ellie's hand hovered over the biscuits as she looked at Carol.

'Are you having one?'

'I don't think I will. I've lost a couple of pounds recently and I'd like to keep it that way.'

Ellie felt disappointed as she didn't want to appear greedy. 'You're right.'

After a lovely browse around the gallery they walked back up to the centre of the village and into the local pub, The Crown, where they sat in the bar area in leather tub chairs. It was a very masculine décor and had a look of a gentleman's club about it with dark walls on to which was painted a giant mural.

When they each had a glass of Chablis in hand, it occurred to Ellie that Carol had changed. She hadn't mentioned Bryan once, for a start. She hadn't sighed like she was totally fed up with life. On the contrary she was positively upbeat. Happy even.

'So?' Ellie decided that now was the right time to broach the subject of Bryan.

'So?'

'So, what's happening in the world of Carol? Enjoying your new job?'

'I am, actually. They are a lovely bunch and I'm working on these recipes now, to show customers how they can use the veg we have in the shop. I'm even going to be cooking some of them in the kitchen as samples for what they might do in the café.'

'That all sounds really great. What sort of hours are you working?'

'I'm doing three days a week. And I've still got my shift at the village shop, of course.'

'So, you feel better, do you? Despite the Bryan situation.'

'I know he's staying at yours. Is that what this is all about? You don't have to feel guilty; I mean he is your friend too.'

'I really don't want him there,' Ellie jumped in to explain. 'I got home from work one day, actually it was around the time that my mum went back to Benton Street, anyway I got home from work and there he was. Roger had already told him he could stay for a few days and, of course, a few days has turned into a few weeks.'

'What I don't understand is, where is Tiffany? I know he thinks her flat is too small but how are they still seeing each other?'

Ellie took a deep breath. 'Ah, well, that's just it. It's over between the two of them.'

Carol looked stunned. 'And do you actually believe that? He said that she was the love of his life; that our marriage had been over for a long time.'

'What a fool he has been. To be honest, I didn't believe him at first, but he has tried so hard to be helpful and the other evening, we had a little speech from him.'

Carol looked perplexed now. 'A speech! Saying what exactly?'

'Well, the bottom line is, Carol, he wants you back.'

Carol threw her head back and laughed. 'You are not serious? I don't believe this is happening.'

Ellie reached out to her friend and placed a warm hand over hers. 'I think he's genuine.' But even as she said it there was a niggling doubt in the back of her mind. 'How do you feel about it?'

There was a long pause. Carol was clearly deep in thought. Had Bryan hurt her so much that she couldn't forgive him? Or did their thirty-five-year marriage stand for something, something worth saving.

'I don't think I want him back.' She was very uneasy rather than sad.

'I do understand the hurt he's caused you, but perhaps think about it?'

'The thing is, I've met someone and I really like him.'

'Really? Who?' Ellie was dumbfounded. Who could Carol have met so soon?

'Bill. Bill at the farm shop.'

'Huuuuh!' Ellie's breath was taken away. 'Wow! He's rather nice. How long has…?'

'We just went for a drink after work last Friday; ended up having dinner and…'

'And?' She couldn't believe her ears.

'And he's coming round to mine tomorrow evening; I'm cooking for him.' Carol was coy now. 'It's a business thing really.'

'Business!' They both laughed out loud. 'How do you make that out? Getting to know your boss better?'

'He wants to sample my cooking.' Everything was funny now.

'I bet he does!'

Eventually the raucous merriment died down and Ellie was left with the disturbing thought that she'd never get rid of her unwanted lodger. 'What am I going to do about Bryan?'

'Throw him out,' Carol said. Did she mean that?

'He's actually beginning to get on my nerves a bit. It would just be nice to find Roger in the kitchen when I get home from work, rather than Bryan.'

'What's he doing in the kitchen? He doesn't cook.'

'He buys takeaways and puts them in the oven to keep warm. Oh Carol, he's going to be gutted when I tell him.'

'What are you going to tell him?'

'I don't know. What do you want me to tell him?'

'Nothing about Bill; it's too early days.'

'Yes, you're right.' Ellie thought about it. 'But you definitely like him, don't you? Is he keen?'

Carol blushed. 'Gosh, this is so silly isn't it? I can't quite believe that it's happening to me. But yes, it was him that made the first move and he actually came out and said, "I like you".' And then she was quick to add, 'but I don't want to rush things and I'm certainly not ready to tell the world.'

'So, I'll have to tell Bryan that you don't want him back.'

Carol looked confused and slightly agitated. 'It's not easy all this, is it? I keep thinking of Rebecca and Megan and what they would want. Certainly, Rebecca would say I should save my marriage.'

'But it's your life, Carol. You have to do what's best for you.'

'I know and the fact is that Bryan has hurt me so badly; I mean how do I ever trust him again?'

'Yes, you have a point.'

'Am I doing the right thing? I mean, seeing Bill.' Carol suddenly seemed to be unsure.

'I think you are. Why not? This could be the start of a beautiful romance.'

'All I know is, I need to find out.'

Roger settled down with a coffee and the local paper. He had already read the headline on the front page: *Local Council Bribe to Agree Cost-Cut Plan* and feared the worst.

He read on to realise that, not only were Cost-Cut offering to gift substantial sums of money to both the church and the village hall, but they were also wanting to sponsor the villages in bloom competition and the Christmas lights in Market Square for the next five years. Roger was impressed with their cunning and worried that the councillors would be swayed by this. He then read that over two hundred locals had objected to the planning permission. Surely, they had to take notice of that? But around fifty had supported the scheme; was Addington amongst them, the covert fat cat? At least it was a point of differentiation between Addington and Ellie. He finished the article and put the paper down. He knew Ellie felt very strongly about this. She had taken an active part in the protest group. He was moved to support her. After all, he had time on his hands and it would get him brownie points. So, he needed to come up with a plan.

He decided to email Joe. It was a long shot but maybe he could get a message to Lady R and get her to help in some way. She must be a woman of influence around here.

Much to his surprise, Joe was very quick to get back to him and had forwarded his email to the woman herself. Roger felt a frisson down his spine when he received a message direct from her and signed Annabelle. She seemed happy to help and was suggesting he phone her on her mobile. Should he? Would she mention the game of golf again?

Ellie found him in the garden room putting the finishing touches to his plan.

'Hi darling, did you have a good time with Carol?'

'Yes, as always. Interesting too.'

'Tell me more. What are Bryan's chances, do we reckon?'

'Roundabout zero as things stand; she's dating Bill from the farm shop.'

'No!' Roger couldn't believe it. 'She didn't hang about!'

'And why should she? I'm really pleased for her.'

'Yes, of course, but Bryan's going to be devastated.'

'You mustn't tell him. She doesn't want him to know. I mean it's early days and she's no idea where it will lead at this point.' She looked down at his scribblings. 'What's this?'

'Ah, well.' He sat back in his chair with a grin on his face. 'This is a cunning plan to stop Cost-Cut. I've actually been talking to Lady R and she—'

'Lady R?'

'Lady R who owns Capel Green Farm.'

'You have her phone number?'

'Yes, well...' Why did he feel guilty? 'I emailed Joe and asked him if he could get her to help with the protest. You know, local figurehead with influence.'

'And you now have her mobile phone number.' Was she jealous?

'Yes, well she suggested we spoke on the phone. It was just easier.'

'I bet it was. Why would she talk to you, anyway? It's not like you're the protest organiser.'

'Well, no, but I'm doing my bit. Anyway, I met her when I was grape picking; I told you.'

'I don't remember that.'

'Yes, you do. She bought us all a drink at The Cock after. You were in a mood because I got home late and we didn't have anything for supper.'

'I remember that but nothing about a Lady R buying drinks.'

'I'm sure I told you but the point is she's happy to help our cause. I thought you'd be pleased.'

'We've managed without her so far.'

'Well, yes, but I've been reading the local paper and you know it's not looking good for us.'

'Really? Even after the meeting.'

'Even after that. Anyway, the point is, Lady R is well connected and she happens to know that some of the key decision-makers on the council are meeting up on the field where Cost-Cut plan to build.'

'That's interesting but haven't there been hundreds of complaints on the planning permission website?'

'Two hundred according to this.' Roger showed her the article on the front page of the paper.

Ellie read it in full, a frown deepening on her forehead.

'Do you think Addington is involved?' Roger asked.

'What makes you say that?' Ellie looked unsure now. 'I sincerely hope not. I'm happy to ask him. So, when is this meeting in the field?'

'Wednesday next week she reckons. She's going to confirm that but the plan is that we get as many protesters along as possible.'

'Sounds like a good idea.'

'Ah but I haven't told you the best bit.' He couldn't help feeling pleased with himself.

'Why am I nervous?'

'No need. It's brilliant. Lady R, herself, is going to turn up!' Ellie was looking uncertain. 'Brilliant, isn't it?'

'I suppose so. She's not the Queen.'

'Oh, come on, she's going to have some sway.'

'How are we going to get everybody along? I think I'm working next Wednesday.' Ellie was checking her mobile calendar.

'Can't you change your day off?'

'Yes, I'll have to. More importantly we better let the farm shop lot know.'

'Ah well, Annabelle said she would let Bill and Joe know.'

'Oh, good. I'll contact Emma.'

There was a moment's pause before Roger said, 'What are we going to do about Bryan?'

Chapter 19

Ellie arrived at Starling Skies to find Kathleen sitting in reception with her smart camel coat on. She looked like she'd had her hair done and was wearing a pale pink lipstick which was actually quite flattering. Larry was sat next to her and he also had his coat on.

'That's a coincidence; are you going for a trip out today, as well?'

'Yes.' Kathleen patted Larry's knee. 'And even more of a coincidence, he's coming with us.' She was triumphant.

'Oh, no, Mum. No, Larry can't come. They are only expecting you and me.'

'I don't want to cause trouble.' Larry looked quite upset.

'Larry wants to look at this place too. I said it would be all right. There's room in the car, isn't there?'

Ellie looked at her watch. If they didn't leave now, they were going to be late. The two of them looked so sweet sitting together, somehow unsure of their destiny but determined to be together.

'All right then. But I make no promises.' Was it worth saying any more than that? Probably not.

Kathleen sat in the back of the car. She never sat in the back always preferring the passenger seat at the front. But today she and Larry sat together like a couple of mischievous children. It took nearly an hour before they reached The Beeches and pulled in to the driveway. They both got out of the car looking around in wonderment and saying nothing. Happily, there was blue in the sky today and some sunshine to boot, enough to brighten any view and the Georgian splendour of The Beeches certainly looked impressive.

'Right.' Ellie led the way through to the hallway which was beautifully warm and housed a smiling receptionist.

'Good morning, how can I help you?'

Ellie went up to the desk and reading Sarah on her name badge, she spoke quietly. 'I have an appointment with my mother, Kathleen Hervey. I'm really sorry but she's brought one of her fellow residents with her.'

Sarah smiled sympathetically. 'These things happen.'

The manager, Pauline, soon appeared and behaved impeccably, giving a warm welcome to all three of them and not batting an eyelid towards the unexpected guest. Ellie considered that Stephanie would not have been so gracious. She watched as Pauline focused her attention on Kathleen, asking her questions about what she wanted from a home.

'We'd like a record player, wouldn't we, Larry?'

'Yes, yes, that would be excellent,' Larry agreed.

'We have one, actually, and one evening a week we play records. Some of our residents even get up and dance.'

Kathleen and Larry exchanged a knowing look.

There were a number of residents in the day room, some with mugs of coffee and four were sat round a table playing a card game. They all looked pretty content and some said hello. Kathleen waved at them in the same way the Queen waves at her subjects. They didn't seem to mind but simply waved back.

As soon as they walked into the orangery Kathleen gasped and went straight up to the door and was out in the garden, a look of enchantment on her face. Larry followed her.

'Isn't it a beautiful garden?'

Her face lit up. 'This is so much better than our place.' She turned to Larry. 'Shall we move here; shall we move here together?'

Bryan walked up to the pub in the village and ordered a pint of bitter from Gavin behind the bar. It was only midday and apart from a couple of the usual suspects, it was pretty empty. He decided to sit away from anybody else and in a quiet corner and mull over his thoughts.

The big question that niggled away at him was, were Ellie and Roger holding something back? Or was he being paranoid? It just didn't make sense. Why didn't Carol want him back? Didn't thirty-five years of marriage mean anything to her? But then he thought back to the last time he'd turned up when Megan was there. Carol had been pretty frosty then. Megan had been cold too, disappearing upstairs. One thing was for sure, he had supremely messed up. He had it in mind that perhaps he should go and see Carol and ask her to her face. That was the only way he was going to know for sure. But then Ellie had said just leave her alone for now;

give her some time. The worry was, the more time that passed, the more likely he was to be too late.

He had spoken to Rebecca last night and she had been fine with him, nice even. When he told her that he wanted to get back together with her mother she had said, '*Brilliant Dad, you must; Mum is really sad and lonely without you, I'm sure she'll take you back.*'

Another problem was he knew he'd outstayed his welcome chez Hardcastle. He seemed to spend his days dancing round Roger, them both trying to think of reasons to go out. It was testing their friendship and friends were thin on the ground these days. But where could he live? He had even checked to see if the Kersey cottage was still on the market for rent but, of course, it had been snapped up. But his gut feeling was that he should stay in the village as close to Carol as possible.

Gavin came over and sat next to him. 'You all right, mate?'

'Not great,' he had to admit. 'I've been a fool, left my wife and now I have nowhere to live.'

'That's a bummer.' Gavin was thoughtful. 'I'm afraid our services don't run to marriage guidance but we do have a room upstairs which we were planning to let out on a B & B basis. There's not going to be much demand through the winter months so we could sort something that suited us both, possibly; I would have to check with the wife.'

'That sounds good. You see I really want to stay in the village.'

'You're retired, aren't you?'

'That's right.'

'Ever done any bar work?'

'A few times at the village fete.'

'We're actually looking for someone to help out. We could come to some sort of arrangement if you were interested.'

'I'm interested. Can I see the room now?'

Ellie had felt uneasy about leaving her mother and Larry in the garden but Pauline had assured her that they would be safe. The two of them were sat in the dining room and Ellie had been given a hot drink and a biscuit.

'I'm sorry about Larry,' she said. 'He wasn't supposed to come.'

'They are obviously fond of each other.' Pauline smiled sympathetically.

'I take it you still just have the one room?' Ellie didn't really want to ask and feared the answer.

'We do, yes.' Pauline sighed. 'However, rooms do come available from time to time.' She paused before adding gently, 'I do need to push you on the room that is available now. Obviously, we need to fill it.'

'I know. I'll have to talk to them both but I really would like my mother to move here. I'm convinced it's the best place for her.'

Ben was in a taxi with five large canvases, two of them he had included reluctantly but he was pleased with the other three. Bella had insisted he shelled out on a cab; she was always referring to *all that money* he had got from his first

262

sale but Ben had seen quite a bit of it disappear already. But if he was honest with himself, it would have been difficult taking them on the tube.

Finally, they arrived on Islington Green and the meter stopped ticking over and bankrupting him. Ben could see the gallery across the road. He struggled to get his artwork out of the cab but a convenient lamppost gave him something to lean the canvases against and he managed to pay the cab with his debit card.

'Sorry, can't afford to tip you,' he said. The driver didn't react.

Jonathan Glover appeared from the other side of the road.

'Ben,' he shouted across the busy street and waved. He crossed the road as soon as he could. 'Need a hand?'

Ben wasn't big on anticipating problems ahead but had to admit that some help at this juncture was useful.

Once inside, Jonathan made him a coffee.

'As you can see this is a pretty busy area of Islington. Footfall's not bad.'

Ben looked around him at the current exhibition. There were just two smallish rooms which were whitewashed to show off the art and perhaps three artists on display tops. He considered he'd have to produce a few more works to equal the numbers of the artists here.

'Shall I start unwrapping?'

'Yeah, great. It will be interesting to see what you want to show me first.' Jonathan had seemed pretty friendly from the first time they met in Suffolk. But Ben still felt nervous. This was the moment of truth. He had already decided that if this didn't go well, he was going back to bar work for a bit.

He unwrapped his favourite which was based on a female jazz singer that he'd seen at Ronnie Scott's recently. She was a really curvaceous red-head and wore a mustard coloured dress which clung to her. It had seemed like there was smoke all around her and he'd tried to depict that in his painting.

Jonathan took his time to explore the new work, standing back and then honing in on the detail. About five long minutes passed before he said excitedly, 'I like it. I hope they're all this good.'

Ellie collapsed in an armchair with a cup of tea when she got home. This was her day off and she was exhausted. Her mobile had been bleeping at her for some time so she took a look. There were seven updates on the new WhatsApp group that Emma had set up to make communication about the Cost-Cut protest easier. There was a lot of excitement about the plan to gatecrash the Cost-Cut meeting on the proposed development field. Some were warning not to post about it on public social media pages which would ruin the element of surprise.

Word was being passed around stealthily to known supporters of the protest. The fact that Lady Rochester was turning up was considered to be a massive point in their favour and Roger had received much praise for bringing off this move.

Ellie's curiosity was pricked and she decided to find out the low down on this Lady; a quick Google search brought up several images of an attractive woman who certainly dressed stylishly. It didn't take long to find out that she was sixty-two. She had to admit that she looked amazing for her age. Did Roger fancy her? She'd never really thought of him as the type to stray. Roger was quick to comment on her relationship with James which, of course, was entirely innocent, if not a little terse since the Cost-Cut issue emerged. Although perhaps James did fancy her. But that wasn't her fault.

She looked through yet more images of Lady R; she was widowed, as it turned out, but really would someone as la-di-dah as her be interested in Roger?

She thought back to the journey home from The Beeches with her precious cargo. Kathleen and Larry had both been thrilled when she had suggested that they stopped for lunch at a pub that she knew they would be passing in the village of Cockfield.

'This is a proper day out!' Kathleen had said.

Ellie was waiting until they had all finished their food before she brought up the subject of The Beeches, but the playful pair couldn't stop talking about it. It was when her mother said, 'How soon can we move?' that Ellie knew she had to break their hearts.

'Mum, I've told you what Pauline said. There's only one room available at the moment.'

'So how long will it be before another one becomes available for Larry?'

'We just don't know. I'm sorry.'

Larry sighed with an air of resignation. 'I will need to consult my son on this matter. Is it expensive, this place? Compared to Starling Skies?'

'Funnily enough, it actually costs less. But Larry, you're absolutely right, you must consult your own family.'

'Graham's not a bad sort. He will want what I want.'

'Precisely,' Kathleen chipped in. She put down her knife and fork. 'Can't you phone them, Ellie dear? Find out how long we need to wait for Larry's room?'

'Until someone pops their clogs,' Larry said. 'They all looked pretty healthy to me.'

'We'll just have to wait,' Kathleen said not hiding her disappointment.

'But Mum, in the meantime, if you don't say you want that room right away, they will give it to someone else.'

'I want it. Make sure I get it.'

Ben wandered down Islington Green. It certainly had a buzz about it: a crepe café, a comedy store, a theatre pub, a business design centre. Upper Street was full of restaurants, cocktail bars, pubs and cafés. It was multicultural and had a trendy vibe. Ben liked it. He looked in an estate agent's window. He knew that house prices here would be extortionate and probably rents too. Two thirds of the window displayed properties that were beyond pie in the sky to Ben. But at the far end there were a few new-build flats which seemed ridiculously cheap in comparison. Then he saw that you were just buying a twenty-five per cent share and wondered how that would work. He imagined Bella's face if he told her they could move to Islington. She'd be ecstatic. He found himself going into the agency even though it seemed like a crazy idea and he felt a bit of a fool when the man behind the desk said, 'Can I help you?'

His words got stuck in his throat at first. He coughed.

'I was just wondering about the flats you've got in the window, the twenty-five per cent share ones.'

'Yes, the shared ownership flats. They are new builds and nicely done though I say so myself.' He pulled some details out of the filing cabinet behind him and put them in front of Ben. 'Would you like to register?'

'How does it work then? Who owns the other seventy-five per cent?'

'Well, the landlord does, so you pay rent.' He pointed to a figure on the details of the one that Ben was looking at which was the cheapest one.

Ben laughed in horror. 'Over a thousand pounds for the rent for this tiny place and the mortgage on top. Sorry mate.' He stood up, 'I've wasted your time.'

'No problem. You renting at the moment?' the agent asked.

'Yeah, big house at Tufnell Park; loads of us in there.'

'And you and your girlfriend would like your own place?' How did he know?

'Yeah, actually, but nah, not at these prices.'

'What brings you to Islington?'

'The gallery up the road; they have just taken on some of my paintings.'

'Is that Jonathan Glover's place?'

'Yeah.' He was in the know this man.

'Well done you. That's a pretty prestigious gallery. Look if you're interested, I could show you some smaller flats for rent in this area. Then you could compare with what you're currently paying.'

Ben was halfway out the door but decided it was worth a look if only to rule Islington out completely. He sat down again. 'Go on then.'

Chapter 20

The Cock Horse was buzzing with anticipation amongst a crowd that seemed to be building fast. The landlord looked confused.

'What you lot doing here on a Wednesday afternoon?'

'Sorry, we had to have a meeting point.' Ellie explained.

'Ramblers, are you?'

'If I were to ask you what you think of the proposed Cost-Cut development, what would you say?'

'Ah, that's what it's about.'

'I need to know, for or against the development?'

'Against. One hundred per cent. I hear they're planning to sell alcohol.' He tutted at the injustice. 'What's the plan, then?'

'We are gatecrashing a meeting due to start in about half an hour.' Her heart skipped a beat. She was nervous about how this was going to go.

'What here, in my pub?'

'No, down on Brett Field. Where they plan to build.'

'So how are you getting down there?'

'There's some with cars but otherwise we thought we could walk from here.'

Roger appeared. 'Made it.' He looked pleased with himself.

'You didn't have to get past James.'

'Was he difficult?'

'He asked me when was I joining the eco warriors.'

'Excellent. Well, I had a hard time convincing Bryan he shouldn't come.'

'Oops. What did you say?'

'Just about everything. Anyway, luckily, he's moving into the pub today, so I said he had enough to do. Although, of course, he's only got to pack his bag. It was all a bit lame. And I can't help feeling a bit bad about chucking him out.'

'We're not chucking him out!'

'He did twig that not coming today might be Carol related.'

They both looked over to Bill with Carol by his side; there was a loved-up woman if ever Ellie saw one.

Bill shouted out, 'Time to go folks!' The noise didn't abate and so he held his arms wide and high until they quieted. 'And remember the element of surprise is everything here. There are placards by the door so, some of you, pick one up on your way out. Keep it peaceful!' People started to filter out as Bill shouted, 'Good luck my friends!'

It was a clear dry day, encouraging people out. The sun was already quite low in the sky and it was at this time of year that Ellie particularly enjoyed the landscape and the pink sunsets. She had three reluctant walkers in her car with placards in the boot and drove down the high street and turned off when she got to the new housing estate, taking the first left down Frogs Hall Lane which ran alongside the field.

She parked, as Bill had advised, behind some tall trees. The four of them exchanged glances before getting out of the car.

'Shhh,' Ellie said as one slammed his door. She took the placards out of the boot. One read *Capel Green Says No* and the other read, *Cost-Cut Ruin Villages*.

Others appeared. Ellie looked for Bill so that she could follow his lead. Roger arrived, walked up the bank and looked through the trees. He came back animated.

'They're there!' he said in a loud whisper. 'About five of them, a couple with clipboards.'

Four more cars pulled up. The last two were exposed to the field; they had run out of tree cover. More were arriving on foot and they made a sizeable group, probably fifty in all.

'Right time to go,' Bill said.

He led the way and they marched up the road to a gate which was closed and a couple of them grappled with it but couldn't get it open. Ellie had visions of them all clambering over it holding their placards; she let out a nervous laugh. Roger got to the front and managed to open the gate. There was a cheer for him. No need to be quiet any more; one of the enemy was walking towards them. Bill strode out confidently to meet him. As the protesters got closer the man pushed a palm towards them. He was unsuitably dressed in a suit with an overcoat and smart shoes which were already covered in mud.

'What's all this?' He seemed immediately angry.

'We're here to make a peaceful protest against Cost-Cut's plans for development on this beautiful field, part of a conservation area.'

'Ah! Well, that's where you're wrong. The boundary for the conservation area ends at Frogs Hall Lane.'

'But the villagers don't want this. It's obvious from the petition many have signed, the two hundred plus objections to the planning permission. Don't you know when you're not wanted?'

The crowd cheered loudly in support. They were holding their banners high, getting more agitated and started walking straight up towards the rest of the suits.

'Look, we're here for a private meeting; you've no right to gatecrash.' Another chap appeared and Ellie recognised him from the village hall meeting; it was Chisel Features, Derek Dunhill.

'Now look here, this is out of order. We are simply going about our business and—'

'Planning to ruin our village and our livelihoods!' Emma shouted out from the crowd.

'We have the right to peaceful protest,' Roger said boldly remembering something he'd read and again those gathered were roused to cheer him.

'We know our rights!' one shouted.

'Fine and you've made your point and it's duly noted. Now I'm asking you nicely to leave.'

'We're not leaving until we have some reassurances from you that you will not go ahead with this development that

Capel Green villagers simply do not want.' Bill was looking his opponents straight in the eye while they glanced around their assembled audience looking nervous. 'This will bring competition which will badly affect existing local services; it will be a blot on our much-loved landscape.'

'You're just frightened of the competition.' Another of the suits appeared. 'Aren't you from that expensive farm shop?' This was beginning to get nasty.

'I am from the farm shop,' Bill said proudly squaring up to his aggressor, 'where we sell high quality local produce and not cheap unhealthy processed foods that you are planning to sell.'

This met raucous approval and the protesters started heading towards the centre of the field chanting, 'Capel Green says no', as they went. Derek was walking backwards so that he could still face the crowd as he shouted, 'You are trespassing! I am going to call the police if you don't leave now.'

Many simply chanted louder or didn't hear him. Ellie worried that this was not going to end well. The suits were getting more red-faced and angrier; the protesters more determined to get their message across. Just then the air was filled with the deafening sound of a helicopter above them in the sky. They all looked up anxiously and only Roger had a broad smile on his face.

'What's this?' Ellie shouted above the noise.

'This, my darling,' Roger announced triumphantly, 'is Lady Rochester dropping in to lend her support.'

The smart black helicopter had gold lettering on the side which read Lady R. It landed safely at the top of the field and Annabelle herself emerged in her customary denim jeans, green wellies and padded gilet. She ran towards them waving to her fellow protesters. A shifty looking man with a camera was following closely behind her.

The suits looked confused and as if they couldn't believe this Lady, a pillar of the community, was supporting the cause of the protesters.

'Good afternoon my friends,' she shouted out to the assembled demonstrators, her hands held high and looking very pleased with herself. 'I hope you don't mind if I join you?'

This met with wild applause. Derek looked like he might spontaneously combust. The cameraman started taking photographs.

'You are trespassing on our land!' Derek raged.

'Do *we* really own the land?' Lady R switched to being an orator delivering her rhetoric in thoughtful tenor.

'Of course, we do!' a suit yelled into her face.

'What rights does that give us?' she continued ignoring him. 'I like to think we are merely guardians of our piece of earth, preserving wildlife and looking after it for the next generation. Ensuring we do right by our fellow humans, our local community.'

'Bollocks!' Derek shouted and stormed off and the crowd were in uproarious mood as the suits made a hurried and undignified exit across the field, one stumbling as he gathered pace in his shiny shoes.

'We have triumphed my friends!' Lady R shouted. She put her hand on the shoulder of the cameraman. 'And this journalist will ensure we're on the front page of the *East Anglian Daily Times* this week!'

'That's brilliant.' Roger shouted.

'Now, back to the pub and celebration drinks on me!'

Ellie had to hand it to Lady R; she certainly made an impact.

By the time they left the pub, Roger and Ellie were both hungry and decided to try their luck at one of the restaurants in the village. They were in luck; the bistro had a table.

'Everything all right?' Roger asked after they had ordered their food. Ellie seemed uninspired by the menu but went for the mushroom risotto in the end. As usual when he opted for the fish and chips, she rolled her eyes at his predictability.

'Yes, I think so.' She was sipping her lime and soda and looking thoughtful.

'You think so? What does that mean? The protest went well, didn't it? Isn't that what you wanted?'

'Of course it is.' She was in no hurry to respond. Then she added, 'You were certainly the hero of the hour after you pulled that stunt off with Annabelle.'

'Yes, it did go down well, didn't it?' He couldn't help grinning as he pictured everyone's faces when the helicopter arrived. 'Annabelle, now, is it?'

'I was chatting to her actually and she said, "Call me Annabelle".'

'She's all right, isn't she? I mean for a Lady. She's not all airs and graces.'

'No, she's not. She's actually really nice.'

'That's what I thought.'

'So, do you fancy her?' Ah. That was what was bugging Ellie. He had to admit Annabelle was a striking woman.

'No! Don't be silly.'

'I'm more likely to believe you if you say you do. At least a bit.'

'Well, she's a good-looking woman, what can I say?'

'So, you do?'

'Oh, for goodness sake!'

'I noticed you and her were talking in quite a huddle for some time.'

'What do you mean by a huddle?'

'Well, you were close together.'

The food arrived and Roger welcomed the intervention.

'This looks good,' he said changing the subject but Ellie had an incredulous expression. She knew him too well.

'Look, it was noisy in the pub,' he explained. 'Especially when that music started up. I mean, it was difficult to be heard.'

'Good excuse.' Ellie smiled ironically. 'So, what were you talking about?'

Roger sat back in his chair. 'Nothing really. I was just saying that I'm looking for a job, locally ideally. She was saying that Joe, her vineyard manager, wants to move down to the winery in Essex.'

'What's that got to do with anything?'

'Well, nothing really.'

'She's not offering you a job, surely? You've got no experience.'

'No, no, of course not. But I did do the grape harvest.'

'I'm sure there's a lot more to it than that.' Ellie was pushing rice around her plate.

'Yes, of course there is. Is your food all right?' Roger asked.

'Yes, it's fine.'

There was a thoughtful pause before Roger said, 'Actually, Annabelle was telling me about an online course in viticulture.'

'Viticulture?'

'Yes, apparently it teaches you everything you need to know, pretty much, to be a vineyard manager.'

'I see. So how much does it cost? You're obviously considering it.'

'Three to four hundred pounds, she reckons. Not much really.'

Ellie went quiet. She did that when she was confused, maybe concerned.

'Look.' Roger realised he needed to explain. After all he'd had various thoughts in his head over the past few weeks that he hadn't shared with his wife. 'I need to do something; get out of the house; have a reason for getting up in the morning. And what that AXA interview taught me was that I'm never going to get back into that world at my age, so maybe it's time for something new.'

'It would certainly be a drastic change. I suspect the salary is pretty low too.'

'Of course, but I think I might really enjoy it. You know out in the open fields.'

'In all weather.'

'That doesn't bother me.'

'I suppose Annabelle is a bit of a draw too. Would she be your boss?'

'Oh, not that again.'

'How long will it take you to do this course?'

'It's a hundred hours, so, if I crack on, I might do it in a month or so.'

'Have you forgotten about Christmas?'

'That's only a day or two.'

'Not really. There's all the shopping and food stuff to worry about.'

'But you do all that.'

Ellie laughed in despair. 'Too right I do. But that was when you were working full time.'

'True, well, this year I'll be studying full time.'

'Great, and have you forgotten that I've got a job now?'

'No, course not. Why don't we have a low-key Christmas? I mean I can't stand all the fuss anyway and the boys won't mind, will they?'

'Oh great! You've already invited Bryan, haven't you?'

'True.' How was he going to get out of this corner? 'Look, this is important to me, can't you see that?'

Ellie looked at him, her expression softened now, her eyes thoughtful. 'Looks like you've made your mind up. And you're right you do need something like this. You should go for it.'

Chapter 21

Bryan sat in the small armchair in the corner of the room. He told himself that it was a reasonable size and there was a smart television he could watch when he wanted to relax. The décor was subdued with lots of pale grey and cushions; clearly the work of Gavin's wife, Zoe. It was quite stark with no paintings on the walls, something that Gavin had said they were going to remedy when they got round to it. Bryan had hung his shirts, trousers and two smart jackets in the wardrobe and filled the drawers with the rest of his clothes; his underwear, T-shirts, two belts and the sports gear Tiffany had persuaded him to buy. Now they were just a reminder of why the relationship had failed.

He had his laptop, his mobile phone and a small Bluetooth speaker he had purchased recently. He also had a couple of Stephen King novels. He had even started one of them, but not got very far. The bookmark was left in the page he was at. If ever he did want to read it, he'd have to start from the beginning to remind himself of the first couple of chapters.

He was surprised at how sad he had felt on leaving Roger and Ellie's home. Although he'd always felt a bit uneasy there, at least he had the run of the house and was able to make a contribution to mealtimes. He had driven first to his own home and knocked on the door in the vain hope that Carol would invite him in. But there was no answer. Her car was missing so she must have been out. He still had a key and thought long and hard about letting himself in. Maybe he would find some clues as to why she didn't want him back; maybe he would find more of his own possessions that would provide some small comfort and he would be able to take them because they were his. He decided in the end that he would come back another time when Carol was home, in the hope that he would be able to talk to her.

Gavin had made a bit of an effort to make him feel welcome at the pub.

'Feel free to use the kitchen and the lounge up here. We are pretty busy downstairs most of the time so it's no problem,' he said with an air of detachment.

'Thanks, I appreciate that,' Bryan had been quick to respond.

But even if they had taken pity on him and now he had a place, albeit just one room, where he was justified in being, there was something extremely sad about the situation that he couldn't ignore. His standing in the community had plummeted from respectable family man in a large four-bedroomed detached home to a tainted reputation and just four walls around him. He told himself to buck his ideas up; he could get through this and win Carol back. He was just at a low point. The only way was up.

He moved over to the window and looked out and down the street. He could actually just see his own home in the distance on the other side of the road. It was the last house in view. So near and yet so far. He peered hoping to catch a glimpse of Carol. And then the absurdity of the situation hit him and tears filled his eyes.

Bella was pacing the studio flat like a caged animal. It was on the first floor of a red-brick Victorian building, the window frames of which had seen better days. Inside it had a high ceiling which helped and the room was an L shape with the kitchen round a corner.

'I told you, it's too small,' Ben said with certainty and resigned to the fact that this whole trip was a non-starter.

She looked thoughtful. 'It's a good size room but it's the only room apart from the bathroom.'

'We'd have to buy furniture,' Ben pointed out and imagined them sitting on the floor with just a mattress they would somehow acquire and his easel in a corner.

'Would you stretch your budget?' The estate agent was not much older than them.

Bella said, 'Yes.' At the same time Ben said, 'No.'

'No, we can't,' Ben reiterated.

'We so could. You're a successful artist now. And my vegan street food is bringing in some cash.'

The estate agent had the sort of expression you might have if you were an ardent carnivore and someone put a vegan falafel in front of you.

'Where are you going to cook all that food for your stalls?'

Bella walked over to the kitchen area. 'Probably at Anna's mainly. I could do a bit here. But would you paint in here?' she asked Ben.

'Yes.' He had to admit the light was good.

'Over here maybe?' She was in front of the large bay window.

'But where would the bed go?'

'Well here, of course,' she said moving about two paces to her right.'

'We've got more space where we are now!'

'Yes, but we're not in Islington which is an awesome stylish place. And I'm fed up of sharing! This would be ours.' She pouted like a child determined to get her own way.

'All five square metres.' Ben raised his eyebrows.

'This will get snapped up. It's an attractive space and very central. Do you want to take it?' The agent was beginning to annoy Ben. Didn't they always use that line?

'We'll let you know,' Ben said grabbing Bella by the hand and persuading her out of the building.

'We will! We'll take it!' she shouted as he coaxed her down the stairs.

In a café down the road they sat opposite each other both checking their mobiles for updates. Bella took a sip of her flat white and looked at Ben.

'I think we should take it.' Her mind was made up. 'Islington is the sort of place an artist should be. Picasso moved to bohemian Paris to paint at an early age. I'm only asking you to move a few miles south in London. You need to be in a happening place, not stuck in boring Tuffers.'

'But it would be down to us to find the rent every month. At least with a house share it's not quite so pressured.'

'But actually, it's the same rent practically.'

'For a tiny space.'

'We'll be out all the time in the bars and restaurants.'

'We'll be broke.'

'All great artists struggle; it's how they produce their best work.'

She was so pretty. Did he love her? It was so easy to fall in love with Bella but he couldn't help a certain reticence; would she hurt him in the end?

'Perhaps we should keep looking. Something better might come up. Maybe something furnished.'

Her shoulders sank in despair. 'We've been looking online. I've looked at everything in our price range. Anyway, I don't want someone else's scuzzy furniture.'

'We can't afford new!'

'Second hand. Upcycling. I'll do all that,' she said as if it would be easy.

Ben sighed.

'I love you,' she said and reached across the table to hold his hand.

'S'pose we'll take it then.' He grinned at her. He did love her.

There had been a frost overnight and a mist was lingering over the fields, softening the landscape. A buzzard took off from a high branch and flew majestically away. Two sets of eyes followed it until it was obscured by the white haze. Despite the cold, Carol felt warm and content. The thermal layer she had on was certainly helping but this blissful time she suddenly found herself experiencing was warming her through to her very heart. Bill was holding her gloved hand and every time she caught his eye he smiled gently. He was such easy company and she couldn't quite believe that this was happening to her at this time of her life.

Before Bryan's indiscretion she had just accepted a mediocre existence as a wife and mother. She was frustrated that Bryan didn't want to go on holiday as much as she did but, somehow, she saw it as her fault; she wasn't interesting enough.

But now she'd started this relationship with Bill she realised that she had a lot to offer. He appreciated her, complimented the way she looked, described her cooking as delicious. They talked for hours, getting to know each other's pasts. It was interesting to hear about Bill's wife, Lisa; there was no need to be jealous of his memory of her. Of course, she was important to him but he had also moved on and knew he wanted more from life; after all, he was only fifty-five.

Fifty-five and so five years younger than Carol. Ellie had teased her, calling him a toy boy, but she was mainly really pleased for her.

And he had been the perfect gentleman and seemed content with cuddles and kisses, at least for now. Although nothing was said, Carol suspected they both knew it would be a big step to make love. Dating was a thing of the past, a simpler age, for them both and it all seemed very different from the first time. She certainly didn't want to rush things; it was so important to her that this wasn't a mistake.

Rebecca had rung last night. It always felt like she had her own agenda which she tried to weave into the conversation by asking certain questions.

'Have you seen Dad?' she asked.

'No, why would I?' Carol reacted.

'Well he is your husband, after all.'

Carol was surprised by this and decided to say nothing.

'Anyway, he's living in a room above the pub in your village. Did you know that?'

'Ellie mentioned it.'

'Mentioned it? Mum, it's an appalling state of affairs. You're living in that huge great house on your own and he's roughing it just up the street. You know it's totally over with Tiffany; he wants you back. So?'

Carol wasn't ready to tell her daughters about Bill, yet. It was stupid really but she actually felt quite guilty.

'Darling, he had an affair and left me. He told me she was the love of his life and our marriage was over. How do you expect me to react?'

'Look Mum, I know he's been an idiot and he admits it too, but surely you can forgive him now? I mean for the sake of the family, for me and Megs.'

Carol couldn't quite believe that her daughter expected her to reunite with her father to please her.

'How's Steve?' she asked unashamedly changing the subject.

'Steve's great. It's going really well. I'm so excited; I think he might be the one.'

'Really? Well that's wonderful, darling.'

'Thanks Mum. You did really like him, didn't you? I mean when we came to stay.'

'Yes, yes I did like him.' She'd been underwhelmed, truth be told, but there was no point in arguing with Rebecca.

'You see and here's the thing...' her daughter went on.

Carol braced herself.

'The thing is that I really want to bring him home for Christmas!'

Carol was sure there was a but coming.

'But, how can I? I mean, I can't say come and stay at mine and by the way it's going to be my parents' first Christmas apart so perhaps we'll spend some of the day with my Dad, oh and by the way he's renting a room above the pub.'

Carol wanted the ground to swallow her up. Rebecca always was a daddy's girl and she always seemed to see everything from his point of view.

'Up to you, darling, if that's what you want to do,' she said knowing full well that this was an obtuse response but not having the will to come up with anything better.

'But Mum?' She didn't hide her horror.

'Now, I'm sorry but I'm going to have to go; I'm expecting a call.'

'Who from?' She sounded outraged.

'A friend,' Carol said.

'Since when have your friends been more important than me?'

'Of course not, darling, but we have been talking for quite a while and, as I said, I am expecting a call. It's to do with this Cost-Cut development protest,' she lied to make it more palatable to her hopping-mad daughter.

'Well I hope it's worth it!' Rebecca ended the call.

Now, out walking with Bill, nothing else seemed to matter. They reached the attractive village of Gem Corner with its magnificently preserved Tudor architecture and pretty little green at its centre, soon arriving at the pub where they planned to have lunch. They walked in to a cosy space with a log fire. It wasn't busy, with only a few other customers, and Carol felt a little exposed. She went for a table in a corner while Bill got some drinks and menus from the bar.

When he sat down, he asked, 'You okay?'

'Yes, of course. It's silly really but it feels like I'm having a secret affair.'

'How exciting!' They both laughed and then he said, 'Does it have to be a secret?' which seemed like a serious question.

'I haven't told my girls yet. Rebecca's hell-bent on me getting back together with her father and rescuing him from his reduced circumstances.'

He was thoughtful, slightly worried. 'What do *you* want?'

'I'm just trying to enjoy this moment; I've not been this happy in a long time.'

He smiled and relaxed a little. 'Me too,' he said.

'What about your girls, have you told them about me?' Was she being too forward?

'I've sown seeds. It's different for me. They both want me to start a new relationship, especially now they are at uni and at home a lot less.'

'That's nice.'

'Yeah they are good girls. In fact, I think they are more worried about me becoming sad and lonely in my old age.'

'I wouldn't have thought there'd be much chance of that,' she flirted.

'Is that a compliment?' He was beaming.

'Yes, I suppose it is.'

'What about telling Megan?' he asked.

'Yes, good idea. I get on so much better with her and she's coming to stay this weekend. The only trouble is she'll probably tell Rebecca.'

Bill looked miffed. Carol realised she was going to have to be brave.

'You're right. I'll tell Megs.'

There was a thoughtful pause before she added, 'Perhaps you could meet her? I mean after I've told her.'

'I'd love to.' His smile was wide, his green eyes shining. Suddenly it seemed like a good idea.

Chapter 22

'Are you going to say goodbye to Larry?' Ellie asked. Her mother just looked a little confused.

'Oh, he'll be coming to The Beeches too, very soon, I'm sure. We've talked about it and decided. His son is making the arrangements.'

Ellie knew that there was still only one room vacant; she had expressly asked the manager, Pauline, to let her know the minute a second one was available. Looking at her mother, Ellie thought perhaps it was better this way. Goodbyes were always difficult.

Kathleen was all packed and Ellie was checking they had everything. 'These cushions, did they come from Benton Street?'

'I don't know, did they?'

'I'll have to ask Stephanie.'

'Oh, don't fuss.'

'But Mum, if they are yours you should take them.'

Kathleen was staring out of the window and seemed quite disinterested in the fact that she was leaving this room which had been her home for over a year now.

Stephanie appeared with a forced smile pinned across her face. 'All done?' she asked breezily.

'These cushions?' Ellie held one up.

'Yours. We don't do tartan.'

'Thank you.'

'I've just come to wish you all the best, Kathleen.' Stephanie raised her voice but the words still fell on deaf ears.

'Thank you, Stephanie,' Ellie answered for her. 'And all the best to you and all your staff. Kathleen has very much enjoyed her stay here at Starling Skies.' They both knew that wasn't entirely true but there was no point in parting with bad feeling. But the expression on Stephanie's face told Ellie that she was wasting her time.

'There is the matter of the final bill to be settled. Perhaps you could do that on your way out?'

'Certainly.'

Stephanie held out her hand and Ellie shook it.

'It has been very nice knowing you.' Was that a tear in her eye? Surely not.

As they drove away it occurred to Ellie that what was left of her mother's possessions fitted neatly in the boot and on the back seat of the car. She felt a mixture of relief and trepidation. How would her mother react to this new home when she was actually there alone? Would she miss Larry terribly? Perhaps she'd make new friends. Please God. She looked across to her mother who had a serene expression. She seemed to be in full possession of her faculties today.

When they got to The Beeches Pauline was there to welcome them. She shook Ellie's hand warmly and held it for a few seconds longer as she looked into her eyes and said, 'I will do everything I can to make your mother's stay a very pleasurable one.'

'Thank you. That's reassuring. You never know how these things are going to go, do you?'

'Do you like dogs?' Pauline asked Kathleen.

'Yes, I love dogs. We had one, didn't we Ellie? A springer spaniel named Saffy. She was a darling.'

'Well good because this afternoon we have a few local residents bringing their pets in while we have tea in the conservatory.'

'How lovely,' Ellie said.

They got to Kathleen's room where there was a lamp on by the bed and a poinsettia with its red flowers cheering up the space. It was warm and cosy and had a good view over the garden.

'I'll leave you to settle in,' Pauline said as she turned to leave.

Ellie set to work unpacking for her mother whilst Kathleen looked wistfully out of the window. Finally, she said, 'Do you think I'll be all right here, darling? When will Larry be able to come?'

'I'm sure you will be all right. I don't know when Larry will be coming.'

As soon as the room was done, Ellie suggested they went downstairs to meet some of the other residents. The conservatory had quite a buzz as they waited in anticipation for the owners and their pets to arrive. Kathleen went straight to the French doors and pushed the handle. To her surprise it opened. A chill wind immediately came through but it didn't wipe the excitement from her face.

'Mum, it's a bit cold for outside today.'

'Yes, it is today.' She shut the door and for a brief moment looked lost and as if she didn't know where she was.

Ellie felt the need to apologise to the other residents for the blast of cold air.

'That's all right,' a friendly face said and she heaved herself out of her chair and came over to them. She wore a blue forget-me-not pin badge and another badge with her name on. 'My name's Nancy.'

'Yes, I can see. Kathleen, pleased to meet you.'

'They'll get you a badge in time. Do you want to come and sit with me and Cynthia?'

'Yes, all right.'

'We're quite a friendly bunch. All help each other. I'd introduce you to everyone but of course I can't remember names but we've all got our badges on.'

'What a brilliant idea.' Ellie was impressed.

It didn't take long for Kathleen to look like she belonged. Pauline appeared and suggested quietly to Ellie that a quick goodbye and then a sharp exit would be a good idea.

Ellie agreed but asked, 'Would you call me later and let me know how she's doing, please?'

'Of course, I will.'

She told herself that this was a good move and her mother would be happier. But still she had a heavy heart as she drove away.

Chapter 23

On Friday morning Bryan was roused by the noise of an early delivery from the brewery. He managed to laugh it off; it was a response that was proving useful these days. He looked at his watch. It was actually just after seven and normally he'd be up and about. He thought back to his first shift working in the bar last night. He'd actually quite enjoyed it. There was a lot of cheerful banter and enough to do to keep him busy, probably the start of the Christmas celebrations. The first half hour dragged with just Paddy propping the bar up in his usual spot but after that it soon filled up. The inevitable questions kept coming: *What are you doing here, Bryan?* Or they might jest, *Fallen on hard times, eh Bryan?* After throwing out some evasive replies he decided to treat it all as a joke and dispense with any attempt at satisfying their curiosity.

He got the hang of the pumps and the optics pretty quickly and Gavin was impressed. From seven-thirty diners were coming in, having booked a table, and he had to do the drinks orders for the waiters as well. It was really quite full-on but he coped. It made him feel a bit better about life.

He looked at himself in the bathroom mirror now. He wasn't a bad-looking chap. Perhaps a shave and a shower would be a good idea. And then it struck him. Carol had her shift at the shop on a Friday morning. He could nonchalantly call in for a paper, maybe even some milk and he might manage to snatch a word with her. Suddenly he felt brighter and smothered his jaw with shaving cream in readiness for a wet shave.

Forty minutes later and wearing his favourite blue jumper over jeans and trainers, and even a splash of aftershave, he walked down to the shop. His heart skipped a beat as he went in. Immediately he could see Carol behind the counter and serving a customer. He smiled across at her but she didn't notice. Grabbing his newspaper and some milk he moved to behind the woman being served. They were exchanging pleasantries and Carol glanced at him, not giving anything away. Finally, the woman left and Bryan stood in front of his wife. This was his moment. Don't cock it up, he told himself.

'Hello Carol,' he said and kept his voice soft, not wanting Jeffrey in the post office to hear.

Carol operated the till efficiently. 'That will be three pounds fifty-five.'

He was staring at her now.

'Three pounds and fifty-five pence,' she repeated.

'Oh, sorry, yes, erm, contactless?'

She pointed to the newly installed card machine and he waved his debit card at it.

He looked around and behind him. Jeffrey was doing a good impression of someone who wasn't listening in so he leant forward, 'Carol, darling, can we talk, please?'

She appeared baffled. 'What about?'

'Carol, please?' He didn't want to plead but it seemed necessary. 'Carol, I really need to talk to you. I've got so much to say.'

Now she looked worried.

'Later today, perhaps? Or over the weekend?'

Another customer walked in. Damn. They headed for the post office counter. Phew.

'Please, I am begging you.'

She nearly went cross-eyed with amazement before sighing deeply and then said, 'If we must.'

'Thank you,' he said and smiled at her, getting nothing back.

Linda appeared. 'Everything all right here?'

'Of course, Linda,' Bryan said. 'Just talking to my wife.'

Carol flinched but then said, 'It's all right Linda,' and she left them alone.

'Later today,' she said turning back to Bryan.

'Great. How about this afternoon?'

'Yes, okay. But I have got things to do, you know.'

'Right. See you then.'

'Where?' she asked.

'Oh sorry, I assumed at our home.'

She looked offended but then said, 'Okay, three o'clock.'

In the next few hours the words he was going to deliver played over and over in his mind, varying the nuances here and there. It needed to be perfect. It needed to win her over. He decided to book a table at The Great House in Capel Green for the following evening, just in case she agreed to let him take her out for dinner. It was pricey there but he knew it was her favourite place. He needed everything aligned in his favour: stars, planets and restaurant tables. He asked Gavin if he could put some washing on and laundered his best shirt, the green one with a thin stripe. He'd wear it tomorrow evening. He even did some online research into holidays in Split in Croatia and discovered a wonderful heritage hotel with suites and a view over the town square. It looked delightful and it was exactly the sort of thing Carol would love. He was tempted to just book it, there and then, but that was probably a bit risky.

With five minutes to go until three o'clock, he was in fighting form and strolling down the street purposefully. Margaret who was ahead of him lingering, expecting to chat no doubt, was brushed off with, *Sorry, can't stop now.*

He got to the back door at the side of his home and rapped the knocker. It was an excruciating thirty seconds until she opened the door. She stood there looking slightly flustered.

'Hello Carol.' He was willing her to invite him in but she didn't.

'Bryan,' she said and then moved back so that he could enter the boot room and then the kitchen. She looked different, younger somehow. Was it her hair? She was wearing a pretty blouse that he didn't recognise, over jeans. Had she lost weight?

'Cup of tea?' she asked.

'Thank you, yes please.' He hovered feeling awkward before deciding to sit at the kitchen table uninvited. As she made the tea he watched her face, looking for clues. He decided she looked attractive but pained. They were happy together once. The tea made she carried the mugs to the table and put one in front of him. She sat on the other side of the table rather than next to him. He forced a smile.

'So, what's all this about?' she asked.

Suddenly words failed him. He was disarmed by her assured stance. She was looking at him now, clearly impatient for an answer.

'I, erm, I, well, I just wanted to say, I mean I did want to say, I do want to say... I'm sorry. I've been a complete idiot and I know I've hurt you and I really want to make it up to you. For things to be like they were before; I mean better than before.'

'You mean better than they were before you had an affair.'

'That's over. Totally. A massive mistake; I know that now. I'm so sorry.'

'It's difficult Bryan, I mean to forgive you, to trust you again.' She seemed very certain of her every word.

'I realise that and I know it will take time but I want to prove to you that I've changed.'

Still no encouragement from her expression.

He continued, 'I've booked a table at The Great House tomorrow evening; I know it's your favourite restaurant and well, I... will you come?' He reached his hand across the table to her but she didn't reciprocate.

'I can't. Megan is coming for the weekend and—'

'That's okay; she could come too; I'd love to see her.'

'I'm sorry but we have plans.'

'Oh? What plans?' Damn, that came out wrong. He looked at her; nothing he said seemed to have much impact. What was going on? 'Perhaps another time then?' As he said it the whole thing seemed hopeless. She was looking at him pitifully and saying nothing as if she couldn't find the words.

'Carol, tell me, please, what's going on?'

'You left me. It was what you wanted. You didn't care that you were hurting my feelings then.' Her eyes were watering. He reached out to her again but she was rigid.

'I'm so sorry. I really am. I want to make it up to you in so many ways. Will you let me at least try?'

She was crying now. It was unbearable. He stood up and walked round to her carefully putting a hand on her shoulder. She threw it off.

'I think you'd better go,' she said bitterly.

'I can't leave you like this.'

'You did before. Before when you were with *her*!' The anger and disdain in her voice shook him.

'So, is that it?' He was broken. 'There's no hope for us? What about the children?'

'Don't you dare play that card!' Fury flashed in her eyes.

'But... but the children; we've always put them first.'

'No Bryan, I've always put them first. And they're not children any more. They are grown adults living their own lives.'

'Rebecca is so upset about this whole thing. She wants us to get back together again more than anything.'

'Rebecca wants what suits her.'

Was this his wife talking? One thing was for sure: Carol had changed; she wasn't the woman he had married. She was frightening him and he just didn't know what to do about it. He needed to think.

'I can't carry on living above the pub indefinitely.' Perhaps he shouldn't have said it but at last she looked troubled.

'No,' she said before blowing her nose on a tissue. He wanted to shake her.

'So, you might like to think about that while you are enjoying this big house, our family home, all on your own.' There he'd said it. It needed saying. There was a lot going on behind those eyes but Bryan hadn't a clue what she was thinking.

'This situation we find ourselves in is of your making so don't blame me.'

'But Carol, why won't you let me put it right?'

'I think you'd better go.'

'What about Christmas? Have I got to spend Christmas at the pub? Rebecca is heartbroken by all this. And Megan too, I'm sure.'

She stood up to meet his gaze and yelled at him, 'Get out!'

He was stunned. She was staring at him through watery eyes.

'Just get out!'

He was shaking as he made his way to the door. 'I don't believe this. I don't believe you can't find it in your heart to forgive me.' He didn't want her to see him crying, but he couldn't help it. He turned. She had collapsed back onto her chair weeping into her arms folded in front of her on the table. He felt like he was being stabbed in the heart as he left her there and walked unsteadily on to the street. What had become of them?

Roger took his reading glasses off and rubbed his eyes. He yawned and stretched. Ellie walked in to what had become his study room.

'Tired, are you?' She sounded sarcastic rather than concerned.

He sighed. 'No, not tired. It's quite technical, this... growing grapes malarkey. You'd be surprised at how complex the whole thing is.' He had to admit that at his age learning didn't come quite so easily.

'Perhaps you should take a break? You're spending every waking hour at that desk.' Why wouldn't she just leave him alone?

'Don't be silly. If I'm to stand any chance of getting this job, I need to get through this.' He didn't mean to raise his voice but she obviously didn't understand.

'So, is the current manager leaving any day soon?'

'January some time. He's not actually leaving, just moving to another area. But Annabelle says they want to interview in January.'

'How far through the course are you now?'

'I've done four modules out of ten.'

'You'll never do it! What with Christmas not far off.'

'Thanks for the encouragement.'

'And what about Christmas? Am I getting no help at all from you?'

He looked at her, slightly confused. 'I thought we were going low key? Anyway, it's a long way off.'

'Oh yes, well if your contribution is going to be the usual zero, then who cares?'

'This is important to me,' he said calmly but firmly.

She picked up the course outline from his in-tray. 'It says here most people take three to six months to complete this.'

'Yes, I know. But most of them are working full time and just doing it at weekends.'

'Most of them are probably a lot younger, too.'

'Twist the knife, why don't you?'

'I'm sorry but I've had a difficult day, what with Mum and everything. I thought you might do supper, this evening.'

'Sorry yes. Your Mum okay? Tell me about it later.' He was staring at the screen. 'Takeaway, okay?'

'No! No, it's not. I'm sick of takeaways. We had enough of those when Bryan was here. Do you know the Chinese in Hadleigh know both our names?'

Roger couldn't help the smile that crept across his face. 'Look, I'll do something in a minute.'

'Oh, don't bother. I'll cook. Again!'

Chapter 24

It was a perfect cold and sunny December day with a beautiful blue sky. As they went into the Really Rather Good coffee shop, in Bury St Edmunds, they walked into a blanket of stuffy warmth. It was packed with customers and the windows were steaming up obscuring the view over Angel Hill and Abbeygate.

The waitress brought over their drinks. Megan could only be persuaded to have an Americano and Carol wondered if her daughter had lost weight.

'Are you sure you don't want a pastry?' Carol asked.

'No, Mum. You have one, if you want.'

'Goodness no. I don't need any extra calories.' She thought about the last encounter with Bill and how he was beginning to want more than a cuddle in their more intimate exchanges. It was her pulling away.

'Dad says you've lost weight.'

'Did he now!' She had and she was pleased about it. Her jeans were so much more comfortable now.

'He told me he'd seen you and it didn't go well. He's gutted, Mum.'

Carol took a sharp intake of breath and steeled herself.

'It's all right.' Megan was reaching across the table. 'Sorry, I know it's difficult for you.' How difficult, she couldn't possibly know.

'Becky keeps phoning me too. I'm actually quite sick of hearing her going on about it. She's very worried about Christmas and us not all being together.'

'Well it's not my fault,' Carol said.

'Of course not, Mum.'

'So why do I feel guilty?' She wished she hadn't said that out loud.

Megan had a puzzled expression. 'You shouldn't. I can understand that it would be difficult to trust him again.'

'Exactly.' Carol sensed a but.

They sipped their coffees.

'I like your hair. And that blouse you're wearing. Very chic. It's nice to see you making the most of yourself.' Megan smiled with surprise. Her eyes were lively.

'Thank you,' Carol said.

'Have you done it just to make yourself feel better?'

Carol decided this was as good a moment as any. 'Actually, you know I said I get on well with Bill at the farm shop?'

'Yes.' Megan's expression was immediately serious.

'Well, we've been seeing each other, I mean dating, I suppose. Sounds so silly at my age.'

Megan's eyes were wide with disbelief. 'Blimey Mum. That's... well... unexpected I suppose. I mean so soon.'

'Well I know and, don't get me wrong, we're taking things slowly. It just happened and we get on so well. But we haven't, you know.'

Megan was deep in thought. 'Gosh. I'm quite shocked actually Mum. I mean not shocked, surprised. Does Dad know?'

'No! You're the first person I've told. Well, apart from my friend Ellie.'

'I see.' It looked like her mind was whirring.

'And I'd like to keep it that way for now.'

'Right. So, I can't tell Becky?'

'Well, you could but, well, I don't know. I suppose I don't want to make a massive deal of it at this stage.' She felt she should downplay the relationship, at least until her daughters were more used to the idea. But the reality was that she was pinning her wildest dreams on one lovely man. Bill.

'Do you think it will probably fizzle out then?'

'I just don't know.' There was a thoughtful pause as they both finished their coffees. Carol did know that it felt like she and Bill were falling in love. The thought of it fizzling out was frankly heart-breaking. How to play this? Where was the manual of life when you needed it?

'So, the way I see it,' Megs seemed to have worked something out, 'if it's not serious then the family, all four of us, could try and have Christmas together. I mean, not all of it, of course, but some of it. Say, Christmas Day, opening prezzies, having lunch. Dad wouldn't have to stay the night but...'

'I'm sorry, Megs, but I just can't do that. I actually do have quite strong feelings for Bill, and him for me.'

'But you said you didn't.'

Carol felt like she was getting tied in knots.

'I didn't actually say that. Look, I'm finding this hard. I'm not the perfect mother, I know, but I do think I deserve this chance of happiness.'

Megs looked down into her lap. 'So, you and Dad, it's really over for good?' She had a tear in her eye which moved Carol.

'Yes, I'm sorry, I think it really is.'

'But what about the house? Dad's got nowhere to live. What will happen?'

'I don't know right now. I just can't work it out.'

The atmosphere was thick around them as they walked out of the café. Carol tried to put an arm around her daughter but she wore a deep frown and moved away. The shopping trip they had planned suddenly seemed like a bad idea.

'Where do you want to go?' Carol asked trying to be upbeat.

'Not sure.'

'There's a Mistral now on Butter Market.'

'Yes, okay. I quite like their stuff.'

Megan found a jumper she liked and Carol persuaded her to try it on.

'It looks lovely on you. That saffron yellow suits you.'

'I like it but I'm a bit strapped for cash at the moment.'

'My treat then.'

Megan took another look in the mirror and said, 'Thanks Mum.'

Whilst she was changing, Carol picked a pretty grey scarf that went with the jumper.

'How about this as well? They go together, don't they?'

'Yes, okay.' Her lack of enthusiasm was hard work.

As they wandered around the streets, dropping into this shop and that, they kept the conversation mundane, avoiding the elephant that was following them around. To think that the plan was for Bill to meet Megan this weekend; that seemed like a crazy idea right now. She would have to text him. But then, how would he take it?

Carol followed her daughter into Garland Interiors and the beautiful fabric and objet d'art seemed to lift both their spirits. Megan giggled when she saw a quirky pair of candlesticks, the bases shaped like monkeys.

'Do you like them?'

'Yes, Mum, but we're not buying them.'

Carol looked closer at them and clocked the price. She decided she might come back and buy them for her daughter as a Christmas present.

By the time they were walking back to the car park they were both in a better mood. Retail therapy had worked its magic. They popped into Waitrose and bought shellfish and the makings of a paella for that evening. As Carol drove them home, she turned up Radio 2 and they sang along to Pharrell Williams' song *Happy* and when she looked across to Megan she was smiling at her.

Ellie found Roger at his desk.

'Fancy a cup of tea in the garden room?'

'Can you bring one up?' His full concentration was fixed on the screen.

'No, I can't. You'll have to come down for it?' He looked at her, his expression confused. He really was on another planet.

'Now,' she said firmly. 'I'm about to pour.'

He didn't move.

'Roger!'

'Yes, yes, I'm coming.'

'Now!'

'What's the matter with you all of a sudden?'

'I'd just like my husband back for half an hour.'

This seemed to register something in that male brain of his. He stood, scratching his uncombed hair and looking slightly bemused.

By the time Roger appeared in the garden room, Ellie had made the tea.

He sat opposite her. 'Right, so what's so bloody important?'

Ellie felt hurt now. 'I was talking to James earlier.'

'Ah. Has he finally admitted he's got the hots for you?'

'Stop it! He's going on about us having dinner; I mean all three of us.'

'Do we have to?'

'Well, no we don't but we sort of do.'

'That's female logic for you.'

'Anyway, the thing is, he's got a plus one to bring.'

'Well I suppose that could make it a bit more interesting.'

'He has suggested The Great House in Capel Green.'

'Blimey, is he paying?'

'We didn't talk about that.'

'Too vulgar to talk about money for the upper classes.' He put on a haughty accent. 'Why didn't you suggest our local?'

'I suppose because I don't want to, well, I mean...'

'You don't want to admit we're poor!'

'But we're not.'

'So, we've got to shell out for The Great House. Marvellous.'

'He's suggested one evening next week.'

'Did you tell him we're busy?'

'No! We're not busy.'

'Well, we could be. We could always invite Bryan over and talk him out of committing suicide.'

'He's not that bad, is he?'

'He looked pretty depressed when I popped into the pub yesterday. A picture of Vincent Van Gogh just before he decided to cut his ear off, only he's staring at a beer pump like it was responsible for all his woes.'

'Oh dear. Perhaps we should have him round this evening.'

'I don't think he can. They have him working at weekends.'

'Well, what about this afternoon.'

'I'm studying! Trying to.' Roger picked up his mobile.

'What are you doing, now?'

'I'm just checking the menu prices at this place to see if we can afford Addington's night out.'

'Actually, I've got my first commission on May Cottage. It will be in our account soon.'

'Really? That's brilliant. So, are we rich now?'

'Trust me, we can afford The Great House.'

Ben had stared at a blank canvas for about half an hour. He had all sorts of thoughts but nothing very creative. He kept telling himself to produce another work on the jazz theme; Jonathan couldn't get enough of them. He had even sold another painting for him. He had some good ideas floating around after he'd been to Ronnie Scott's for a second trip the other evening. Bella had been too busy planning her next vegan stall to go with him so he'd taken Adam, even though he'd said that jazz wasn't really his thing. Ben told him the women who went to the club were hot, and so desperate was he for a girlfriend, that was enough to persuade him.

The image of the black singer that evening stayed with him. She was tall and thin, with the grace of a gazelle, her head shaved accentuating big bright ebony eyes and full rouge lips. But still nothing came to him. Perhaps he should just paint her. He couldn't be bothered.

He stood up, put down his mug and stretched his arms out. Looking across the room, he couldn't quite believe how small this place was. Ridiculous. Bella, true to her word, had managed to get some furniture second hand. Anna's boyfriend had been getting rid of a sofa so that was good timing. It wasn't really their thing but Bella got some throws to cover it. It was also a little big for the space and he kept walking into it and banging his knee.

The worst thing was there was nowhere to go apart from the bathroom. Bella was out at the moment which helped especially as she complained about the smell of the turpentine that he used to thin his oil paints. But still he couldn't focus. He wondered if this was what claustrophobia felt like. The street scene below the bay window was always enticing. Islington definitely had a buzz about it. He put on a coat, grabbed his phone and wallet and left in a hurry.

It felt good to hit the pavement and stride out. Every other shop seemed to be a café of some sort on Upper Street, whether you wanted coffee, juice, gluten-free, sugar-free or vegan. Ben liked Kobo's. It had an unpretentious, Scandi-style and the Americano was good. He always smiled as he walked past the Ministry of Waxing. Bella thought it was a great name for a beauty salon while Ben thought it sounded painful. He ended up wandering into Fat Face and buying a grey jumper. It was pricey but they couldn't afford heating so it was essential for keeping warm. He felt more relaxed, just taking in the local vibe, and was in no rush to get back to the confines of their studio flat. Eventually he had sauntered as far as Jonathan's art gallery. One of his paintings was in the window. That was amazing. He went in.

'Ben, how you doing mate?' Jonathan came over.

'Not bad.'

'Enjoying Islington?'

'Yeah, it's great.'

'So, to what do I owe this visit? Got a work of art hidden about your person?'

'Nah, just chilling. Needed to get out of the flat.'

'Settling in okay?'

'Actually, it's so bloody small I'm finding it difficult.'

'Not good. Zapping your creative juices, is it?'

'Yeah, seems to be.'

'We can't have that.' He looked troubled.

Ben sighed. 'Oh well, Bella's never been happier.'

'She's a stunning girl, but my friend, you need to paint.'

'You got it in one.'

'Perhaps it's time to rent a studio, somewhere local?'

'Huh! You must be kidding.'

'Well I've got someone coming to look at what you've got here currently, an American guy as it happens. Minted he is.'

'Great.'

'Yeah, great, but not so good if you don't keep painting. This is your livelihood now, Ben! Am I right?'

'Well, that's the idea. I don't know.' Suddenly it all seemed like an impossible dream. How was he going to paint in that bloody place?

Jonathan put a friendly arm round his shoulder. 'Look, mate, you need to sort this. What about that not-for-profit place, not far from here; they have studios from about four hundred a month, I think. Or you can do this co-worker desk thing, but that probably wouldn't work with oil paint.'

'What are they like, then, these studios, apart from pricey?'

'Pretty good. I've seen them actually. One of my other artists hung out there for a while.'

'Nah, I just can't afford it.'

'But you're earning good money now. Ben, you need to take this seriously. You've got talent. Do you want to hit the big time or end up working in some soulless call centre?'

He had a point. Four hundred a month. Perhaps it was doable. Ben couldn't believe that he was seriously considering it. Bella would go mad. But what else could he do?

The text from Bill was asking what the plan was, the plan for him to meet Megan. Carol didn't know what to do and felt on edge. She couldn't ignore him forever.

'Shall I pour a glass of wine for us?' Megan asked. 'Cooking is always more fun with a drink.'

'Yes, good idea.' Carol was looking at the recipe Megs had found and it said the preparation took an hour. Looking at the list of ingredients she could see why. 'Not sure if I've got everything for this.'

'Doesn't matter. We can improvise.'

'Yeah, sure.'

They seemed to be getting on a lot better by the time the paella was simmering away and smelling gorgeous. Carol topped both their glasses up.

'Why do you keep checking your phone?' Megs asked.

'Am I?'

'You know you are.'

Should she tell her?

'Is it Bill? Are you expecting to hear from him?' Megs went up to her mother and gave her a hug. 'Sorry about earlier. It was just a bit of a surprise. Of course I want you to be happy.'

'Thank you, darling.'

'So?'

'Well, the thing is, and you don't have to, you really don't have to, but Bill would like to meet you.'

'Oh. Right. Well, I suppose I might as well.'

'Are you sure?'

'Yes, I think so.' She put a spoon through the paella.

Carol decided to go for it. 'We could invite him to help us with all this food this evening, or...'

'This evening?'

'Well maybe. But then he may have other plans. I would have to check.' She knew full well he was waiting for her call.

'Yes, well, ask him, if you want.'

'Are you sure? Really sure?'

'Why not? I'm actually quite intrigued to see what he's like.'

'Okay.'

Megan went upstairs with the excuse that she wanted to change. Carol phoned and he answered straightaway.

'Sorry, I've left it so late.'

'That's okay.' He sounded hurt.

'Would you like to come for supper? We've made paella.'

'Yes, that would be lovely. I've actually got something in the oven but it will keep.'

'Yes, sorry. It's not been straightforward but she's okay with it.'

'I see. Had I better wear battle armour?'

Carol laughed with relief. 'No, you'll be fine. I've actually had a hug from her and she said I deserve to be happy.'

'That's nice.'

'Anyway, we've had a couple of glasses of wine which always helps.'

'Indeed. See you soon, then.'

'Can't wait,' she said and realised she meant it.

Bill arrived with a beautiful bunch of white lilies and a bottle of chilled white wine. Megan couldn't take her eyes off him at first. He was wearing a navy linen shirt loose over a pair of jeans. Carol decided he was definitely fanciable.

'Hello Megan, it's good to meet you.'

'Yes, and you,' she said uncertainly. She looked at the bottle. 'Capel Green Farm?'

'Yes, it's where I work so... well, it's a decent wine anyway.'

'And Mum. She works there too.'

'Part time,' Carol chipped in.

'I didn't think she'd ever have another job when she retired from teaching. Her and Dad were looking forward to having more holidays.'

'Your mother's still relatively young and she's proving to be a great asset at the farm shop. Has she told you she's creating recipes and providing ideas for dishes in the café?'

'Yes, she mentioned that. She's always been a good cook.' Megan wasn't actually nasty but Carol sensed a strong resentment from her daughter. Carol sighed. Nothing was easy.

As the evening went on, Megan seemed to thaw, relax even. The conversation got lighter and they laughed together.

'I've applied for the management training programme at work,' Megan announced.

'Oh good.' Carol was so pleased. It was nice that she had shared this with Bill too.

'What's this, then?' Bill asked.

'It's so I can get into the fund management side of things. Fiona, she's a fund manager, well, she persuaded me to go for it.'

'That was good,' Carol smiled with pride. 'She obviously thinks a lot of you.'

'Yes.' Megan blushed. 'Yes, I think she does.'

'Well, well done you,' Bill said raising a glass to her.

'Coffee anyone?' Carol asked while the going was good.

Later Bill waited for a cab to arrive and Megan went through to the lounge. Carol was trying to figure out if the evening had gone okay or not.

'What do you reckon?' she asked Bill.

He swept over to her and took her in his arms. They kissed and it felt heady and wonderful.

'It's never easy, this situation,' Bill said still holding her.

'So I'm finding out.'

'But I think we did all right.'

'Yes, yes, I think she's okay with it all.'

'Are you going to the jazz evening in your village hall next weekend?' he asked and Carol immediately felt panicked.

'Well, I've got two tickets but...'

'You don't want to be seen in public with me.' He kept his tone light hearted.

It must have been the alcohol that made her say, 'To hell with the gossip; let's go together.'

He kissed her again just as Megan appeared. She looked embarrassed. 'The cab's here.'

'Thanks Megan and lovely to meet you.'

Chapter 25

Bryan looked a bit awkward sitting in their garden room drinking coffee; to think he had lived here for a while.

'So, how's it going?' Roger asked.

'I did another shift at the pub last night. I quite enjoy it. Anything to keep me busy.'

'Are they paying you for all this work?'

'No. The idea is that the room's free. Otherwise they could potentially be hiring it out for B & B.'

'I see. So, do you have some sort of agreement as to how many shifts you have to do a week?'

'Not really. They just ask me if I'll do it. They're busiest at weekends of course.'

'Bit unsociable for you then.'

'Yeah.' Bryan sighed. He made no attempt to sugar-coat the situation. 'Not that I have a social life.'

'We wanted you to come round here last night, but of course...'

'Yeah, thanks. You've been a good friend to me. Actually, serving at the pub is helping me to reconnect with people in the village a bit. It's like I'm getting brownie points for good behaviour. Community service almost.' He smiled at that.

'But Bryan you haven't committed a crime.'

'You'd think so if you saw Carol the other day.'

Roger bit his lip. 'Sorry to hear that.'

'I think it's really over between us. I can't quite believe it. Rebecca's really upset. Even Megan was trying to organise that we all had Christmas Day together but apparently that's definitely not on.'

'As I said before, you must come here. You know you're welcome,' Roger said without hesitation.

'Thanks mate. The pub opens for a couple of hours...'

'Surely you don't have to work Christmas Day? Sounds to me like they're taking liberties.'

'Well I don't say no because I think, what else would I be doing? Anyway, Gavin did say that come the spring they will want the room back for B & B guests. Apparently, they already have a booking.'

'Well you don't want to stay there any longer than you have to, do you?'

'No. And if it really is over with Carol, I want my share of the house. She'll have to swallow that. It's not fair as things stand.'

'Actually, mate, I agree with you.'

Ellie had to smile at the scene before her when she arrived at The Beeches. There was ballroom dancing in the main lounge. Residents had coupled up and were doing their best to keep up with Gloria and Marvin, who were leading them in full-sequined regalia, as they waltzed to *Que Sera Sera*, playing out through the speakers. The couple were nimble on their feet, defying their age and swirled elegantly around the dance floor. Gloria was wearing an emerald green dress, with a fitted bodice down to the hips embellished with chiffon and gold leaf. The skirt was long and silky and fanned out at her calves. Her lined and tanned face was heavily painted and she wore ruby red lipstick which accentuated her rapturous smile. Her partner was more demurely dressed in a dark grey tail suit with a matching emerald bow tie. They came to a graceful end with a bow and a curtsy and everyone clapped. It was then that Ellie spotted her mother sitting on her own in the far corner. She made her way over, careful not to draw too much attention to herself and sat down next to her.

'Hello Mum,' she said and took her hand gently in hers. 'Not dancing?'

Her mother had a sadness about her. 'I'm waiting for Larry to ask me.'

'Oh Mum, Larry's not here, is he?'

'Didn't you bring him with you? Why didn't you?'

Nancy came over. 'We're doing a cha cha cha next. Do you want to dance with me?' she asked. 'We're short of men, you know,' she said to Ellie laughing it off.

'Go on, Mum, you can do the cha cha.'

'No!' Her face was a picture of defiance. 'I want to dance with Larry.'

Nancy simply drifted away to find another partner.

'Shall we go and get a cup of tea?' Ellie suggested as the music started up again. Kathleen rose to her feet. She had that lost look today.

Ellie made her mother a cup of tea using the facility they had in the corner of the dining room. Kathleen had just looked blankly at her when she asked her if she wanted a drink. The mug was now sitting in front of her, the tea going cold.

'Do you remember the lobby at The Swan Hotel in Southwold?' No response. 'You could make yourself a drink there. They said that rather than do it in your room you could be more sociable. You liked that.'

Kathleen's expression softened.

'The beach huts were always pretty, painted pastel shades. I used to love the names some of them had. Hunky Dory; Auntie Bong Bong; Linga Longa!' Was that a smile of recognition? 'Do you remember Mum?'

She nodded. 'You loved the pier especially the funny mirrors that made you look short and fat.' There was a pause. 'We always got fish and chips and sat on a bench to eat them.'

'That's right, Mum.' She still hadn't touched her tea. 'Do you like it here, Mum?'

Her mother looked confused. She looked around her as if she was trying to work out where she was. 'I prefer Benton Street,' she said.

'But it is okay? I mean, are the staff nice to you?'

She was anxious now. 'Staff?'

'Yes, the carers.'

'I don't know where Larry is. Do you?'

Ellie sighed and squeezed her mother's hand.

On her way out she asked if she could have a word with Pauline.

'As you probably know, in the early days of dementia, you have days when you're not so good; quite confused and fuzzy headed. Other days are better,' Pauline explained. 'I know it's difficult to experience but your mother has settled in well.'

Ellie's mind was churning as she drove home. Halfway through Capel Green, she decided to do a slight detour and drive up to the market square to see the Christmas lights which were always magical. As soon as she entered the square, the fairy tale scene that made her gasp every year was before her. The crooked medieval timber-framed houses, painted in various muted shades, were lit up with pretty white lights. A fir tree stood tall in the centre also sprinkled with white illumination. She parked up and got out of the car walking round in wonderment until she saw a sign.

Your Christmas Magic with the compliments of Cost-Cut.

How dare they! How could this beautiful sight be marred by such an ugly outfit? She checked her WhatsApp messages on her mobile and saw that several in the protest group had realised the same thing. It made Ellie fearful that the battle was not won. Had they been complacent of late? Did they really need to protest even more to stop the development going ahead? Suddenly she wondered what there was to look forward to and made up her mind to head straight to Starling Skies.

It was five-thirty when she went into reception. Angela was behind the reception desk and immediately raised her eyebrows.

'Did you forget something?' she asked.

'No! No, I would like to see Larry.'

'Why do you want to see him? I take it you're still not a relative of his?'

'No, of course I'm not.'

Angela had a wide-eyed enquiring look on her face which wouldn't budge.

'Please. Just for ten minutes. I'll see him here in reception.'

'I'm sorry Mrs Hardcastle but this is most inappropriate. Why do you want to see him?'

'Because my mother misses him!' It spurted out before Ellie thought through the consequences.

'The answer remains no,' Angela said calmly in that infuriating way.

'Listen, please will you ask Larry if he would come to reception and talk with me just for ten minutes? I promise I won't cause trouble. If he says, no, then fine, I'll go.'

The receptionist seemed to be lost for words now. She made a call and Stephanie appeared.

'Ellie! To what do we owe this pleasure?'

'I'd like to speak with Larry. Please will you at least tell him I'm here.'

'I'm sorry but that won't be possible. We can't have anyone coming in here demanding to see one of our residents at any time of the day or night.'

'It's quarter to six on a Tuesday evening for goodness sake. And I'm not anyone! My mother was a resident here for over a year.'

'I'm sorry we would be breaking protocol; it's out of the question.'

'To hell with protocol!' Ellie cried meeting a stunned expression from Stephanie. It was hopeless. 'I'm clearly wasting my time.' She left the building, defeated and distraught, her hands shaking as she fumbled to get the car key from her bag. The final insult was a note under her windscreen telling her not to park in front of the building where ambulances might need access. She tore it up and let the pieces fall to the ground.

*

Roger was sat back in his chair, his legs stretched out and crossed at the ankles, looking around the restaurant. He couldn't help smiling at the opulence of the place. It was all starched white table cloths and every shade of pale grey imaginable. Even the Christmas decorations were tasteful and low key with just a hint here and there: a long thin ivory candle in a shiny silver holder, festive greenery with silver additions. In defiance of the sombre look there were some bright red exotic-looking flowers in a very tall vase, probably flown in from Sri Lanka. It all looked very expensive.

'Roger, sit up at least.' Ellie had been on edge from the moment they were getting ready to come out. He had been told off about his choice of outfit and was now wearing a rapidly ironed pale blue shirt and casual navy-blue jacket. Why all this fuss just for Addington and his latest fling, he didn't know. She was giving him one of her stares from across the table.

'All right, but they're not even here yet.'

'They will be any minute. We were a bit early.'

'Why?'

'For goodness sake, just behave. Don't ruin this whole evening because you've got a thing about James.'

Just then Lady R appeared. So, this was where she hung out. She looked amazing in silky black trousers, a frilly cream blouse and a longline blazer. Wow! To think that he might be working for this woman one day. And she was heading over to their table.

Roger quickly stood up. 'Fancy seeing you here.' He beamed at her.

'Good evening Roger.' She nodded to him and then turned to Ellie. 'So lovely to see you.' Ellie stood up and they kissed, both cheeks, just as Addington appeared and came over.

'Ah, I see you've already met,' he said, his blue eyes positively twinkling with delight. Surely not. Surely Annabelle wasn't his plus one? Perhaps a last-minute stand-in? The upper classes operated in strange ways. James sat next to Ellie and so at least Roger had Annabelle by his side. She smelt divine.

'Well, first things first, we need some drinks.' James beckoned a waiter over. 'An aperitif; some Champagne seems appropriate. What would you recommend?'

'The Rosé Gruet, sir.'

'Excellent. May as well have a bottle,' he said clearly not concerned with the bill.

'Oh, James, you're just showing off now aren't you, darling?' Lady R was playful.

Darling?! Just how long had these two known each other?

No one looked at the menu. They were all just sipping their fizz and James was praising Ellie to the skies. It was as if she was his little protégé when the reality was that Ellie had stumbled into being an estate agent accidently.

'I believe she will be a real asset.' Will be? How long was she going to be working for this man? 'You must be very proud?' James continued, eyeballing Roger.

'Yes, of course.' No point in saying anything else.

'What have you been up to, Roger?' Annabelle smiled as she turned to him.

'I've been studying viticulture. I found this course online, Wine Academy...'

'Ah, so you took my advice.' James looked very pleased with himself. Did a mention of Capel Green Farm constitute advice?

'I've heard the Academy are very good,' Annabelle was quick to add. 'So, you'll definitely be applying for Joe's job, will you?'

'If he finishes it in time,' Ellie chipped in. 'He's cramming it all in, in just a couple of months, I don't know...'

Why did she have to scupper his chances? 'It's fine; I'm giving it my full attention and I'm nearly through it. Just a couple more assessments to pass. And,' he gave this word emphasis, 'I am really enjoying it.'

Ellie looked doubtful.

'Sounds like a very industrious household,' James said cheerily.

'Well, I hope you do apply.' Annabelle smiled at him again and that made Roger's evening.

He was halfway through his Gressingham Duck with some strange-looking carrots when it occurred to him that this couple must be on opposing sides of the Cost-Cut debate. Like a dream Ellie opened up the subject for him. James had been waxing lyrical about how the market square looked so splendid with the festive lights.

'But have you seen the posters? It's Cost-Cut who are sponsoring them this year. Can you believe it? How low will they stoop?'

'They've just paid for this year's lights; what's wrong with that?' James was defensive.

'Bribery and corruption is what is wrong; they clearly want to influence the council's decision on their proposed development.'

James looked nonplussed; he didn't care if the development went ahead.

'Actually, I happen to know there is a meeting this week where they are going to decide whether to grant planning permission,' Annabelle said calmly. 'The feeling is it will go in Cost-Cut's favour, subject to certain conditions which they may, or may not, be prepared to meet.'

James sat back in his chair and sipped his classy wine looking unmoved while Ellie was beside herself.

'Such as what?' she demanded. 'What conditions would stop them?'

'Well, they will probably be asked to provide the money needed to create the access road for a start.'

'Will that be enough to put them off?'

Annabelle looked apologetic. 'We'll just have to wait and see.'

'Whatever happens I'm sure it will be all right in the end,' James said with the sort of tone you might use to tell a child they won't be getting the bike they had always wanted.

'Well I think it's very sad especially after the protest group have worked so hard.' Ellie put her knife and fork down even though she hadn't finished her meal. Did she know how much the wild turbot, with additions he couldn't even pronounce, cost?

'I agree, Ellie,' Annabelle said firmly.

After that the atmosphere turned to lighter subjects and forced jollity. It was like finding out your dining companions had voted the other way over Brexit and then limping through the next half hour before it was a respectable time to go home. Roger decided to keep Annabelle sweet even if his wife was scowling at him. He had studied bloody hard for this vineyard job; he wasn't going to wreck his chances.

*

Ellie was trying to find the Christmas decorations in the loft. She hated going up there; it was some sort of phobia she had. She started feeling breathless. Where were they? Perhaps they wouldn't bother this year and make do with the odd wreath and a tree. But then what would they put on the tree?

Something gold caught her eye. That was probably the box. If only it wasn't over the far side of the attic.

'Roger,' she called out as loud as she could. She knew he was not far away, at his desk where he was glued these days. No answer. How dare he ignore her.

'Roger!' She was angry now. 'Roger! I need your help.'

He appeared at the bottom of the steps. 'What?' he shouted back, as if he was put out by this intrusion into his studying.

'The Christmas decs; they are right over there. Can you come up and get them for me?'

'Will it wait? I'm in the middle of something.'

'No! No, it won't bloody wait. Christmas is next bloody week!'

'All right. Keep your hair on.'

'Don't you dare! I've put up with enough from you lately. What with you, Mum, those sneery bastards at Starling Skies; I'm fed up with it all!'

'Steady on. You know how important this opportunity is to me. Give me a break.'

'It's not fair!' Her mouth was dry; she had lost her nerve. She had to get out of here. It took all her effort to manoeuvre her way down the steps; she was clinging to the handrails for dear life, her whole body shaking now. Slowly and deliberately she placed one foot on the rung below followed by the next. She was sweating; this was horrible. Halfway down she could feel Roger's large hands holding her hips. He held her firmly and she found the final rungs a little easier. With her feet securely on the floor she began to calm her breathing. Roger put his arms round her fully and held her close.

'I'm sorry,' he said and she burst into tears.

He had made them both coffee and they were sat in the garden room when he asked, 'What's all this about Starling Skies?'

Ellie took a sip from her mug. 'I went there; the other night.'

'You didn't tell me.'

'No, well it's been so busy and you've been so preoccupied.'

'I'm sorry,' he said again and she knew he meant it. 'So, tell me now.'

'Well, the thing is I saw Mum and I was worried about her; you know she really misses Larry.'

'Right.'

'Anyway, when I left The Beeches the other day, I drove straight to Starling Skies in the hope of being able to see Larry; just to talk to him for ten minutes. I was going to invite him here for Christmas Day. I thought it would please Mum.'

'That's a lovely thought. We should invite him.'

'Yes, but that Gestapo receptionist and then stuck-up Stephanie, who probably hasn't had sex for a very long time, well, she kept saying that seeing Larry, even for ten measly minutes was, "out of the question," in that stupid haughty voice she's got. It was ridiculous! They really are prisoners in that place!'

Roger was smiling now. He said gently, 'Poor you. You should have told me. I'm sorry, I've been a bit one-track recently.'

'I know this job means a lot to you,'

'Not as much as you do.' He looked thoughtful. 'Larry's got a son, hasn't he?'

'Yes, Graham, I think his name is.'

'Perhaps we could track him down.'

'How on earth?'

'Not sure. But I'll find a way.' Roger stood up. 'Now you stay there; I'm going to get those decs down.'

Chapter 26

Jeffrey was flustered but refused to process his customers any quicker. He had told Carol on more than one occasion that if he rushed, he was likely to make mistakes. He complained that the Royal Mail chap was late again for picking up the mail bags and they were crammed in around him behind the counter making it very difficult to carry out his duties.

Carol meanwhile had a nice steady flow of customers, just as she liked it. She had decided a few times that she should give this voluntary shift up, now that she was working at the farm shop. But even a hint of this to Linda and she faced a lecture on the importance of keeping this community shop going and how the village relied so heavily on volunteers and wouldn't it be tragic if the place had to close? By the time she was halfway through Carol was already waving her white flag. But since she had been seeing Bill, and what with Christmas coming very soon, she really could not spare the time.

Her mobile rang and, as she didn't have a customer at that very moment and it was her daughter, she answered.

'Hello Rebecca.'

'Mum, at last! Where are you?'

'I'm in the shop, darling. Why, what's so urgent?'

'I'm in the shop and you're not here!' Rebecca sounded like she might explode.

Carol looked around her. This place was far too small to miss someone, especially her own daughter. 'I can't see you, darling.'

'I'm by the tills. I spoke to someone called Emma and she said you're not in today.'

'Oh, you're in the farm shop. What are you doing there?'

'Looking for you, stupid.'

'There's no need for that. So, you've come all the way from London? How did you get from the station?'

'I got a taxi at great expense.'

'I see. Well I'm in the village shop, just down from where I live.'

'Oh, well thank goodness I'm not wasting my time completely. Will you come and get me?'

'Sorry, hang on a minute.' A customer was trying to buy one of Susan's cakes delivered that morning. 'I'm stuck here for now. You'll have to ring your dad.'

Rebecca was ranting away but Carol ended the call.

'Sorry about that,' she said.

'That's okay,' Margaret was grinning at her. 'I hear you're a busy woman these days.'

Carol pressed the wrong button on the till. 'Damn! Sorry, erm, wait a minute.' She was trying to think. She was having a hot flush. Was it the void button to clear a transaction? Margaret lent over the counter.

'You need to press the cancel button and then it's that one there for cakes.'

'Oh yes. There. Two pounds fifty.'

She looked up. Margaret was smiling at her. 'Are you going to the jazz evening tomorrow?' she asked.

'Oh, yes, I think so.' Carol had lain awake last night worrying about it. She was having second thoughts.

'You think so? But it's sold out. Do you have tickets?'

'Yes, I have tickets.'

'Oh.' Margaret looked confused.

Carol smiled benignly even though she wanted to scream.

'Bye then,' Margaret said somewhat deflated and left.

What on earth did Rebecca want? And why couldn't she just phone like a normal daughter?

Back at Hill View, Rebecca was huddled in the doorway. There was no sign of Bryan.

'Hello darling, this is unexpected.' She didn't look like she might accept a hug.

'Well everything is a bit unexpected at the moment, isn't it?'

Carol took a deep breath and carefully put her key in the door, unlocking it and letting them in.

'Cup of tea?' she asked.

'Something stronger might be more appropriate.'

'Well it's tea on offer.' Carol was firm. She didn't wait for an answer and put the kettle on.

Rebecca sat down at the kitchen table. The tea made, Carol sat down next to her daughter, her movements gentle. 'So?' she asked.

Rebecca was obviously making some attempt to calm herself. She took a deep breath. 'Mum, I'm hearing things that are really worrying me. The situation is, Steve and I, well it's looking serious and I think he might be the one for me.'

'It's still early days, isn't it?' Carol dared to point out.

'Nearly six months actually.'

'Right.'

'But when you know you just know. And the thing is I really want to bring him home for Christmas but he's saying that if you and Dad aren't together it would be better if he didn't come.' The tragic consequences of this scenario were written across her face.

'What will he do if he doesn't come here?' Carol wondered if perhaps Steve would be on his own.

'He's threatening to go to his family. He says I could go with him but they live all the way up in York and I'm too worried about you and Dad to...' She started crying.

Carol tried to comfort her but she threw her off.

'I'm sorry to hear that,' Carol said. 'You're both very welcome here but I won't be inviting your dad. Perhaps it would be better if you went to York this year?'

'I don't know; I've not met any of his family yet and they seem, well, different. There are loads of them too; apparently, we might have to sleep in a caravan. Can you imagine?'

337

Carol had to stifle a smile. 'That might be fun,' she said lightly.

'Not my idea of fun! Not in the freezing cold without a proper toilet in the middle of the night.'

'No, I take your point.'

'Megs says that there's something else you need to tell me. She wouldn't say what it was and I've been so worried.'

'Did she now.' Carol looked around the room wondering how she was going to get out of this corner. 'Are you planning to stay tonight?' she asked.

'To be honest I haven't really planned any of this. I did chuck a few things in a bag just in case. But I really need to get back to London.'

'I see.' She didn't see at all.

'Mum, what is it? What do I need to know?'

It was no good. 'I'm seeing someone. A chap called Bill. He's the manager at the farm shop.'

'What, so you're dating?'

'Yes, that's right. Megs actually met him when she came up for the weekend.'

'She met him!'

'Yes.'

'And what did she think of this Bill?'

'She liked him, I think.'

'But surely this isn't serious? I mean it must be ruining your chances of getting Dad back. I really feel very strongly, Mum, that you and Dad should be together. I couldn't bear it if it was all over for good. And what are Steve and his family going to think?'

Carol's phone rang and she saw it was Bill. She answered, walking away from the kitchen and into the lounge.

'Are you okay?' he asked sounding concerned. 'I hear your daughter was here looking for you.'

'Yes, I'm all right. Rebecca is here now; she's tricky at the best of times.'

'Oh dear. Have you told her?'

'Yes, just now.'

'And?'

'Not the best of responses.'

'Do you want me to come over?'

'That would be like putting a match to a bonfire.'

'Oh Carol, I'm so sorry. I wish I could do something.'

'Don't worry. I can handle my own daughter.'

'Look it's probably not the best moment to suggest this but actually my girls really want to meet you and I suggested Sunday, here at my place.'

'That's nice. Why can't my family be as civilised about all this as yours are?'

'It's still raw for yours I suppose. But I do hope they don't put you off. Carol, you mean the world to me.'

She had a tear in her eye. 'I feel the same way,' she said.

'So, Sunday?'

'Yes, that should be okay. I'd better go now. Face the music.'

'Call me later, will you. I'm thinking of you.'

Carol felt a rush of love for this wonderful man. He was so considerate.

Back in the kitchen Rebecca was standing now. 'That was him, wasn't it?'

'Yes, it was.'

She was putting her coat on and picked up her bag. 'I'm going back to London,' she said playing the victim, tears across her face.

Carol's first thought was that she should persuade her to stay but she knew there was no chance of them reconciling the situation at this moment in time.

'Do you want a lift to the station?'

'No. No thanks, I'll get Dad to take me.'

'Okay.'

She was outside the back door when she turned to say, 'You don't care about me! You are so selfish! All you care about is you and this Bill. I suppose he'll be coming for bloody Christmas!'

'Becca, darling, I do care about you. I'm really pleased you've found the right man for you.'

'I am not spending Christmas in a sodding caravan!' she yelled and Jeffrey, who was walking down the street across from them, glanced over, a look of horror on his face as he quickened his pace.

Rebecca kept walking, heading in the direction of the village pub. Carol closed the back door on the cold and went to find a cardigan. It occurred to her that Rebecca would tell her father about Bill; her guilty secret would be out. But instead of feeling anxious, she felt a warm sense of relief. It was as if this was the first day of a new life that she now knew she absolutely wanted.

Bryan was stood behind the bar at The Dog and Duck. He had decided some time ago that it was one up from sitting in his room. Although there were times when he was just too tired to do anything and he might want to watch a bit of television; then his room sufficed. At least when he was playing at being bartender, he felt useful and Gavin was always grateful for the help. The fact that they weren't busy at lunchtimes made it quite tedious but the lone drinkers you tended to get, like Paddy, were always up for some banter.

He was surprised to see Rebecca again so soon. She looked like she'd been crying.

'Hey Becs, you okay?'

'I am but I really need to talk to you.'

'Oh, I see. Well I'm stuck here until Gavin gets back.'

'But Dad, there's virtually no one in here. Surely you can take ten minutes out?'

Bryan looked at Paddy who nodded. 'Don't worry, mate, I'll keep an eye.'

He really didn't want Rebecca to see his room but it was the only place that was private.

'God, Dad, this is tiny. How on earth do you live in here? Has Mum seen it?'

He offered her the only chair and sat on the bed. 'I manage. Have you seen your mum?'

'Yes, I have. Do you know, I can't believe how selfish she has become? She doesn't care about us, Dad. Not a jot.'

Bryan was thoughtful. 'There's something she's not telling me. That's what I sense.'

'Too right there is. She's got a new man; this Bill chap from the farm shop.'

A wave of realisation hit him. Had he known all along, but not dared to admit it to himself?

'Oh no! I should have guessed.' He covered his eyes; he didn't want to cry in front of his daughter. 'It's not serious though, is it?'

'Megan seems to think it is. I mean she's actually seen them together which I've only just found out. Mum has completely ruled out a family Christmas.'

Bryan was struggling to take all this in. He felt paralysed in fear; fear of what his future would hold.

'Dad... Dad are you all right?'

'No, not really.' He stared into oblivion. 'I had my suspicions when I saw them together at the protest meeting.'

'But that was ages ago, Dad. How long has this been going on?'

His face crumpled. 'I don't know,' he said feebly and blinked a tear away. He stood up and turned to look out of the window.

'Dad, you absolutely mustn't give up. Surely it won't last with Bill; apparently he's quite a bit younger than Mum.'

Bryan couldn't help smiling at the irony of it all. 'I've tried, Becca, darling, believe me, it's no good. I'm never going to get her back.'

'Oh Dad, I'm so sorry.' There was just a short pause before her fighting spirit reared again. 'Right, well if that's the case, you need to get the house back. You can't possibly stay here.'

Chapter 27

Carol wriggled into her new dress making sure she didn't brush her face with the fabric; she had carefully applied her make-up. Was it too dressy for a village hall event? Ellie had said she was wearing a dress. Red seemed a little daring but the shop assistant had talked her into it. It was amazing that it actually looked good on, despite the fact that it seemed to cling to her; something about ruching the woman had said. Looking in the mirror she only saw a startled Bryan staring back. Should she wear something else? Too late, that was the doorbell; Bill must be early. She rushed downstairs, running her fingers through her hair and straightening her fringe.

There he was and it was like he couldn't help himself; he smiled at her with longing in his eyes and took her in his arms. His embrace was firm and passionate and she knew that tonight would be the night.

Extracting herself she said, 'Fancy a quick drink?' She took the chilled bottle of Prosecco out of the fridge.

'Ooh, we celebrating?' Bill asked. He looked serenely happy as if nothing could rock his boat.

'Just thought it would be nice,' she said pouring two glasses. 'Anyway, Dutch courage and all that.'

'You're still worried about Bryan being there?'

'I keep telling myself to hell with him.'

'It's me that should be worried. What's his left hook like?'

'Dear God, I hope it doesn't come to that.'

He took her in his arms and kissed her again. 'Do you think I might not be driving home later?' he asked with a cheeky smile.

They must have been the last to arrive; the hall was packed and loud with chatter and anticipation. They found the round table where Ellie and Roger were sat, at the far end.

'Come and sit here; we've saved you some seats.'

There were canapes and nuts to nibble in the centre of the table. Roger was looking at Bill curiously. In fact, as Carol scanned the hall, which was brightly lit, she noticed several eyes trained on her date.

'Anyone want a drink?' Bill asked standing up. Ellie looked uncertain. Carol glanced over to the far side of the room where the bar was; she could just make out Bryan serving with Zoe from the pub.

Roger stood up. 'You're all right, mate; I'll get them in.'

'No, no, I insist. You've obviously got the first round in.'

Carol was standing now. 'Tell you what, I'll go. Women's lib and all that.'

Bill handed her a twenty-pound note. 'If you're sure.'

Carol resigned herself to an awkward encounter and decided in some ways it was better to get it over and done with. There were quite a few waiting at the bar hoping for attention and holding notes up in readiness. She kept her eyes down until she reached the front.

'Bottle of white, please?' she asked Bryan as Zoe was busy with another customer.

'Ah, yes, the final humiliation; serving my wife when she's out on a date with her new man.'

Zoe glanced over. Her face was willing Bryan to behave.

Carol waited as her husband just stood and stared. 'Just look at you. You never made that kind of effort for me, did you?'

'That's enough,' Zoe admonished him. The air was thick with hurt and embarrassment. What were people thinking?

'I just want a bottle of white wine, please?' Suddenly the red dress seemed like the worst idea imaginable.

Zoe produced a bottle. 'Two glasses enough for you?'

'Yes, thanks.'

'It's hard to believe that this woman is my wife!' It was like he was addressing an audience. Was he drunk?

'Bryan, enough,' Zoe said sternly.

'You certainly didn't hang about, did you? First bloke to come along and you're in there.'

Carol fought to hide her outrage. Thirty-five years of marriage and he dared to talk to her like this, and in public. His behaviour tainted every memory she had of their life together. She walked away clutching the bottle and glasses, close to tears. All eyes were on her now.

Bill had an anxious stare as she sat down. 'Are you okay?' he asked.

She muttered under her breath, 'Bryan has just said some dreadful things. I can't quite believe it.'

Roger and Bill both stood up. 'I'll sort him out,' Roger said.

'No, you won't. Sit down, both of you.' Carol didn't want to be even more of a public spectacle.

'Here, Roger, let's swap seats.' Ellie was now next to her friend. 'What on earth has happened?'

'It's Bryan. I think he must be drunk.'

Ellie looked horrified. 'Someone needs to say something to him.'

Just then, the lights were dimmed and the compère for the evening appeared on the stage to introduce the band. The audience was hushed. Carol took a deep breath to calm herself and didn't hear a word that was said. She just wanted to cry. How dare he make out she was the guilty party? She would never forgive him for embarrassing her in this way.

After a while she sighed and smiled at Bill. He was wonderful; she was very lucky. The band was playing familiar tunes, covers of Fats Waller, Duke Ellington and Gershwin, so it said on the programme that she found on the table. They looked like they modelled themselves on Chas and Dave, wearing trilbies and all with ill-fitting dark suits, off-white shirts and loosened ties creating a casual, friendly look.

There was huge applause before the interval. Ellie was peering over to the bar area to see if Bryan was there. She couldn't see him.

'Are you all right?' She squeezed her friend's hand.

'Yes, I'm okay.'

'Do you want to go home?' Bill asked. It was a tempting thought.

'Hang on a minute,' Ellie said and went off to the bar. It wasn't long before she had made it back.

'Bryan's gone.'

'Are you sure?' Bill asked.

'Yes, he's definitely gone. I spoke to Zoe. She actually sent him home. Gavin's turned up to help out.'

'Less than he deserves,' Carol said.

'Darling, don't let him ruin your evening,' Ellie pleaded.

'I think he already has.' Her time spent with Bill was normally such a joy, so relaxed. But then, they had been totally secretive up until now. Were the locals shocked? Was this a big mistake?

By the time she was walking back home, with Bill beside her, she told herself, to hell with them all and she felt better. There was a full moon and a starry sky. She had quite enjoyed the second half, reasoning that in many ways Bryan was making it easy for her to leave her old life behind. She shivered in the cold night air, but didn't care that she only had a wool shawl to keep her warm. Bill held her close.

As they approached Hill View, she could hear music.

'Someone's having a party,' Bill commented.

'It's a bit late for that kind of noise, surely? Even if it is Saturday night.'

As they got closer it dawned on them that the noise was coming from Carol's own home. They looked at each other in horror. The music was so loud it was almost shaking the building. It was familiar. Verdi's *Requiem*. Angry, shocking, instilling fear; everything that Bryan had been to her this evening.

'Oh my God. Bryan still has a key.'

'Should we call the police?'

'And say what? My husband is in his own home playing loud music?'

'Perhaps I should go in first?' Bill asked although he looked distinctly nervous.

'I can't believe this is happening. He's invaded my home!'

'He can't do that. What kind of man is he?'

'He's angry. He blames me for our break-up. I don't know him any more.' Carol braced herself. 'I think we should go in together.' Bill caught her hand just as she was about to put her key in the back door.

'Why don't you come over to my place? I don't think it's safe here.'

She couldn't think straight. She just wanted to be in her own home. 'Let's just see what he has to say for himself.' She went in, Bill right behind her. The first thing they were confronted with was her daughter casually taking a bottle of wine from the fridge, as if she was in residence.

'Rebecca? What on earth?' She had to shout to be heard above the noise. At least her daughter had the decency to look embarrassed.

'Mum?' she froze, bottle in hand.

'What the hell is going on? Will you turn that racket down?' Her head was beginning to ache.

Bryan appeared. 'Come home to your cosy love nest, have you? Shame. Looks like you've got squatters.' He flashed her a sarcastic smile.

Carol walked purposefully past Bryan and into the living room to turn off the speaker. Bryan followed her.

'I was listening to that. You never did like my music, did you?' The bottle of Prosecco that she and Bill had enjoyed earlier had been finished off and another bottle of wine beside it. Bryan was obviously on some sort of belligerent mission to hurt and destroy.

'As if it is not enough to insult me in public, you then invade my home. Let me remind you, how this started, Bryan. You left me!' She was shrieking at him, shaking with anger. Her head was throbbing now; this was a nightmare.

'Well, you've more than made up for that little misdemeanour, haven't you? Anyway, this is my home too and I'm fed up living in that pokey room above the pub.'

'So, you thought you'd break in uninvited and at night! What am I supposed to do?'

'Your problem, darling, you can stay or you can go.'

What a monster he'd turned into.

She went up to the bathroom to find some pain killers and swallowed them down with water. Then she froze for a moment and tried to think clearly. What should she do? Her mobile rang; it was Bill.

'I'm outside. I'm going to call a cab. I think you should come with me.'

'Yes... Yes, I think you're right. I can't deal with this now. I'm sorry, Bill.'

'Don't be silly. Grab some things and come out. I will worry until you do.'

'Right.'

She found a holdall and started throwing stuff in there. Anything she might need. How long would it be? Just one night. She couldn't move in with Bill; that wouldn't be right. She grabbed toiletries, clothes, her glasses, her mobile charger. What else did she need? Bryan appeared at the door.

'Pack plenty.' He sneered. 'I'm not planning to go anywhere.'

She looked at him and it saddened her deeply that their marriage was ending in this way. There was no point in saying anything. Her bag packed, she walked back through the kitchen where her daughter stood sheepishly.

'I'm surprised at you Rebecca, stooping to your father's low levels.'

'I'm sorry Mum, but Dad has a right to live here too,' she protested.

'No, he doesn't! Not after what he did to me!' Her anger clearly shocked Rebecca.

She put on a coat and slammed the door behind her.

Bill put his arms around her. 'You're shaking.' He held her tighter and she started to cry, unable to hold it together any longer. 'The cab will be here soon.'

Chapter 28

Ellie took a wrong turn and swore under her breath. She had done this journey to The Beeches a few times now. Of course, it was much further than Starling Skies but she didn't mind that. The voice of the satnav stayed calm and determined and told her to take an unlikely right turn. She put her faith in it and, after a couple of miles on a narrow country lane and one close encounter with a tractor, she emerged on to what was possibly a familiar road which at least had two lanes. Back on track she sighed with relief.

She pulled into the driveway of The Beeches and, with the relief of having finally made it, felt moved to pause and take a moment before getting out of the car. Over the last few days she had been trying to defeat a to-do list, which only seemed to get longer. The Christmas presents were not all bought yet, let alone wrapped; the house just seemed to get more and more untidy, it just looked overly cluttered rather than festive with decorations everywhere. She had commented to Roger only last night what a mess the place was and he'd just looked slightly puzzled and said, 'Looks fine to me; you worry too much.'

On top of all that she couldn't believe how many people were still viewing houses and one of her client's was actually trying to exchange contracts before Christmas Day. Did they want to spend the holiday packing? Mrs Bradshaw phoned her at least once a day. She knew more about this woman's life and all the machinations of her family than she did her own life.

If only they had managed to track down Larry's son. But it was hopeless. They didn't even have a surname for him; they just knew he was called Graham and worked in insurance. Why were they even bothering?

She felt frazzled but gathered herself and walked into reception. 'You all right, Ellie?' The receptionist smiled at her.

'I've been better,' she said truthfully and a sympathetic face gazed gently back at her.

'Ooh, Pauline would like to see you,' she said as if just remembering something.

'Not bad news, I hope.'

'I'm sure it won't be. Wait there; I'll just tell her you're here.' She went off and came back with the woman herself.

'Ellie, so lovely to see you. Would you like a coffee?'

With the coffee made, they were sat at a table in the corner of the dining area.

'Now, let me get straight to the point,' Pauline said.

'I hope my mother has not been difficult.'

'No! Don't be silly. Kathleen is a joy; she would be one of my favourite residents if I was allowed to have them.' She laughed nervously as if this was a reckless thing to say. But then composed herself.

'Larry Taylor,' she said quite deliberately, 'we now have a room for him here.'

Ellie's jaw dropped. 'Really?'

'We do. His son, Graham, has been informed and is happy for the transfer to go ahead.'

'Oh, Pauline,' tears burst from Ellie's eyes, 'that is such brilliant news.' She pulled a tissue out of her handbag and dabbed her face.

Pauline reached across the table and squeezed her hand. 'I'm so pleased for you and your mother,' she said and Ellie wanted to hug her.

'When is it likely to happen?' she blurted out so desperate to know the answer.

'Graham is seeing what he can do but I think it will be just after Christmas.'

'I so wanted to invite Larry to ours on Christmas Day so he could be with Mum.' She sighed. Perhaps this wouldn't be possible.

'I'm happy to pass Graham's contact details to you. He actually gave me permission the last time we spoke.'

'Wonderful. This is the best Christmas present anyone could want.'

'Buy goose, Dad, not turkey. Turkey's always dry.' Rebecca was proving to be quite demanding now that she had decided that she and Steve would be coming to spend Christmas at Hill View with him. Bryan had protested against the ludicrous idea of him actually producing a meal on the big day, saying, 'Becky, darling, you'll have to do the cooking.'

'Of course, I'll help out.' She'd sounded a little indignant.

They still didn't know if Megan was going to join them. All she had said was how difficult it was having to choose. That was swiftly followed by her implying that she really didn't want to spend the day with near strangers just so that she could see her mother.

'Can't Mum pop over for an hour or two?' she'd asked.

Bryan hadn't even answered that. What was the point?

Now, in Waitrose, he seemed to have a ridiculously long list which Rebecca had emailed over last night. There were things on here that he wasn't sure about at all. What did she mean by spices for mulled wine? And stuffing? Didn't Carol make that? Where would he find it? The store was packed with frantic shoppers all grabbing things here and everywhere and ending up with trollies spilling over with items for the big over-eating festival. He began to think he should book the pub for Christmas lunch and have done with it, but actually he had a strong feeling that they were already fully booked. He decided to start with the goose and fought his way to the butcher's counter where there was a long queue. Eventually he got to the front.

'I'd like a goose, please.'

'When did you order?' the chap asked.

'I haven't. Is that necessary? Can I not just buy one now?'

'Sorry, sir, we only have enough to fulfil the orders.'

'Well can I order one then, please?'

'Not possible. The closing date for orders was two weeks ago.'

'Really?' Bryan knew this was an omen; Christmas was going to be a disaster.

'We have a few turkeys left.'

'I'll take one,' he said. He couldn't go home empty handed.

'They are over on aisle twelve.' The butcher pointed.

'Thank you,' Bryan called out as he hot footed it over there.

He was trying to find a member of staff so that he could ask where he might find stuffing, when he saw Tiffany out of the corner of his eye. At first, he dared to think that maybe she was alone and they might have a reasonable exchange but then some body builder type with a triangular torso in a tight-fitting leather jacket approached the same trolley. They were laughing together, clearly in the first flush of romance.

Bryan quickly headed in the opposite direction and made for the tills. A scan of his list told him he didn't have everything but he was past caring; this was not a pleasurable experience. He was quite relieved when he had all the shopping loaded in the car and he was sat in the driver's seat. He took a moment to reflect on what a mess he'd made of his life. This season of joy and goodwill to all men just left him feeling depressed and lonely. His mobile rang and he saw it was Megan. Would this be more bad news?

'Hello Megs, darling. How are you?'

'Dad, you okay?'

'Yes, yes, I'm in Waitrose car park; just done the shopping. Well, tried to.'

'Is it all right if I come to you for Christmas?'

'Of course it is, darling.' The tears swelled from his eyes now.

'Dad, what's happening? You sound upset.'

'No, no, well, yes, I'm a bit emotional. It's this stupid time of year but I'll be fine. When will you be coming?'

'Christmas Eve. We finish work at lunchtime so I'll be there late afternoon.'

'That's wonderful.'

'Yeah, Mum's going to be mainly at Bill's so...'

'Mainly? Isn't she living with him now?'

'No, apparently she's got some flat of his.'

'Really? Where's that then?'

'I don't know Dad, but it's local so I'll hopefully be able to see her at some point while I'm there.'

'Right.'

'Becks says she told you to get goose.' She laughed.

'Yes, well, I tried but they don't have any so I've got turkey instead.'

'Oh good. I prefer turkey.'

'Yes, well your sister will just have to compromise for once. Anyway, now I know you're coming, it will be two against one.'

Megan giggled. 'What about Steve? He won't dare side against her.'

Bryan laughed now too and felt a little bit better about life.

Ben stood back from his painting, brush still in hand. Was it finished?

'You've captured her now.' It was the woman from the studio next door. She was not much younger than his mum, wore long skirts all the time and had scruffy, curly hair.

'Thanks, he said not really wanting her opinion. She was hovering on the threshold.

'May I?' she asked and came into his studio, approaching the painting. She tilted her head this way and that and screwed up her eyes. 'Yes, you've definitely got her. I love the fact that you've elongated her limbs to fill the length of the canvas. And everything else in the club is a blur.'

He was pleased that she had used the word club. 'Thanks,' he tried again, hoping she'd leave now.

'Your work's up at Glover's place, isn't it?'

'Yes, that's right.'

'Is he expecting this?'

'He's expecting something. This has taken a few weeks.'

'Takes a bit of time to settle in here,' she said and it occurred to him that she was right. It hadn't helped that Bella had put so much pressure on him to sell more paintings to cover the rent. Was he ready to let this go now?

'So, you taking it up to the gallery this afternoon?'

'Oh, I'm not sure about that.' He looked at his watch. It was only four o'clock.

'I've got a car outside if you want a hand?'

That was interesting. Cabs were pricey even over short distances. 'Are you sure?'

'Of course. Happy to help.' Turned out she was not a bad person to have on side.

Roger was grappling with his last assignment when he could see that Annabelle was calling his mobile.

'Hi Annabelle,' he said affecting a confident air.

'Roger, how are you? About this job.' She wasn't a woman to mince her words.

'Yes?'

'The thing is that Joe's keen to move down to the winery asap after Christmas.'

Surely this wasn't bad news? Maybe she'd found someone else fully qualified with experience and ready to go.

'Yes, well I'm very close to finishing this viticulture course.' It didn't feel like it at this moment, what with Ellie on his back about helping out with Christmas.

'Good, good. So you'll be fully qualified by first Jan?'

He daren't say no. 'Yes,' he blurted out uncertainly.

'You sure? I mean if you need longer...' You'll be out of the game, mate.

'No, I'm sure. I mean, yes, I'm sure I'll be ready by the first.'

'Great, so let's get your interview date in the diary. How about the second?'

It was going to be an interesting Christmas.

Ben got to the Little Bat just before happy hour ended.

'Benny boy!' Bella shouted out.

'Quick, I'm getting a round in while it's still half price,' Anna jumped down from her bar stool. 'What do you want?'

Ben couldn't think.

'We're on the Flamingos,' Bella said. 'Awesome.'

'Okay, Flamingo it is.' He took a perch and looked around. It was all warm wood and purple banquettes this place, sort of old fashioned but somehow with a trendy vibe. It was certainly popular.

'So, you took your painting, huh?'

'Yes, I did. He loves it, actually. Says it's my best one yet.'

Bella threw her arms round him. 'You are a genius!'

'Maybe.' Ben smiled.

'So, how much does he reckon?'

'He's going to let me know. He's thinking about framing options.'

'Well, it better cover the damn rent on that studio of yours.'

'Yeah, and leave a bit over for cocktail nights, hey.'

Her back stiffened. 'Don't be like that. We're living in Islington; we have to make the most of it.'

'Yeah, of course, but...'

'But nothing...' She smothered his head with kisses and he felt nothing but embarrassed.

Back at the flat Bella started cooking pasta. Anna sat on the sofa. They had made a sort of table out of a box covering it in some random piece of colourful fabric, probably a shawl. Ben made himself comfy on the bed by rearranging the pillows.

'Bella tells me you're going back to Suffolk for Christmas?'

'Yeah, that's the plan. I go every year actually. It's a kind of family thing. We all make the effort.'

'That's nice. My family aren't like that at all. We can't go five minutes without a row.' She laughed at this. 'So, what you doing, Bella?'

Ben was actually quite pleased that she'd asked her because he wasn't sure himself.

'Hang on a minute!' She drained the pasta and poured it into the tuna sauce she'd knocked up. She was serving up into three bowls when she said, 'Well, Anna, you know that I want to stay in London but...' Her voice trailed off.

'Yeah, well, Jason says you two are very welcome to come to us. You can stay over and we can party all night.'

'Woo hoo,' Bella cried out. 'Right, now, come and get your bowl. Oh no, my glass is empty; where's the wine?'

The food tasted good. This girl could certainly cook.

'So, Ben, the thing is,' Bella put on her slightly whiny voice and he knew what was coming. 'Wouldn't it be totally awesome if we both went to Anna and Jase's for Christmas?'

'Well, yeah, of course, but I'm committed to going to Suffolk.'

'Soooo boring that place, don't you think?'

'I dunno; it's where I was brought up so I'm sort of used to it. Anyway, I'll see Matt so that will be cool.'

Anna smiled at him. 'Look babes,' she said to Bella, 'you should go and do this Suffolk thing. It's only a few days. We'll party on New Year's Eve. Wha' do yah say?'

Bella had her sulky face on. 'Don't know.'

Chapter 29

'Why are we having coffee out here?'

'The sun is shining, it's a beautiful day and if you wrap up warm...' He held up a blanket and handed it to her. 'For you, my love.'

Against her better judgement, Ellie wrapped the blanket round her shoulders and sat on the terrace looking over the garden. It was a pretty scene even in winter with the hellebores hanging their muted ivory and purple heads and the expanse of snowdrops drifting down to the river.

'Anyway, we should make the most of this time while the boys are out.' Roger made a good point. It had been frantic for days. She reclined back in her chair and closed her eyes for a dreamy moment.

'Remind me, where have the boys gone?' she asked.

'They've gone to boring Capel Green in deadly dull Suffolk.' He was making a vague attempt to mimic Bella.

'At least we got through Christmas Day relatively unscathed... and Mum and Larry seemed to enjoy themselves.' She could picture their sweet faces now. Who says you're too old to fall in love in your eighties?

'Yeah, it was good to see them reunited. I think it really perked your mum up. Especially when he went back to The Beeches with her and with a twinkle in his eye.'

'Can you imagine Stephanie's face when she found out? She must have been beside herself.' Sweet revenge! Ellie sat upright. 'I'm surprised that you're not straight back to your desk.'

'Ah, well, good news on that front. I had an email this morning; I have passed my final assessment - with flying colours, of course!'

'You heard today? Boxing Day?

'Not everyone celebrates Christmas. Anyway, it was probably one of those automated thingies.'

'What, so your assessment was marked by a robot?'

'Very funny.'

'Is that it, then? You have your qualification?'

'Yes! And a good job too as I've got my interview in a few days.'

'Really? When was that decided?'

'Oh, when Annabelle rang me, I think.' He always sounded vague when he had something to hide.

Ellie decided to let it go. 'I must admit, it is good news. Even if it was painful getting here.'

They both sipped their coffee.

Ellie had a thought that made her smile. 'Did you see Ben's face when Bella turned up?'

'Even if it was nearly midnight on Christmas Eve; trust her to get the last train.'

'She was working until six at Camden Lock.' Ellie wondered why she was defending the girl.

'Yeah, I know.' Roger obviously wasn't impressed.

'She'll break his heart one day.' Ellie always felt she needed to brace herself for this inevitable eventuality.

'Maybe.' Roger would be very *c'est la vie* when it actually happened.

'Funny that Matt turned up without what's her name and didn't even mention her.' She racked her brain. 'What was her name?'

'I can't remember either; my heads full of viticulture. Let's call her Vegan 3.'

Ellie laughed. 'Was she vegan?'

'Who cares? She's a has-been in Matt's world.'

Carol had slept well and, realising where she was, she awoke with a smile on her face. She wrapped herself in her velour dressing gown and went into the living area which had a small kitchen at one end of the room. When she had first seen this apartment above the farm shop she had been wowed by the height of the vaulted ceiling. The wooden beams were exposed and it was painted in a warm cream. The picture window overlooked the car park, but beyond that there was a pretty row of poplars and green fields with alpacas grazing.

'Do you really only use this for the occasional night?' she had asked Bill.

'Yes, it forms part of the farm's estate so I don't actually own it.'

'Are you sure it's okay for me to stay here?'

'Yes, of course. I've cleared it with Lady R.'

That explained the décor and the feel of the place. It was chic with stylish furniture; open shelving in the kitchen displayed some exquisite ceramic pieces as well as French style plates and bowls. It was so different to Bill's own home, which definitely lacked a woman's touch and was more of a refuge for a man who had been stricken by grief and thrown himself into his work.

'You don't have to move in here,' he had said. 'You know you're very welcome to stay with me.'

'I know but it is too soon. I need my own space.' She tried to be gentle with this assertion but he still had a look of longing about him. Carol knew that she was falling in love, but she didn't want to free-fall; she wanted to float gently knowing she was doing the right thing every drift of the way.

'Well I might have to join you every now and then,' he said with a mischievous smile and they had embraced and kissed and every time it was magical.

The night of Bryan's angry Verdi moment she had been so upset when they finally lay together, her head on his chest, he simply held her gently in his arms.

'I understand if you just want to sleep.'

She turned her head up to his and they kissed and she knew then, that this was the moment.

Now, she was enjoying her first coffee of the day, sat looking out of the window and she smiled to herself and felt very fortunate. The idea of spending Christmas Day with Bill and his two girls had felt odd, but Naomi and Elise had been a joy. They were truly lovely and so tactile from the off, wanting to hug her, accepting of her, almost as if they had longed for a mother figure. The day was so relaxing and full of laughs. There was no pretence, just genuine joy. It didn't matter that the turkey was a bit overcooked; it didn't matter that it started to rain on the way back from their walk, and everyone at Bill's local pub was so welcoming of her without question.

Megan had called. It had been good to talk to her. Carol had conveyed with honesty how happy her day was; it was a shame that her daughter seemed to be struggling with the situation.

'Becky is so annoying when she's with Steve. She seems to think she can control everything. And she went mad when she found out we weren't having goose!'

Carol blurted out a giggle. 'Oh dear,' she tried to sound sympathetic. As they ended the call, she asked Megan if she would get Rebecca to phone her. She had tried earlier and got her voicemail. Later in the day she wished she hadn't bothered. Rebecca was clearly still mad with her. Finally, at around nine in the evening she called.

'Happy Christmas, Mum.' Her tone was flat and forced.

'Have you had a good day?' Carol asked trying to be upbeat.

'It's been special to be here at Hill View and with Steve. Dad has done his best and the meal wasn't too bad.

Obviously, we've missed you. It feels weird that you're spending Christmas Day with a man I've barely met.'

Carol felt too tired to respond. She realised that her daughter would forever blame her for the break-up of her marriage. 'Well, I've had a lovely day.' She left it at that.

'Where are you living now? At Bill's place, are you?' Rebecca demanded.

'I'm here for Christmas Day, but I'm actually living in an apartment.'

'Where's that then?' she sounded affronted.

'I'm happy to tell you but I'd rather you didn't tell your father where it is.'

'Why the hell not?'

'The last time I saw him he was drunk, angry and out of order. I can't just overlook that kind of behaviour.'

'Well, yes, he'd had a few drinks, but Mum, you couldn't expect him to live over the pub forever.'

'I didn't expect that. But I was shocked by what he did that night.'

'What you don't realise, Mum, is that Dad is really distraught about the whole thing. He really misses you.'

'It is, what it is.' She wasn't going to argue.

'So, are you going to tell me where you are?'

She had already told Megan so it was only a matter of time before they all knew.

'How about you come on the walk with Roger and Ellie's family tomorrow?' Carol suggested as a diversion.

'I'll think about it,' Rebecca said coldly.

Now, as Carol gazed out of the window holding an empty mug, she considered that here, in this little sanctuary of her own, she could be totally selfish and lazy when the mood took her. She would have a shower and get ready to go out.

Later that morning there was a knock at her door. It would be Megan; how nice. She opened up with a smile on her face only to see Bryan standing there alone. Her impulse was to slam the door shut on him. He looked different, vulnerable and forlorn and held up a surrendering palm to her.

'Please, Carol, I promise I come in peace.'

She stood back. 'I'm going out shortly so you'll have to be quick.'

They sat opposite each other, either side of the picture window. She didn't offer him a drink.

'This is a nice place you've got.' He was looking round but sounded deflated.

'I like it.'

There was a long pause, his eyes downward. She feared he might suggest a reconciliation. Then he looked straight into her eyes.

'Carol, I want to apologise for my behaviour of late. I have been out of order and you didn't deserve any of it.'

She managed a half smile. It was good to hear him say that.

'I know I've made mistakes,' he continued, 'and I need to make amends. I accept that you have a new relationship with Bill and I'm pleased for you, genuinely I am.'

This was surprising. 'Thank you.'

'I just want us to be able to get on together, for the sake of the girls.'

'That seems reasonable.'

'Good. I know it won't be as before but...' He trailed off his expression pained. 'I know this possibly sounds ridiculous but I'd like us to be friends. Friendly, at least, in each other's company.'

'Well, it would make life easier.' He had a cheek really, after what he'd done but he did seem sincere.

'Yes, and I know it's what Rebecca and Megan want.' He relaxed a little in his chair now.

Carol wondered if this declaration was Rebecca's idea.

'Are you okay living here, for now?' he asked, glancing around the place. 'I mean, I was going to suggest that we put Hill View on the market if that's what you want?'

'I'm fine here for now but I suppose we'll have to think about all of that sometime soon.'

'So, is it okay for me to stay there for the time being?'

'Yes, Bryan, it is.'

'Thank you.'

There was another awkward pause. Carol looked at him. He had aged in the short time they had been apart and was a shadow of his former self. She found herself concerned for his welfare.

'What are your plans?' she asked gently hoping for a spark of something positive.

'No plans.' He looked brighter perhaps simply because she'd asked the question. 'I've thought vaguely about going abroad.' He was staring out of the window now. 'France, probably; starting again; somewhere I can put all this behind me.'

'Another country. That seems drastic. You still have the girls, you know. And your friends.'

He raised his eyebrows in surprise.

'Have you seen Roger and Ellie recently?' she asked.

His brow knitted together now and he sighed. 'I'm the bad guy; why would they want to see me?'

'I'm sure they do. Ellie mentioned the other day that they were quite concerned about you. Why don't you pop round there?'

'Yes, I might do that.' He stood up. 'Nothing to lose.' As he made his way over to the door he added, 'Megan's in the car so I'll send her up.' He didn't look back, just kept going leaving Carol at the door.

It took a lot of persuading to get the boys out but, surprisingly, Bella was keen.

'Well if we don't do the walk, what are we going to do?' she'd asked as if she was at her wits' end. Ben didn't seem to react to anything she said. It was obviously all too familiar to him.

They were congregated on The Street outside the pub. Carol appeared with Megan. They were full of cheerful conversation.

'I've invited Bryan; he should be along shortly.' Roger came clean to Carol straightaway.

'Oh!' She seemed shocked. Surely, they could manage a walk together? 'Okay then,' she said.

'That's nice,' Megan said. 'He needs a boost.'

Ellie hugged her friend. 'So lovely to see you. I can't wait to see this new place of yours.' They were all smiles. 'No Bill?' she asked.

'No, he's gone to visit his mum, taken the girls.'

Roger decided to phone Bryan. 'Where are you mate?'

'At home. You don't want me there.'

'We do! Get yourself down here.'

'Are you sure? What do you think Carol will think?'

Roger moved away from the others and said quietly, 'Carol knows you're coming and Bill's not here so the coast is clear.'

'Right.' He still wasn't enthusiastic.

'So? You coming?'

'Give me a few minutes.'

Roger addressed the group. 'Right, when we're all here, we are going to head up to the causeway and then up Swingleton Hill. Everyone warm enough?' Bella looked woefully underdressed and her delicate pink hands, frozen.

'Do you not have any gloves?' Ellie asked her.

'No, I always forget.' She giggled.

Ellie pulled a spare pair out of her rucksack. 'Here.' She held Bella's hands together in hers to warm them first.

'They're mittens!' she cried with delight.

'You're such a girly,' Ben said, a look of fondness about him.

Bryan appeared in the distance scurrying up the street. As he got nearer they could see that he'd thrown on any old gear, boots and bobble hat. He must have rushed out of the house.

'Thanks, mate,' he said to Roger. Roger put a manly arm around him and patted his shoulder.

'Right, we're off.' Roger led the way up The Street.

'Sure you know where we're going, Dad?' Matt had a cheeky grin.

'Yes, son, I do. I've done this walk quite a few times.'

'Any vineyards on route?' he goaded despite trying to sound innocent.

'No, son, we're going up to the Capel Rose pub.' Roger looked at Bryan and raised his eyebrows; Bryan looked a bit lost and Roger couldn't help thinking back to the last time they had done this walk and how different Bryan was then, when he was deluded enough to think that he was about to start some sort of new life with Tiffany.

'You stick with me, Bryan. Just in case I do forget a turn here or there.'

He smiled now. 'It's nice to get out. Gets me out of whatever Rebecca thinks I *should* be doing.'

'Did she not fancy the walk?'

'No. I don't really know what it is. She blames her mother. I must admit I don't argue with her but perhaps I should.'

'So, she hasn't seen Carol this Christmas?'

'No, she seems to be more worried about what this new man, Steve, thinks than anything else. Somehow if they went to see Carol it would make the split seem more obvious.'

'Complicated, women, aren't they?'

'You did well with Ellie.'

'Yeah.' He paused for a moment at the bottom of Mill Lane where they were going to turn. 'Perhaps I don't appreciate her enough.' It was something to think about.

They moved into single file as they entered the causeway where the canopy of trees and hedges formed a darkened pathway which the stream meandered over in places.

'Er, it's wet!' Bella complained.

'Told you, you need proper walking boots,' Matt said laughing at her.

Back out into the daylight of Back Lane Roger considered that it was a murky day at best. Greyish clouds were thick and omnipresent and the air was still. Not the most uplifting scene. He turned to Bryan.

'It must feel good to be back in your own home.'

'Well it's a big improvement on the pub, but somehow it seems big without, you know...'

'What do you think you'll do now?' Roger asked. He couldn't help thinking they'd have to sell.

'Go and live in some village in the Dordogne; get out of here.'

Roger was taken aback. 'Bit drastic mate. When did you dream up that idea?'

'Probably on my way home from a disastrous Waitrose shop.'

'Blimey, what happened?'

'Oh, nothing really, it just all went wrong and I began to think maybe I don't fit in here any more.'

'Don't be silly. You were a hit at the pub in the end. I didn't know you had those skills.'

'Yeah, but I don't want to be a barman for the rest of my life.'

'So, what makes you say the Dordogne?'

'Property is cheap. I can see myself wandering round the markets, having a coffee with the old men of a morning; taking my turn to sit in the square and gaze out aimlessly contemplating my life.'

'You've really thought about this, haven't you?'

'Not really. I'm not sure I'll actually do it. I mean I'd probably live in some run-down gîte and drink cheap vino in an attempt to keep my spirits up. And then one day I'd die and no one would notice until I didn't turn up to sit in the square.'

Roger looked at him properly. 'Mate, you've got to stop thinking like that. Maybe you need to talk to someone. Or read one of those books, you know, *you-might-think-life-is-abysmal-but-it's-not* type of book.' Bryan laughed at that, at least.

Roger reached the top of Swingleton Hill and looked back to see that some had slowed down and others were struggling with the gradient. They all stopped to catch their breath. Mist hung over the fields in the distance so you could only guess at where the horizon was. There was blackthorn in the hedgerow with its blue-black berries attracting redwings looking for food.

'Where's the pub?' Bella asked.

'We're probably about halfway,' Bryan said and she looked as if she'd rather be anywhere else. 'It's flat from here so we'll probably pick up the pace,' he added as if to compensate for the bad news. She pulled a face as if anything to do with the countryside was just weird.

As they approached the Capel Rose, there was a cheer from the younger contingent. It was always a welcoming sight, a pretty little pub set on a green. They piled in and Roger started ordering drinks. Bryan joined in getting his wallet out. 'I'll get some of them.'

Ellie spotted Annabelle on the other side of the pub and waved. She was surprised when Lady R came straight over.

'Happy Christmas one and all,' Annabelle said chirpily.

'Well we got through it,' Ellie added keeping her tone light.

'Not a fan?'

She quite liked this woman. 'Not really.'

'Ooh! Ellie, I have some news,' Annabelle said. 'Only found out the other day. Cost-Cut were granted permission to go ahead at that meeting but with lots of stipulations and, would you believe it, they've decided to pull out!'

'Are you sure?' Ellie was astonished.

'Yes, it was going to cost them far too much. But, you know, I think the protest group had a big impact on their decision.' Annabelle looked very pleased with herself.

'I should think so. We put a lot of time and effort into that.'

'They knew that local feeling was against them so they were unlikely to run a successful store even if they went ahead.'

'Cost-Cut aren't going ahead?' Carol had overheard.

'That's right.' Ellie was so thrilled she wanted to shout it from the roof tops.

'Fantastic, Bill will be pleased.'

'Well done, darling,' Roger said nodding to his wife.

'All thanks to your hard work,' Bryan added toasting the group with his beer and Carol actually smiled back at him.

They walked the shorter way back past the equine centre at Boyton Hall. Bella seemed to think that the horses grazing was a redeeming feature of this otherwise wet and muddy place. Bryan seemed more relaxed and actually walked with Carol and Megan for a while.

Ellie was quite happy to bring up the rear; she had a good feeling about the year ahead. Roger appeared by her side.

'I thought you were leading this walk?' she said knowing full well they all knew the way back.

Roger tutted. 'Even Ben could get home from here.'

'I heard you talking to Annabelle about the vineyard job. Sounds like you're a shoo-in. Is she bothering with that interview?'

'Of course! It's all above board. Joe's going to be there, anyway. I've got to impress him.'

'But you've already left quite an impression on Annabelle.' She knew she was teasing him and it was fun to see him squirm momentarily.

'A bit like the impression you made on James.' He looked pleased with himself for that retort.

She laughed. 'Looks like we're both going to be working full time soon. Makes me feel younger, knowing I'm not being put out to grass yet.'

'Too right. Anyway, we are young,' he insisted.

'It will be good to get back to something like normal.'

'Ooh, no, it's far from normal. Working out in the fields amongst the vines in all weathers, muddy boots, sun on my face; it will be brilliant.'

She beamed at him. 'I might even have a new and improved husband on my hands.'

'Play your cards right.' He put an arm round her and as they looked into each other's eyes she could see that he was happier than he had been for a long time.

About the Author

Looking back at my life I can honestly say that it has never been dull.

After I got my degree, I had a career in marketing, never staying with one company for too long. There were highs as well as lows and being a woman in a male dominated environment was not easy.

At the same time, I had one disastrous relationship after another but at least I maintained my independence throughout. I've never been one to just accept the status quo; I'm always looking for new adventures.

I started writing in my forties and soon realised that being at my keyboard, creating characters and storylines, was where life became thrilling and fun.

By then I had had finally met the right man, my husband, Tony. Thank goodness! We moved to Suffolk and I started a new life as a writer and author.

When I'm out and about I am always fascinated to get into conversation with new people, especially if we have shared experiences. Even better if they are a little bit different, eccentric even. It makes for a richer life and feeds my creative mind.

Please be in touch through my website: gillbuchanan.co.uk

or my Facebook page: facebook.com/literallyforwomen/

Printed in Poland
by Amazon Fulfillment
Poland Sp. z o.o., Wrocław

62280785R00230